RINGMASTER!

KRISTOPHER ANTEKEIER
and Greg Aunapu

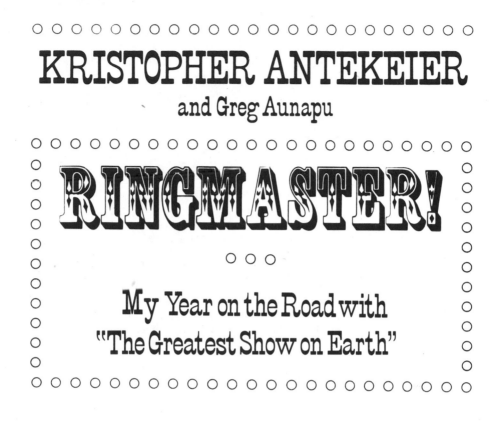

RINGMASTER!

My Year on the Road with "The Greatest Show on Earth"

E. P. DUTTON NEW YORK

Published in the United States by E. P. Dutton,
a division of Penguin Books USA Inc.,
2 Park Avenue, New York, N.Y. 10016.

Published simultaneously in Canada
by Fitzhenry and Whiteside, Limited, Toronto.

Library of Congress Cataloging-in-Publication Data

Antekeier, Kristopher.
Ringmaster! : my year on the road with "The Greatest Show on Earth"
/ Kristopher Antekeier and Greg Aunapu. — 1st ed.
p.   cm.
ISBN 0-525-24757-2
1. Antekeier, Kristopher.   2. Circus performers—United States—
Biography.   I. Aunapu, Greg.   II. Title
GV1811.A58A3 1989
791.3'092'2—dc19
[B]   88-28278
CIP

DESIGNED BY EARL TIDWELL

1   3   5   7   9   10   8   6   4   2

First Edition

To my "gremlins"—
the motivating force behind my success.

"We are the music makers, and we are the dreamers of dreams."

—Gene Wilder in
Willy Wonka and the Chocolate Factory

CONTENTS

ACKNOWLEDGMENTS

The writing of a book is much more work than I ever fathomed it to be. The day I declared, "I'm going to write a book!" I knew with my tenaciousness and perseverance I'd get it published. In hindsight, however, if I had actually known of the time and effort and obstacles I would encounter, I don't honestly know whether I would have embarked on such a venture. I've always been known for my impatience, and, if nothing else, the creation of this book has taught me the art of being patient. I've also learned a lot about publishing.

Besides perseverance, there is an elite group of people I would like to thank for the specific roles they played, sometimes unknowingly, in the creation of my book:

My longtime dear friend, Michael Sartor, for always keeping me laughing and helping me to discover my specific performing "product."

Terry Woods, for helping me produce the initial audition demo tape.

The Live Entertainment Staff at Cedar Point Amusement Park, for grooming my talents.

The late Charles R. Meeker, Jr., for my first professional break.

Amy Mintzer, for truly loving the circus.

Bart Andrews, for his personal support and genuine excitement about this book.

The Muskegon Chronicle, for the superior photos.

Greg Aunapu, for his patience and understanding.

All those who were involved in any way with the 115th Edition of "The Greatest Show on Earth," whom this story is about, and without whom there would be no story.

My friends who put up with my difficult ways during the writing of this book: Rene "Martha" Rodriguez, Phillip H. Colglazier, Pamela Dayton, David Sinkler, Steve Morgan, Chris Kraft, and Susie Turcot.

My family: Jerome, Constance Elaine, Kimberly, Kirk, Kelly, and Kip.

My stepmother, Andrewina, "Andi."

My dear Alberta "Memere" Antekeier, the matriarch of the Antekeier name who didn't quite live long enough to read my story. And to Arnold "Pepere" Antekeier, the patriarch.

Frank and Leone Cereska, "Nana & Gramps," for taking me to shows and circuses as a child.

Thanks especially to the Lord for my God-given talents, which I've been able to use in all of the special events He's allowed to enter into my life.

And finally, *The Yellow Pages*.

CALLIOPE NOTES FROM THE RINGMASTER

What would we do without our dreams? Seeing some of our most sought after dreams come true makes life truly worthwhile. For as long as I can remember, I've dreamed of landing a starring role in an old-fashioned Broadway musical, like *The Music Man* or *Bye, Bye Birdie*. Unfortunately, today's musical theater doesn't produce vehicles appropriate for a young song-and-dance man like me. I often tell folks I was "born too late." I like to think I might have been a major personality in the days of vaudeville or the days of the happy-ever-after endings of the early musicals had I arrived on this planet forty years earlier than I did.

So what does an aspiring song-and-dance man do? Continue hoping and dreaming of that "one big break"?

Enter Ringling Brothers and Barnum & Bailey Circus. The largest touring big show left on the face of the earth. A show packed with elements of vaudeville, glitz, music, and the starring role—the ringmaster, of course.

I spotted an advertisement in *Backstage*, the actor's trade paper, in New York City when I was "between engagements." The ad announced the first-ever nationwide search for a new ringmaster for this American institution—namely, the twenty-seventh ringmaster in their 115-year history.

At the time, I didn't think it would be the ultimate role of my career, but I hoped it might be a unique theatrical opportunity. Any performer would kill for that chance, and anyone who won't admit it is probably lying!

After several auditions during the national search and major publicity hoopla put out by the circus corporation, I was chosen by Kenneth Feld, the producer, to be the ringmaster—youngest man ever to don the top hat, white gloves, tails, and whistle.

I've chronicled the year that ensued, making it as personal and close to reality as I can. I wanted to share the exact feelings this outsider felt being flung into a bizarre and wacky world that only twenty-six men before him had seen from his vantage point, the center of the center ring. I kept an extensive journal throughout my year with the circus and can honestly say that every story and every event recounted in this book is totally true. The only minor changes I've made are the names of some of the clowns. It's a good thing I have that journal to look back to, because even to me the story sometimes reads like fiction, and I still can't believe that much of what took place actually happened, but it did.

You'll read about how the transition from legitimate theater to circusdom was not too easy for me. I learned to dodge llamas and horses and living unicorns. You'll read about the excitement of becoming a "star" for a year, traveling across our country on the old circus train.

One particular aspect of writing this book was difficult for me. The fun I get from performing is knowing that my audience might forget their troubles and escape reality—even if it's only for an hour or two. But in this case, to keep the story honest and intact, I've had to go against my grain at times and report everything without a rose-colored filter—as it actually happened. At times the pictures aren't very pretty or positive. But I think there are enough sequins and rhinestones and magical moments throughout to make this story shine.

Just to set the record straight, I'll help you out with the pronunciation of my last name since it appears throughout the book and isn't the easiest to decipher at first glance: Antekeier (an-ta-kire).

So now, "Laaaaaadies and Gentlemen, Children of Aaaaall ages!" Join me on a thrilling adventure under the Big Top, a journey to a world like no other . . .

Kristopher Antekeier
New York City
May 1988

RINGMASTER!

1

A MAGNIFICENT MELDING OF MAN AND MEDIA

The Audition

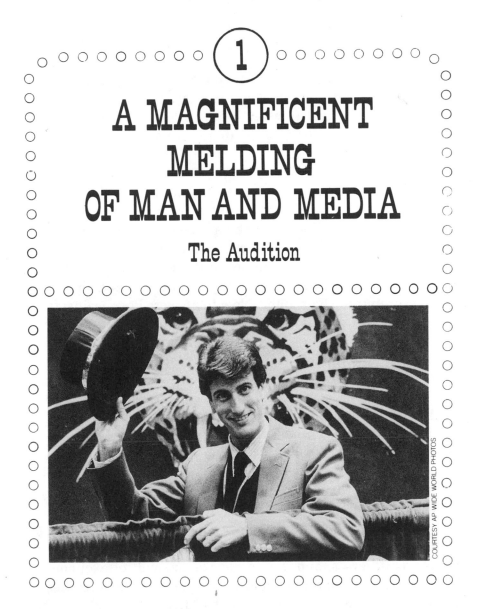

COURTESY AP WIDE WORLD PHOTOS

It was April of 1985 in New York City. The breeze was still cool, yet carried a hint of warm weather to come. You could smell the first blossoms from Central Park mixed with the mouth-watering vapors of hotdogs and pretzels from street-corner vendors. In New York, spring ushers in many things: tourists, new Broadway shows, and street people. But one of the most exciting events is the appearance of "The Greatest Show on Earth" at Madison Square Garden.

Every year the papers are full of articles and advertisements

about this fantastic extravaganza. Such a spectacle has little competition—except itself. Every time it comes to town it must seem
bigger, better, and more mysterious than before. This year, the
hype was enormous. Ringling Brothers and Barnum & Bailey
Circus had outdone themselves. In all of history, no circus had
ever exhibited a unicorn.

Until now.

It was something you had to see if you had the tiniest scrap
of imagination. Unicorns were a myth, we had learned, a fabri-
cation of old storytellers. No one had seen one—ever. Yet there
it was: on subway posters, TV, and in newspapers. No one knew
where Kenneth Feld—the circus producer—had obtained the
fabled creature. But this wasn't the old days when a showman
could say anything he wanted. Now there were laws against false
advertising. How could Feld have found a unicorn? Could he say
he had if he hadn't? I decided to see for myself.

My grandmother happened to be visiting me, and she wanted
to go, too, along with a few friends of mine. Everyone was excited,
and having my grandmother with me somehow accentuated the
feeling of being a kid again, when she used to take me to the
circuses that came through Muskegon, Michigan, where I was
raised. Only now, it was I taking the money out of my pocket
instead of her. But the thrill was the same. Especially since I had
never actually attended "The Greatest Show on Earth," though
I had wanted to virtually all my life.

The air in the arena was heavy with the urinous smell of
elephants and hay, the musk of jungle cats, the musty odor of
chimps and horses, and the unmistakable smell of excitement.
Children laughed and cried and wailed. Some were already ter-
rified by the crowd, and the show had not yet started. Parents
tried keeping their offspring in check by filling their mouths with
cotton candy.

The four of us found our seats, looking down on the empty
rings, thousands of people staring back from around the arena.

"Well, who's running for goodies?" I asked.

"I'm full," my friend Jon said. "We had dinner before we
came."

"You can't come to the circus and not eat something," I
replied. "That's sacrilegious!"

Jon shook his head. "Cotton candy makes me sick."

"Not me," I said. "I love it!"

My grandmother wanted a soda. As soon as I stood up, my friends decided they did indeed want a few things too. Since I was already going, they said, I might as well get some of this and some of that.

"You wanted cotton candy all along," I said. "You just didn't want to admit it!"

"My legs are tired. I worked all day!" my friend complained.

I waited on line forever and heard the orchestra break into its resounding overture. I was getting nervous now, because I didn't want to miss a second of the show. Finally I got to the front, ordered, and started back to the seats juggling a few greasy hotdogs and other assorted delicacies in a cardboard tray, while trying not to spill the drinks.

Scurrying back to the aisle, I excused myself a dozen times squeezing past children's bony knees, seeing their faces alive with anticipation, black kids, white kids, kids with expectant eyes and missing teeth. Families ranging from wrinkled old grandmothers to infants. Spanish and Chinese battled with English, charging the air with a buzz like a giant beehive.

Just as I sat down and passed out the food, what seemed like twenty spotlights hit a tall, husky blond man standing center ring. He was dazzling, with his high top hat and long-tailed tuxedo flashing with rhinestones, piercing eyes, and a persona that reached up into the highest seat. I thought every kid in the arena must want to grow up and be just like him.

He was the ringmaster.

Bringing his microphone up to his mouth, he held the moment in silence. Then his lips moved, sending his voice booming through the air. "Laaaaaadies and Gentlemen! Children of aaall aaaages . . ." I think the heart of everyone there must have skipped a beat. His voice was mellow, and I picked up on his laid-back style right away.

He was what I considered to be a traditional ringmaster: a big man, a leader, a man who could and would jump into a cage full of lions to help the tamer if needed.

They brought out the elephants and clowns. They brought out the showgirls and horses. Gunther Gebel Williams, the great-

est animal trainer on earth, commanded the menagerie in a
breathtaking parade. Yet through it all, my eyes were on the
ringmaster.

"What kind of life does he lead?" I asked myself.

Soon—like any actor!—I was imagining myself in his role,
thinking, "I know just how I would perform this . . ."

I saw the ringmaster as a character to play. I had worked as
a singer and dancer and also as a professional master of cere-
monies for a wonderful amusement park in Sandusky, Ohio,
called Cedar Point, and had eventually worked my way up to
Disney World itself. So I wasn't off base thinking I could do this
job.

Then it was time. At the end of the first act came "the spectacle," where amid great fanfare they introduced the unicorn.

First came a royal procession, with men and women dressed
in courtly, Renaissance garb: colorful silks and satins, high-peaked
hats with veils. There were jesters and musicians and a gilded
float. On the float was a beautiful woman stroking a white, fleecy
animal standing on all fours, holding its one horn nobly in the
air: the unicorn.

"It's a goat!" a friend said.

In high, piping voices I could hear the children around me.
"That's a goat, Mommy. Isn't that a goat?"

And I heard the parents answer. "No, it's not a goat. It's a
unicorn. Can't you see its horn? Only unicorns have only one
horn."

I sat there thinking. "Okay, the unicorn is a goat with a horn
growing out of its forehead. But I know what they're doing. It's
like Mary Poppins or the Wizard of Oz. It's there to believe in—
if you let yourself."

Not all the children were skeptical, and many were squealing
with delight. I couldn't help feeling that no harm was being done,
as long as the goat was not in pain.

I didn't feel in the least let down because what we happily
called a unicorn, others might have called a goat. I began to
understand that the circus was merely following a long tradition
started by P. T. Barnum himself: find something unusual and
sell it as something bizarre.

From my earliest days I had always loved variety shows of

any kind—especially ice shows and circuses. I remember when
I was a kid staring at the empty field that had been the site of
the Clyde Beatty–Cole Brothers circus which came through Muskegon, unable to contain my sadness that it was now gone. My
bedroom was decorated with red-and-white-striped wallpaper
like a circus tent. Hundreds of clowns adorned the room in pictures and statuettes.

My parents had noticed my interest in puppetry, the circus,
and carnivals and encouraged me to audition for community-
theater musicals. Anything to get me on stage. They had great
difficulty at first, too, because I was extremely shy at the time,
though it's hard for me to believe that now!

At the age of twelve, I put together my own one-man production, singing and doing a puppet act, which I toured in my
home state. Then I worked for Cedar Point and Disney World
before doing regional theater and cruise ship entertainment. Finally, I was ready for the big city.

Now, a New York actor, I lived scarcely three blocks from
the trainyard where the Ringling Brothers Circus train parked
every year during the run at the Garden. When I took the subway
into Manhattan, I'd pass directly over the circus train. I couldn't
help wondering about the life-style. What would it be like? What
kind of people actually *lived* that way?

In June, two months after my visit to the circus, I was leafing
through *Backstage*, the actor's trade paper. It comes out every
Thursday and is instantly grabbed up by thousands of out-of-
work performers looking for their next job. It lists all upcoming
auditions for stage, screen, and television. It is also full of advertisements. One thing I always found annoying were ads showing photos of actors who had just been cast in some great part.

Unless it's you, of course.

I had found several things I could go for in that week's *Backstage* and circled them, when I noticed an ad announcing auditions for THE MOST EXCLUSIVE JOB IN THE WORLD. RINGMASTER
FOR THE RINGLING BROS. AND BARNUM & BAILEY CIRCUS.

My hand hovered over the listing while I thought about it.
"Do I want to try for this? Do I *dare* try for this?" I gritted my
teeth and drew a big circle around the ad.

The ad was a preliminary "feeler" by Kenneth Feld, the

circus producer. It said to send a demo tape of three circus announcements and two songs. I called the man who was musical
arranger of the nightclub act I'd done on four cruise ships and
at a club in New York City. We hastily put together what we
hoped was a clever tape.

We wrote our own circus annoucements after listening to
the original cast recording of the Broadway show *Barnum*, which
Kenneth Feld had coproduced. We made up names for our imag-
inary performers and preceded it with the trill of a whistle.

"Walter Winslow Gathers," I bellowed, "faces the most ferocious of jungle beasts! And on the dangerous trapeze, high in
the air . . . behold, the Fabulous, Flying Zucchini Brothers!"

We laughed so hard that we had trouble taping it. The two
songs I chose to sing were already in my repertoire: "There's a
Sucker Born Every Minute" from *Barnum*, and "Pure Imagination," from the children's movie *Willy Wonka and the Chocolate
Factory*. I thought both were extremely appropriate, especially
after having seen the "unicorn" in April. Then that quickly produced tape was off in the mail to the executive offices of Ringling.

About three weeks later, in July, I received a phone call from
a fellow who identified himself as Tim Holst. He said he was the
performance director of the Red Unit of "The Greatest Show on
Earth."

"I liked your tape," he said. "It gave us all a laugh."

"Thanks," I replied. "It was fun to make."

He cleared his throat. "The reason why I'm calling is this.
Mr. Feld wants to see what type of people sent us tapes, and
how interested they are in actually being ringmaster."

I drew in a breath and thought about it. "It interests me," I
said. "I've been an emcee for years. It's just sort of a bigger job.
I think it would be fascinating."

"It is," he agreed, his voice sounding weary over the phone,
"but circus life is hard, and it's a grueling pace. You're on the
road forty-seven weeks out of the year. Ringmaster is a very
important job, and you have to be *on* every night. You don't have
an understudy. Before I moved into management I was ringmaster
myself, and I was glad to retire."

Without thinking about whether or not I really wanted the

job, I couldn't help selling myself. I always want people to think
the best of me, and it's a crucial part of trying to be a working
performer. "I could do it; I'm a professional. I spent years at
Cedar Point doing live shows and then going out on the road. It
was never easy. Then I was at Disney, and they don't set an easy
pace either!"

"Okay," he said. "That's what circus people like to hear.
We'll be auditioning in L.A. and New York, so we'll be in touch."

I went up to Connecticut for the rest of the summer to appear
in a Broadway revue at a dinner theater. The show closed in
September, and on returning to the city I again picked up the
newest *Backstage*.

One of the first things I saw was a new ad for the ringmaster
job. This time, the ad was much larger, informing everyone that
a national search was being conducted by Kenneth Feld. Open-
call auditions were to be held on October 2 at the Minskoff Stu-
dios, a place every professional stage actor in New York knows
well. I had myself acquired several jobs after auditioning there.

I was a little surprised to see the ad, because I had never
heard anything further from Holst and figured they had scrapped
their audition idea. But apparently this was not the case, and
since my conversation with the circus man had been so positive,
I decided to audition for him.

It turned out to be a crazy day for me. I had three different
auditions to tackle: one for a part in *Hamelin* (a new off-Broadway
show, which ended up getting horrible reviews and closed in
five weeks), another for an industrial show (an in-house production for a corporation), and the ringmaster audition stuck in
between them.

When I got to Minskoff, the first thing I noticed was a lot of
people hanging around who did *not* look like actors. They had
cameras and notepads and recording devices. I quickly learned
they were members of the press eager to get news of the next
ringmaster. This was the first time in history that the circus had
held mass auditions for the position, and it had sparked the
interest of newspapers and television stations around the country.

I waited to hear my name called. After you've been auditioning for as many years as I have, you stop feeling nervous, but the presence of all those media people—evidence of all the attention focused on the event—brought back the queasy stomach I thought I had left behind. As soon as somebody would exit, the reporters would converge on him and blast questions in his direction.

The monitor ushered out the fellow before me.

"Kristopher Antekeier!" she called.

I rose from the plastic chair. "I'm ready," I said.

"I hope so," she told me. "You've been waiting long enough."

Inside, leaning on the walls, were over a dozen press people talking among themselves and jostling each other. Three other men were seated in front of a small stage. They turned to face me.

"Is Tim Holst here?" I asked.

A short, balding man nodded his head and spoke. "That's me."

"We talked on the phone," I said.

"I remember. You're the one who invented the Flying Zucchini Brothers." He stood up and we shook hands. "I'm glad you could make it. I was going to call and make sure you came in so I could meet you."

He introduced the other men. Neither was Kenneth Feld. These were still preliminary auditions, and not important enough for the big man himself.

I gave my music to the piano player, then stood up on stage.

"I'm Kristopher Antekeier," I said. "And I'll start with 'There's a Sucker Born Every Minute.' "

Several people around the room chuckled. It was unnerving to audition in front of so many people. I stood there looking out at them, knowing that a major mishap would not be forgotten. It would be remembered and perhaps written about and published.

I motioned to the piano player and started the song.

The first thing I realized was that the tempo was way off. Too slow—horribly slow. I tried picking it up, but the piano player squinting at the music couldn't keep up with me.

The experience of hundreds of auditions under my belt made me keep on going. You don't stop for anything. I plugged on, noticing a strained look on Tim Holst's face.

Then on the second line, the piano quit altogether.

Inwardly I groaned. Outwardly I kept going, hoping the pianist would catch up. Occasionally I would hear some sparse accompaniment, and then it would peter out again. I finished, knowing it had not sounded good. The reporters were scribbling things on their pads.

One of the men with Holst cleared his throat, eyebrows raising. "Do you happen to have that song on tape?"

"It's on the one I sent to Mr. Holst," I replied.

He nodded his head. "Good. We'll listen to it later. What else do you have for us?"

I was glad he realized how poor the piano player was. "Yes," I told him. "I've got a ballad."

"Do it," he said.

This song was easier for the pianist to play, and this time the piece went better. They seemed to enjoy the way I did the song and then asked me to do some actual announcements from the 115th Edition of "The Greatest Show on Earth."

Reading from the script they supplied, I did my best, using my grandest voice, letting the r's roll and the consonants crack, trying to make the names sound wonderfully interesting.

"Sorry, Kristopher," Mr. Holst said. "No Zucchini Brothers in this show—or any other vegetables for that matter!"

We all laughed. His joke was a double entendre encompassing the tape I had sent him and an item on my resume that showed I had played a carrot in the Robert Altman film *Health*.

"Thank you," he continued. "We'll let you know."

The age-old statement all actors grow to hate.

I swallowed, feeling let down. "Thank you," I said, and I left the room.

I quickly realized the audition must not have been a total disaster when the press followed me out the door and were joined by those who had waited in the hall. I stood there as they shoved microphones in my face and shouted questions at me. The big cyclops eyes of TV cameras rolled above their heads. I warmed to it quickly, straightening my posture, trying to answer their questions in an authoritative voice.

"You sound like a ringmaster," one said. "Have you ever been one before?"

"Only in my dreams," I answered.

"So you dream of it?" another shot back. "Has it been a lifelong ambition?"

"One of many," I replied. What else could I say?

New York was only the first stop on the audition trail. Tim Holst went to several major cities, including Chicago and L.A., and concluded with Boston. Their last tryouts were on October 16. The day after that, my phone rang. It was Tim Holst.

"Well, Kristopher, are you still interested?" he asked.

For a long minute I wondered about it. All the attention at the audition had made me realize what sort of position ringmaster was: not private.

"You bet," I said, trying to sound sure.

His tone of voice was friendly, but businesslike. "Okay, then. We've never had national auditions before, and I don't know quite how everything will be handled. But I wanted to let you know you're still being considered for the final auditions. The Red Unit will be performing in Chicago soon, and we'll have the callbacks in the actual ring there."

"In the circus itself?" I asked, wondering whether I'd have to do it with wild animals running around me.

"Yes, sir. We'll have to see how you'll look under the proper circumstances," came the answer, jokingly.

I laughed, but the idea of being surrounded by big cats made the laugh a little high.

We exchanged a few more pleasantries, and I learned there would be no more acts in the ring. I would be doing the announcements for performers who would not be present; that relieved me a bit.

I was still not at all sure that I would take the job if it were offered. But a friend of mine whom I wanted to see lived in Chicago, so I could at least go that far. When the publicity department of Ringling Brothers called me toward the end of October, they told me I was one of seven finalists vying for the job. Kenneth Feld was holding an "announce off" in a few weeks, and they were flying us all out to Chicago.

Actually, taking this job would be a big decision for me. It would mean putting my musical theater career on hold and leaving the contacts I'd built up in three years of living and working in New York. I also wondered whether I could live with animals and make friends with a bunch of "carnies." My friends, however, told me to go for it. They said I was perfect. And thinking it over, I had to agree. Everything I'd done in my career so far seemed to lead to this position.

I had not yet told my family about this particular audition. Sometimes I go to hundreds in a year, three or more a day in the hottest season, and they never know how many times I audition before finally landing a job.

On Halloween I received a call from my father, who was living in Florida.

"I got a call from Michigan," he told me. "They say they read in the newspaper that you're a finalist for ringmaster!"

"In the newspaper?"

"That's right. You'd be great for the job. I hope you get it."

"Thanks. We'll see what happens."

After we hung up, I started feeling unsettled. I couldn't believe I was already being written about in the papers, and I was only a finalist. Evidently, Ringling was putting their all into publicity for this shindig.

The day to fly out to Chicago arrived. It was November 3. Just before I walked out the door, something told me to grab the bright red sport coat I had worn in an industrial show. I got in touch with my friend on arrival, and we walked down Madison Avenue. I had all three circus announcements memorized, so I could enjoy the evening.

The next morning, I went to the lobby of the Sheraton Hotel about a mile from the arena, where I met two of the other six finalists. One was a little guy with wide eyes. Though he wore a tuxedo, he looked too young to be ringmaster. Another fellow was greater competition. He was tall and authoritative, with the right look and bearing, and a strong voice to boot.

A man with a pompadour, his hair greased back, introduced himself as Robin Frye, assistant performance director for the Red Unit of the circus. He drove us to the arena, where we met the other candidates. A few of them looked particularly suited for the job.

The first thing I noticed when we entered the building was the stench of animals. I was thankful, however, that the culprits were nowhere to be seen. The three circus rings were all empty.

As we walked past the closed concession stands, the smell got worse. Robin Frye noticed the expression on my face. "You get used to the smell after a while," he said.

"I hope so!" I told him, smiling bravely. "It's all right though. It wouldn't be the circus if it smelled like a hospital, now would it?"

Tim Holst was there to greet us. We followed his bobbing bald head toward the rings, where we sat. One by one we were called into the office to be interviewed by the Kenneth Feld.

The two other men who had been with Holst during the New York auditions were also sitting in the arena. I went over and introduced myself and found out they were the director/choreographers of the show.

One man was Crandall Diehl, who, as I was informed by another auditioner, had been in the original company of *My Fair Lady* on Broadway. The other man was Bill Bradley, who also had a long list of New York credits. It made me feel better knowing that these talented men were now working for the circus. It seemed to give the job a greater legitimacy.

I went back to the group of auditioners. All of us, it turned out, were apprehensive about the thing. In actuality, we were all stage performers, not quite sure what this opportunity would mean for our careers, or what it would be like to travel in this foreign atmosphere.

Tim Holst entered the arena and beckoned to me.

"It's your turn, Kristopher. Time to meet Mr. Feld."

I took a deep breath and followed him into the office.

Inside was a smallish man who seemed very young for such a position of authority. His father, Irvin Feld, had acquired the circus in 1967 and, upon his death in September of 1984, left it to his son.

I learned later that the Felds were known as crafty businessmen. If the financial world was an ocean, both father and son were sharks in it. The legend is that at the age of thirteen, the father made $8,000 selling snake oil at a summer carnival. A lot of money for a thirteen-year-old in any year, and back in those days it was a fortune!

In 1956, Irvin began a partnership with John Ringling North, then owner of the failing circus. Ringling continued to produce "The Big Show," but Irvin took over the promotion and itinerary. After scrapping the old way of performing under a giant tent, for which "The Greatest Show on Earth" was famous, and booking the circus into city arenas, coliseums, and convention sites, Feld saved the circus $50,000 on the first week's booking alone.

In 1967, Feld put together an investment group that bought the circus for $8 million. He fired the older performers, bringing the average age down from forty-six to twenty-three. He liked the frenetic energy of clowns, so he hired more of them. He knew audiences were entranced by big cats, so he bought a circus belonging to the famous animal trainer Gunther Gebel Williams, who stayed on and became the focus of Feld's advertising. Crowds flocked to see the charismatic blond German snap his whip and command dangerous, snarling tigers to dance and jump through flaming hoops.

After his father passed away Kenneth was intent on making his own mark on the circus—and he was known as being a cut-throat businessman who did not have the same, great love for the circus as his father.

Without standing up, Kenneth Feld shook my hand. The first words out of his mouth were, "So you want to be ringmaster?"

I grinned, liking the bold affront. I figured I had nothing to lose. "I *am* going to be ringmaster, Mr. Feld."

He chuckled, his eyes crinkling, as he leaned back in his chair. "I like that confidence," he replied. "It's something a ring-master has to have."

I smiled. I had been right about him. He *wanted* that sort of aggressiveness. The ringmaster had to excite an arena of fifteen thousand people. A timid person could never be trusted with such a position. In any audition, you have to leave them knowing you can do the job should they give it to you.

As we conversed, he made a point of telling me just how

hard circus life was. I could see they didn't want someone who
would burn out on them. There were no backups or understudies
to go on should a ringmaster suddenly quit, though I imagined
the performance director could do the job in an emergency.

After we got through all that, with my assuring him I could
stand up to it all, he sat forward and rested his elbow on the
desk. "What we're looking for, Kristopher, is a younger ringmaster. Someone around twenty-eight or twenty-nine to zip up
the show. Keep that in mind when you audition for me. I need
to know you're the man."

"I am," I replied. I was twenty-seven years old, just shy of
the age he mentioned, and I thought I had just the sort of spunk
he wanted.

We looked at each other for a minute, and I could feel him
try to probe my brain. He was no paper pusher. He coordinated
a giant enterprise and could read men as easily as newspapers.
I left feeling pummeled.

After the interview, I went directly over to the pianist and
gave him my music to look over. I was determined to sing the
same numbers I had done in New York and was equally determined not to repeat the musical fiasco as well.

By this time, Dinny McGuire, the retiring ringmaster, had
entered the arena in full costume and seated himself beside Tim
Holst and the other directors. I remembered him distinctly from
the show I saw in April. Up close he was an even more impressive
figure than I had remembered: well over six feet, with a proud
bearing and a sure, smooth manner.

All seven hopefuls were seated in alphabetical order between the rings. Kenneth Feld walked into the arena and sat with
Dinny and the others.

"Okay, Kristopher," Mr. Holst said. "You're on!"

I pushed out of my seat and headed toward the "bull tub,"
an upside-down can in the center of the ring. I was at a disad-
vantage here. Being first, I could not see how the other candidates
were going to do their acts. I had to be my most dynamic and
become the one for others to match.

I shook myself into a spry trot and bounded to the bull tub,
jumping theatrically to the top. I picked up the microphone, put

it to my lips, and told myself, "Make it big. Make it exciting!" I mean, the circus is anything but subtle.

I looked into the rows of empty seats and imagined them to be full of faces, young and old. I had to impress not only the kids but the jaded adults as well.

Pulling my voice from deep in my diaphragm, I launched it into the microphone. Amplified hundreds of times, it resounded through the arena. "Laaadies and Gentlemen. Children of aaalll aages! Producer Kenneth Feld proudly presents the one hundred and fifteenth edition of the Ringling Brothers and Barnum & Bailey Circus. The Greatest Show on Eaaaarth!" The echo from the empty arena was overwhelming.

Sitting to one side incognito, in jeans and a fisherman's cap, was none other than Gunther Gebel Williams, the world-renowned animal trainer. I knew it was Williams, because I had seen the circus in New York, but I don't think any of the other candidates realized he was watching.

I proceeded through the memorized announcements, making them grand and interesting, modulating my voice as well as I could. When I came to "The Greatest Show on Earth takes great pride in once again presenting the living legend of the circus, Gunther Gebel Williams," I made a big, swooping gesture to acknowledge Gunther sitting there. Everyone looked his way, and he yanked off his hat and waved it to me, smiling.

He was a charismatic figure, and his brief acknowledgment gave me a boost of energy. I finished with enthusiasm, bowed, and returned to my seat.

Then, one by one, each of the contestants performed for Mr. Feld. All seven of us watched intently to see what worked and didn't work; what to add to our own rendition and what to throw away.

After the seventh finalist completed his work, Mr. Feld withdrew from the arena and the press was allowed in. They stormed inside, fought for strategic positions, then set up lights, cameras, and sound equipment. We were told we would go through the whole process again. This time, Mr. Feld would be watching how we worked in front of the buzzing cameras and flashing bulbs.

While Mr. Feld was away, the press interviewed each of us

separately. There were two Chicago boys in the group, so the local reporters were keenly interested in them. Soon, it was my turn.

The main question was the same as it had been during the first audition in New York: "Is this something you dreamed of doing when you were a little boy?"

It seemed none of the contenders responded with a definite yes. This wasn't anybody's idea of the ultimate role, as some great Broadway part might be. I gave as forthright a response as I could, while trying to seem genuinely positive.

Kenneth Feld came back into the arena to begin the big "announce off" in front of the press. But first, Dinny McGuire, the retiring ringmaster of four years, performed the opening announcement with his mellow, bass voice. Four years of practice was evident. The fellow next to me remarked, "Wow, try to follow that!"

I thought to myself, "Watch me!" I figured if the guy didn't have confidence in himself, he was no competition for the job.

As I watched Dinny, I realized it wouldn't do to re-create his style. Mr. Feld wanted something more intense, more youthful and exuberant. He wanted a Disney flair, and I had that kind of experience.

I went first again. This time when I got up there, it was in front of the cameras. I could either blot them from my mind or play to them. I decided on the latter choice. With a real audience now, I think I did better than the first time. Many people applauded when I took my bow.

Then it was time to sing.

My ballad was the haunting "Pure Imagination," from *Willy Wonka and the Chocolate Factory.*

"Come with me and you'll be in a world of pure imagination!
Take a look and you'll see into your imagination!
We'll begin with a spin, travelling in the world of my
*   creation!*
What we'll see will defy explanation!"

The lyrics were similar to the original song the new ringmaster would have to sing about the fantasy of seeing a "real live unicorn" after the "Ladies and Gentlemen" opening announcement:

"Producer Kenneth Feld invites you to an event unparalleled in circus history. A stupendous spectacle where myth becomes reality, and the unbelievable and inconceivable pass before your very eyes. Join us as we celebrate the fantasy!"

Both had the same theme: take the audience on a trip to escape reality for a few hours. That was why I was an entertainer in the first place. I loved taking people away from themselves, seeing smiles turn to laughter.

I was wearing the red jacket with padded shoulders for the audition. Everyone else was wearing sport coats and sweaters in subdued colors. So I knew I stood out among them visually. I was hoping I could outperform them as well.

My competitors followed one by one again. One guy had a similar quality voice to Dinny McGuire's and did the best rendition of "76 Trombones" I'd ever heard. Even though I had done a good job out there, it seemed the general consensus of the group that he would get the job, because he was so like the retiring ringmaster. I did not know what Mr. Feld had told them, but if he were genuinely interested in getting a fresh, high-energy, Broadway style, this was not his man.

As Kenneth Feld once again left the arena to concentrate on what was for him a major business decision, I could only cross my fingers. The seven of us huddled together, wishing each other luck, though it was obvious everyone's best bet was the Dinny McGuire sound-alike.

Mr. Feld opened the door to his office and strode into the arena as the television cameras rolled. He hopped onto the bull tub in center ring.

"The ringmaster's job," he said, "is extremely important. He must be the embodiment of the circus. It is the most exclusive job on earth. In the entire one hundred and fifteen years of Ringling Brothers and Barnum & Bailey's Greatest Show on Earth, there have been only twenty-six ringmasters. The United States has had more presidents.

"During the year, we will perform a thousand shows in over eighty different cities. Of course, every arena is unique, with different ambiance and acoustics. The ringmaster must have the stamina, talent, and flexibility to make it work. He must sing, project authority, and display immense stage presence. The gentleman I've selected has all those requirements and more!"

I was remembering to smile, but I was so tense I could barely make sense of the words coming out of his mouth. The next thing I knew, he was saying, "and the twenty-seventh man to take his place amongst the elite group of men as ringmaster and uphold the tradition for The Greatest Show on Earth is . . ."

He looked straight at me. Adrenaline flooded my body. My heart leaped into high gear, pounding so loud it almost drowned out his words. I thought to myself, "I have this. I think I have this. I *can't believe* I have this!"

". . . Kristopher Antekeier!" Mr. Feld announced.

All the cameras turned and focused on me. My mind froze. Only one thought was inside it. "What the heck have I gotten myself into now?"

I saw myself reach out and shake hands with the losing contenders, and then I was running up to stand beside Mr. Feld.

Dinny McGuire handed me the famous black top hat and hung a whistle around my neck: clearly the tools of the trade for this unique position. I struggled for something to say, and then the showman inside pushed to the surface. I became suave and personable as the cameras recorded my words to be shown all over the United States on the evening news.

First I thanked Mr. Feld, ending up with, "In show business perseverance pays off. You just never know how an instant can change a person's life so dramatically. I'm proud to be the twenty-seventh person in history honored with the responsibilities of The Greatest Show on Earth. The circus is so exciting and magical!"

After that, I walked closer to the press people, and they started shouting questions at me, some of a less than intelligent nature.

"Did you know you were going to get it?"

"Was it the red jacket?"

"Have you ever done this sort of job before?"

After all the excitement died down and the press finally left,

Kenneth Feld took me into his office, wanting to negotiate the contract right there and then. Interestingly, he had seven different contracts prepared, one for each possible ringmaster, and all at the same salary.

I begged off, asking him to call me in a week, when I would be in a calmer state of mind. I did not tell him that I was still unsure of the offer.

Later that day, Mr. Feld flew to Las Vegas on business, leaving me with the publicity people, who put me on the phone for a few hours talking to various reporters. My hometown newspaper was very excited and ran long articles on me.

I flew back to New York on the same plane as Crandall Diehl and Bill Bradley, the directors. They told me to expect a lot of attention, but I was not prepared for what awaited.

Though I didn't know it at the time, because I was on the flight, I made national news. When I got home there was a message from my agent on my answering machine. Her voice was frantic.

"Kristopher, what is this thing with the circus I just saw on the news? Call me!"

I laughed. My contract with her agency was up, and I wasn't planning to renew because I was getting more work on my own. I called her at home and told her I could handle this by myself. She was very upset she wasn't going to make her 10 percent.

First thing in the morning, I called my mother, who was in Muskegon at the time. She said the phone had been ringing steadily. The whole city was buzzing.

The phone was rarely in its cradle that day. People called from all over the country. As soon as I put down the receiver, it rang again. ABC News wanted to come to my home in Long Island City to do an interview. So did their competition. *Time* magazine interviewed me, saying that an article would run in the coming issue. I suddenly knew how overnight celebrities felt. It was like being crowned Mr. America. I was so excited I drew three exclamation points at the end of every sentence I wrote in my journal.

The next few days found my face on every television network. New York anchorwoman Kaity Tong began: "Now anyone who ever wanted to run away and join the circus, here's the story of an almost overnight success." Cut to—me singing "Top Banana," on the streets of Long Island City with the elevated train passing behind me and the Manhattan skyline in the background. Reporter John David Kline's voice-over concluded: "It's The Big Top now for Kristopher, but in a few years—you can look for him on Broadway!"

It was strange to see this small image of myself prancing around on television, hearing words through the speakers that I had spoken the day before.

The news blitz became even bigger than I could have imagined. I went international on "The Voice of America." I turned on the "Today" show, and there I was. Congratulatory cards and articles came to me from all over America.

Getting those cards was the best. People don't realize the hours spent waiting at auditions, the hours and years of your life you put into the final product of a show, without getting any feedback from the audience after they leave the theater.

A few days later, I was sitting with some friends in a little restaurant in Manhattan, and a woman got up from her table across the room. She came running up to me.

"Aren't you the new ringmaster?"

"Yes," I replied, amazed this was happening.

"Will you sign my napkin? I just have to have your autograph!"

My friends slapped me on the back when she left. I was particularly happy that one of my companions was my old director from Cedar Point, who had drilled me endlessly.

"You're too casual with your announcements, Kristopher," he would say. "Stand there, very strong and sturdy—like the ringmaster of the circus."

Little did he know he was actually training me for the job. It felt good to have him see how well I had taken his instruction.

People recognized me everywhere I went. As I walked down Broadway the next day people were calling: "Hey, Mr. Barnum and Bailey!" "Ringmaster! Ringmaster!"

Without actually making a decision, I had been forced into the job. There was no way I could turn it down after all this publicity. I had to break several commitments to do industrial shows in the spring, and not everyone was understanding.

To clinch it, Kenneth Feld called me. We argued for over half an hour before we came to terms. I'd start out at $500 a week with a $50 raise in April if I proved worthy of it. He told me the contract would be in the mail.

The Red Unit of the circus had since moved to the Meadowlands arena in New Jersey. I was invited by Tim Holst to see the show, to help ease my transition into ringmaster. It was opening day in New Jersey, and I'd taken a bus out to the arena. I found out that each edition of the circus—known as the Red Unit and the Blue Unit—tours for two years, and I'd be coming in on the second year of the tour.

It was different seeing the circus this time. I was not going there just to enjoy myself, but to learn about my job. This time I noticed different things. I was especially impressed by the co-ordination of the event: it was seemingly a cast of thousands, all choreographed into a tight, suspenseful show.

This time I studied Dinny McGuire's ringmaster technique, trying to define exactly how I would be different. I came to realize that in one important way we would be the same. To do the job you had to magnify your persona and project yourself until you filled the arena every show. I knew right then, this was going to be a tiring job.

Before the show the New York publicist took me backstage and introduced me to some of the cast members.

There were sequins everywhere. Every costume glittered in gold, pink, yellow, and magenta. Performers were running up and down the halls, and electricity almost crackled in the air as they prepared for the opening performance. Every arena is different, and getting used to the new place is always chaotic. Opening nights are hectic for any show, but for the circus they're magnified.

People were toweling dry, changing clothes, watering the animals, and doing a thousand little jobs to get ready for the show. A few children were running around, getting in the way, adding to the general chaos.

The first person who could stop long enough to talk was Mrs.

Sigrid Gebel, Gunther's wife. She was a statuesque woman with blond hair piled on top of her head. She wore garish circus makeup, but you could tell how pretty she was without it. She had once been a successful model.

"It's good to meet you," she said. "But you can't be ringmaster. You're too thin to be *ringmaster*."

Her tone was jocular, but there was a hint of a challenge. I knew instantly this would be a problem with many people there. They were used to Dinny McGuire, his age, size, and authority. That was something I did not have until the lights hit me and I was under the spotlight. I imagined myself in the middle of that great melee of performers, elephants, horses, and music, standing there in sequined tails and top hat. I knew my lanky form would be much more imposing then.

"You wait and see how I look. I won't disappoint you," I told her.

She smiled. But there was a "wait and see" attitude in her bearing.

We ambled around, me shaking hands with various clowns, acrobats, and tightrope walkers, all in a hurry to be somewhere else, but all necessarily interested in the new ringmaster. At five feet eleven inches I towered above a few smaller fellows from Latin America and Europe, but also had to look up many a time as well.

We found Gunther. He was busy instructing one of his workers how to position the camels and horses correctly for the opening number. He was a platinum-haired, wiry man, with an undeniable charisma, which has made him the circus celebrity he is. His smile was wider than Martha Raye's, with more imposing teeth. He cocked a fierce blue eye at me as he shook my hand and spoke with a German accent.

"I saw you audition in Chicago. I didn't stay for all the others, but I told Kenny Feld that you were my choice."

"Thank you," I said. "Coming from you that means a lot."

An elephant trumpeted and shied away from a worker behind us. Gunther's worn face remained calm as he jumped away and yelled something in German at the elephant, which stomped back into its place. It was obvious the great animal trainer had plenty to do, so we wandered off.

I met a hundred people with names from a dozen different countries. After the show, I finally plugged homeward with a souvenir program in hand to help me remember the names of the acts.

Leafing through the pages I couldn't help but think, "This is the world I love. The dreamworld of vaudeville, colors, children, carnivals, and the spectacle. It's all here. In a matter of weeks I'll be a part of it."

A week later I had an appointment at the Eaves-Brooks Costume Company for a fitting. When I got to the massive warehouse, I realized that the place used to be Brooks–Van Horne. When I was a child doing civic theater we rented our costumes from here. I spoke with the secretary at the front desk, telling her how I had worn their costumes as a child in *Flower Drum Song* and as the Artful Dodger in *Oliver!*

Soon I was called in again to put on a makeshift ringmaster costume for publicity photos. When I walked down the hall in my tails to where the photos would be shot, I was greeted with oohs and ahhs. All of a sudden a feeling of authority crept in and gave me my first inkling of what it meant to be ringmaster.

I didn't have to report to the circus's winter quarters until January, so I spent a nervous month of December in New York not going to all the auditions I would normally have attended, obviously not getting jobs I might have had. Though some friends thought I was doing the right thing, others thought I was crazy.

"You'll get bored in a couple of months," they told me. "This isn't going to help your career at all!"

The only thing I could do was trust my instincts, and I'm glad I did. The year I was about to experience would be unlike anything I had ever encountered in all my years as a professional entertainer.

2

PRODIGIOUS PRODUCTION PREPARATION

Winter Quarters

BRIAN MASCK / THE MUSKEGON CHRONICLE

On January 9, 1986, I reported to Venice, Florida, where the winter quarters for "The Greatest Show on Earth" are now located. The traditional home of the Ringling Brothers circus had been in Baraboo, Wisconsin, until the winter of 1917–18. At that time, John Ringling moved to Bridgeport, Connecticut, when the great merger with Barnum & Bailey occurred. The home base for the show remained in Bridgeport until after the 1927 tour, when Ringling decided to move to warm weather and brought the circus to Sarasota, Florida. In the 1940s, winter quarters were relocated by John Ringling North, Ringling's nephew, to the sleepy town of Venice, a few miles south of Sarasota.

The decision to move from Connecticut must have been a major dilemma for Ringling. His associates probably thought he was crazy to move to the mosquito-infested swampland of Florida. But, as usual, Ringling had been right. Performers could practice outdoors, and the animals, many from hot climates, did not suffer from cold weather.

Most performers, I was told, lived on the circus train, in claustrophobic rooms made by dividing each car into sections. The more important you were, the larger room you got. I had learned, however, that many people traveled more comfortably in motor homes and trailers, driving along the circus's itinerary. I didn't know what my room might be like on the train, so when my uncle suggested I borrow his motor home for a few months, I agreed.

I had traveled to Florida a few days early, visited my father in Clearwater—a town near Venice—and picked up the trailer there.

My first day in Clearwater, I woke up coughing, with my sinuses completely clogged. The change in weather from northern winter to moist Florida air had joined forces to inflict me with a cold. It also triggered a recurring allergy condition.

By breakfast I could hardly speak, managing only a hoarse conversation with my father. When the illness got worse during the day, I started to panic. First impressions being what they are, I was worried about starting rehearsals sounding like a frog. It would be sad if the fellow hired for his golden throat couldn't talk or sing.

On January 8, I drove the motor home south to Venice. It was a cool, sunny morning, and it was a wonderful drive down the coast. Even my voice was making a small comeback. At least I didn't sound like "the Godfather" anymore.

When I got to town, though, it was not the sleepy retirement village I was expecting. The main street was bumper to bumper with station wagons and Winnebagos, filled with northern families heading for the beaches. This seemed more like Orlando, where I had lived while working as an entertainer for Walt Disney World.

It wasn't difficult to find the arena. It was a massive building with giant letters spelling out RINGLING BROTHERS AND BARNUM & BAILEY CIRCUS on the side facing the road. It had been an airplane hangar before Ringling had made the purchase. At first glance it looked like a pretty dismal place, yet the sight of it got my adrenaline flowing.

From the road I could see tiger cages and colorful floats behind it, and men running around setting up various types of rigging. Right away, I knew this old building had seen the great acts honing their talents, tyros walking their first shaky steps on the high wire, and the high jinks of a thousand clowns.

Pulling up to the gate, I was greeted by a wizened old man with darkly tanned skin who was sitting in the guard booth. I rolled down my window and leaned out, looking down onto his liver-spotted skull.

"I'm the new ringmaster," I told him.

The crusty old fellow cocked a clear eye, probed my features, and mouthed his words around the stub of a cigarette held between two crooked, yellow rows of teeth. "Ringmaster? I've seen them all come and go, and you don't look like no ringmaster to me!"

I chuckled. "Well, that's what it says on my contract."

His voice had the gravelly, wheezing sound that only years of smoking a few packs of cigarettes a day can produce. "You know Count Nicholas? Now there was a ringmaster!"

I nodded my head, though I had never heard of the man before in my life. "Yeah, the Count was great," I said.

The lines in his leathered face smoothed out a small fraction. "You like the Count, kid? Well then you can't be all bad!" He pointed a wrinkled hand in the general direction of the arena. "Park over by those other trailers at the side entrance. See you around." He showed me his back and hobbled to the booth.

I parked the trailer by the others, hopped out, and walked into the old arena. There I found a few riggers, and they directed me to Tim Holst's office.

The performance director, however, was not in, and I was welcomed instead by his assistant, Robin Frye. He was a narrow-shouldered man with a wry smile and a wide nose. His light brown hair was parted in the middle over a high forehead.

He shook my hand energetically and spoke with a down-home North Carolina drawl. "Hello, Kristopher, it's so good to see you again. Remember, I met you at the Chicago auditions?"

"That's right," I said. "I remember you perfectly. That whole scene is engraved in my mind forever."

He laughed. "I bet it is."

We discussed the circus, and he gave me pointers about etiquette. In a while, we got around to train life.

"You'll be in my old room I've had for two years. It's pretty nice," he said. "As train rooms go, anyway."

I cleared my throat, still a little hoarse. "I . . . ah . . . borrowed my uncle's motor home. I sort of thought I'd live in that."

He patted me on the shoulder paternally.

"You don't want to do that," he said.

"Why not? I hear a lot of people do it."

He shook his head. "A few. Mostly families and entire acts. They can share driving and expenses. Believe me, it would be pretty time-consuming to do it yourself. Not to mention the money. Traveling on the train is free. All you've got is a ten-dollar-a-week porter fee. No gas money to pay out or anything."

"It doesn't sound like that great an idea then?"

Again he shook his head.

I sat back in my seat, wondering how I was going to fit into this new life. "I guess I have a lot to learn," I told him.

He smiled. "We all do, don't we? It just takes a while."

I rocked back in my chair and took a deep breath. "Yeah. But that's one thing about me. I'm a very impatient person. I want to learn everything right away. I don't want to take a year to learn the circus ropes."

"Kristopher," he said, his voice sympathetic, yet humorous, "it would take a lifetime in The Big Show."

I looked him straight in the eye, and he held my gaze firmly. Finally I shook my head and chuckled. "That just won't satisfy me."

Rehearsals weren't to begin until the next day, and I was happy that my voice and sinuses would have more time to recuperate. So I trotted off to the motor home to hook up the water and electricity. My grandfather had given me a crash course on motor home care just before I left, but I wasn't sure about any of it.

First I turned on the gas. Nothing.

I went outside, twisted the valve to open, and once inside tried to light the stove again. Still nothing.

Suddenly the train didn't seem so bad after all.

Since there were several other motor homes parked there, I figured someone could help me out. I wasn't comfortable enough to go pound on doors, but thought someone might be outside performing some chore or another.

I put my jacket back on and stepped outside. Playing in the branches of a tree next to the big trailer nearby were two children I'd seen in the show up in New York. I walked over to them and looked up. They peered back down like monkeys eyeing a carnivorous beast.

"I'm Kristopher, the new ringmaster," I called up.

They laughed. "We know," they said in unison, in tones that implied I was stupid not to realize this. "We saw you in New York!"

"I didn't know whether you'd remember," I said.

"Of course, we do," said the boy. "We don't get a new ringmaster every day!"

I nodded. "I guess not. I'm looking forward to working with you, but in all honesty I can't remember which act you're with."

They sat comfortably on a high branch and swung their legs. "Eric Braun's our father. We help him."

Braun, I remembered. He was the head of a dog act in which the entire family participated. Their lineage had been connected with the circus for generations in one way or another. Eric himself had been a clown for years, before he had started training his dogs.

"Almost any kid in America would envy you," I said. "It must be exciting to grow up in the middle of a circus, especially The Greatest Show on Earth!"

They shrugged. "It's all right, I guess," said the girl.

———

I decided against trying to find help with the trailer and thought I would just call my grandfather later on. I walked around the property, watching the riggers for a bit. I called my father, but he wasn't home, so I went back to the motor home to watch TV. I spent a restless night, my sleep broken every few minutes by the barking of dogs in the Braun trailer home.

The next morning, feeling bleary and tired, I took a freezing shower. I finally realized there was no propane in the tank to heat the water: the same reason there was no gas for the stove. The icy water, of course, did my cold no good at all.

Feeling mean, I was off to my first day of rehearsals as ringmaster.

There was much more activity this morning when I entered the arena. I spotted the table where Bill Bradley and Crandall Diehl sat and walked across the floor dodging cables and wires. Around them, in the arena stands, were all the performers. As I picked my way around the obstacle course, I looked at these people with whom I would be working. The ones who noticed me did not look happy.

They had been touring for a full year already and were in no mood to spend two weeks rehearsing a show they knew intimately. But they had no choice. Not only was I new here, but several clowns and showgirls had to be introduced into the production numbers as well, since some of the performers had not renewed their contracts after the 1985 tour—or simply, had not been offered the chance. Putting the circus together is not like anything else. It's a major undertaking, encompassing not only performers, lighting, sound, and all the other technical aspects of a show, but also hundreds of animals of many species.

I reached the table.

"Good morning," said Bill Bradley, looking up from a bunch of papers spread before him. He was a ruddy, round-faced guy about sixty, with thinning, silvery hair and devilish blue eyes.

"Likewise," I said. "Good to see you. Got a script for me?"

Both production directors looked at me quizzically.

"Script?" Crandall asked. He was in his fifties, brown-haired, with a sharp chin and a narrow mustache. His blue eyes were more serious then Bill's, but still held a touch of playfulness.

"Yeah. I was told I would get it down here."

Crandall and Bill looked at each other and grinned. "The young man wants a script," Crandall said to Bill. "You got one on you?"

Bill shook his head and frowned, then spoke, forming the words in the side of his mouth. "Never carry one. Don't have any use for it."

Crandall shrugged and looked back up to me. "No scripts here, pal. Maybe one of the performers has one you could borrow."

I looked at them, feeling foolish. I knew they were just having fun, but I was not in the mood for shenanigans.

"Seriously, gentlemen, I don't have a script yet. All I got was a videotape of the production numbers."

Crandall's face took on a more compassionate look. "It's been a year since we put the show together. Tim Holst would be the one to talk to. He carries the entire script up here." He tapped himself on the head. "Better go find him."

I went in search of Tim Holst. Eventually, I cornered him, and we went back to his office. He had written out a few announcements, but no official script or musical score was available. He went over the main lines with me, but I would have to piece things together during the week. After I had what I needed, I walked back to the rings.

When I got there, I found that Kenneth Feld had come down from his office, which overlooked the arena. On this first day of rehearsals he called each act to appear before him. They had been on vacation for five weeks, and he was checking whether they looked sharp.

I took a seat at the table with Diehl and Bradley and watched. Feld was standing in front of a microphone doing roll call, yelling out a bunch of strange-sounding names that I would eventually have to learn to pronounce correctly.

"Okay," Mr. Feld said. "The Kis Faludi from Hungary."

Several fellows jumped from their seats, ran into the ring, and lined up. I was amazed at their youth; some seemed barely teenaged.

Feld continued: "The Dukovi from Bulgaria! From Romania, the Constantins."

Each time, a group of performers leaped from their chairs and hustled into the center ring, lining up. Finally, everyone was down there, and the seats were empty.

After that, Mr. Feld walked up the line inspecting the individuals. Occasionally he gave notes, asking someone to trim his hair, or to make sure he took off a few pounds.

When he was finished, he gestured at me.

"Now I want everyone to meet our new ringmaster, Kristopher Antekeier!"

I stood up and waved to everyone. They all applauded. Though they were clapping, I could feel a few hundred eyes scrutinizing me. I was not the sort of ringmaster they were used to. Dinny was a big, blond man in his late thirties. There I was, a young, dark-haired fellow, on the skinny side, still in my twenties.

Later in the year, one performer confided in me: "The first time I saw you I said to myself, 'This little guy is the ringmaster? They've got to be putting us on!' "

After a short break, we began rehearsal on the opening number, "The Circus Has It All." It was a catchy tune and right in my best range. Dinny had sung it almost casually. I pepped it up, singing with more energy and flair.

My opening dialogue introducing the showgirls was not drawn out as the previous ringmaster's was, and the dancers had to move faster. All morning, they were giving me nasty looks.

A foreign girl took me aside during a break. "Can't you slow it down a little bit?"

I shook my head. "I'm sorry. This is the way the directors want it. They need the show jazzed up; they specifically told me to do it this way."

She gritted her teeth, looking mad, but didn't reply.

All during the day, one person or another took me aside to complain, but I said the same thing. Every so often I looked up at Mr. Feld's office, which loomed over the arena, to see him watching me from the other side of the picture window. I hoped he was satisfied with what he saw.

I had some trouble keeping my lines straight, and my voice was still fairly harsh, but I blustered through the rehearsal. Exhausted at the end of the day, I had dinner, then stumbled into the motor home and fell into bed. I was so tired that not even Braun's yelping dogs could wake me during the night.

The second day of rehearsals was similar to the first, though everything ran smoother. I had my dialogue down pat, and the performers were becoming more accustomed to my style. Every once in a while someone would smile and nod, and I could see they were growing to appreciate my energy.

It was great to be in the middle of such a vast extravaganza with showgirls kicking, clowns juggling, people flipping and tumbling. It was magnificent, and we still had the animals to bring in. Before we could rehearse with them, the humans had to be in perfect sync.

It was another long, hard day. But this time I did not get a rest. Tim Holst had other plans—he was driving me up to St. Petersburg to see the 116th Edition of the circus, which had just debuted there.

This edition was the Blue Unit, equal in size and wealth of entertainment, but with a totally different setup than the Red Unit I was in. Instead of Gunther Gebel Williams's great animal training, this show highlighted the first Chinese acts Kenneth Feld had acquired for an American circus.

But even here, the show revolved around the ringmaster. In this case the man was Jim Ragona. I had read about him in *People* magazine in 1985. His style was very traditional and smooth, as he had been ringmaster for a few years. I was planning to be a very different sort of ringmaster.

After the show, we went backstage.

Tim Holst charged up to the ringmaster. They had known each other for years. "Jim! I want you to meet Kristopher Antekeier."

We shook hands. "That was a great show," I said. "It must be exciting to start out with a new edition after traveling for two years with the same show."

He was still charged up from the performance and spoke in a theatrical manner. "The new acts are great, and I love doing it. All the new stuff really is refreshing."

"Even so," I said, "you've been doing the circus for years

now, hundreds of shows a year. How can you keep the energy up?"

He smiled at me, and in that smile and in his eyes I could see a little boy peering out, the same little boy who had probably sneaked under the tent to see a show. "I'll do it as long as they let me," he said.

Marveling at his enthusiasm, I wondered whether I would be like him at the end of my contract—the circus in my blood, believing I was incredibly fortunate to be living this life. Or would I be like the Braun children, letting it become a grind, unable to appreciate its excitement?

There was only one way to find out. I would have to live it.

A few days later we had progressed through the first act and now were to rehearse the "Unicorn Spec." The "Spec"—short for *Spectacle*—is a traditional part of Ringling Brothers and Barnum & Bailey, and it usually comes at the end of the first act. In past years, this was when Gargantua the Great, an immense gorilla, had been introduced; another Spec was the first giraffe in America, which had caused a sensation in the 1800s. Jumbo, the famous elephant, had premiered here, as had Goliath, the monster sea elephant.

Now, in the 115th Edition of the circus, our Spectacle featured a unicorn. Here, a cast of hundreds paraded around in Renaissance garb as they guided the float with the unicorn perched on top, being stroked by his keeper. This rehearsal, too, was minus the animal in question.

The song I had to sing was a complicated patter song, which I thought I would never learn. To make matters worse, the Braun children stood beside me in this segment of the production. Since they already knew every detail of the show, they would giggle, talk, and make fun of various people who were parading around.

Since I couldn't concentrate and was forgetting my lines, I finally had to grab one of their little arms and say: "Listen, I know you two could do this show in your sleep, but I can't! All I ask is that you let me get through rehearsals, and in a few weeks we can enjoy ourselves a little! All right?"

The tone of my voice was a little rough, and took them by surprise. But it got their attention, and they quieted down.

I could see Mr. Feld watching from his office. He was frowning. Finally, his face disappeared and his body emerged, walking down between the rows of seats. He strode out to me.

"Kristopher," he said, "this has got to be more dramatic! Make the announcement like it's the most important and fascinating thing in the world. Make people scoot to the edge of their seats on this one!" He motioned to Bill Bradley. "Do it again," he said.

But I was nervous now. My palms were sweating, and perspiration dropped from my forehead into my eyes as I repeated the announcement. Kenneth Feld was still not pleased. He made me come into his office and practice with Tim Holst until he thought I was giving the words the proper "oomph." Then we went back into the ring.

The spotlight hit me. I swallowed the bile that rose in my throat and tried to smooth out my voice as best I could. I imagined that I was announcing the most incredible event ever witnessed, something truly wondrous, making the consonants crisp and the vowels long and breathy.

"Ladies and Gentlemen! Children of aaall aaages! In the tradition of Jumbo the Elephant, General Tom Thumb, and Gargantua the Great, Ringling Brothers and Barnum & Bailey Circus once again stretches fantasy to the limits of imaaaagination! As The Greaaatest Show on Earth presents that elusive creature of fable and legend, the sensation of the ages—the living unicorn!"

Then the band struck up a grandiose march, and the lights went dark except for ten spotlights focused on the float where the unicorn would be.

I sang a song extolling the virtue and rarity of the unicorn, while the entire cast of the circus paraded in spectacular regalia. It was an uproarious melee in which a single man in the center could easily be lost, so I tried to make everything I did extraordinarily exciting. When the house lights came back on, I saw Mr. Feld standing next to Bill Bradley and Crandall Diehl. He smiled wryly, seeming pleased, though it was hard to read the man.

Throughout the day, people would come up to me, now with compliments instead of complaints, which made me feel much better. But even so, none of them hung around for conversation, and I was beginning to wonder whether it would be a lonely year.

After rehearsal in the evening, I wandered around the winter quarters again. I found there were designated times in each ring for the different acts to practice. So far, I hadn't seen the individual acts, as we'd only been staging the production numbers. As of yet, no run-throughs of the entire show had taken place.

This evening I watched the teeterboard troupes sharpening their skills. These consisted of the Constantins from Romania, who included several former members of that country's gymnastics team; the Dukovi Troupe from Bulgaria, which had won Grand Prize as Best Foreign Act at a recent International Circus Competition in Warsaw; and the Kis Faludi Troupe from Hungary, an energetic bunch with particularly handsome costumes who had performed all over the world.

My attention was mostly focused on this last troupe. One after the other, they would bounce off the seesaw apparatus, fly through the air, and land upright on their comrades' shoulders until they were stacked in a three-man high. In the climax of the act a boy, the youngest and smallest of the troupe, did a double backward somersault onto a five-man high. The daring and professionalism of such a young performer amazed me.

Afterward, the boy rode up to me on his bike. He stopped beside me and leaned forward, reaching out a hand which I shook.

"Hi, I'm Attila," he said.

He had light hair in a pageboy cut and looked very American to me: not at all my idea of Eastern Bloc European. But his thick Hungarian accent gave him away.

"Nice to meet you," I said. "You're pretty good out there."

His smile fell, and his eyes widened. He rammed a finger against his lips and said, "Ssshhh! No let anyvone hear you say dat!"

"They might get jealous?"

He nodded, and replied with absolute conviction in his voice, "De Hungarians are de best in de worl!"

"I'll remember that," I told him.

He smiled widely, showing perfect teeth. There was a peculiar elfin quality about him. "Somevone's got to teach you dese t'ings!"

I laughed. "Usually my teachers are older."

"But not alvays," he said, winking at me.

I nodded thoughtfully, thinking to myself that he was a lucky kid to be so worldly at such an early age.

Sigrid Gebel approached me while I was sitting in the stands watching the teeterboard troupes practice. Her movement was regal and graceful. She wore large, glittery earrings and a new pair of designer jeans, looking a little too classy and out of place around these circus folks.

"You seem much more like a ringmaster now," she said, smiling. "Did you gain any weight?"

I chuckled and motioned her to sit beside me. "I told you not to worry!"

She clucked her tongue. "I know, but it was just too hard to imagine. But you're doing good work." Instead of sitting down she took my hand and tugged on it. "Come with me. I want you to meet my family."

She took me outside to where her daughter, Tina, a young woman in her twenties, was commanding a pack of wolfhounds, and Mark Oliver Gebel, only sixteen, was tending to the elephants. His nickname, I learned, was Buffy. He did not have quite the smile of his father, but he tried to hard emulate his father's charisma.

It was good meeting them like this, Sigrid commanding the honors, obviously giving me her approval. Now, at least, I was beginning to feel less like an outsider.

At the end of the first week, I received exactly seventy-five dollars for rehearsal pay and was further surprised to have it paid in two-dollar bills. Apparently, the city of Venice had been complaining about having the circus in town, declaring the old arena an eyesore and the influx of circus people an annual plague. Kenneth Feld decided to pay everyone in two-dollar bills so local merchants could see exactly how much money Ringling would bring to the area each year. All complaints were quickly retired. This was the first incident that demonstrated Feld's particular brilliance to me.

Things became more kinetic over the next few days, with smoothing out the routines, getting cues more snappy, repairing props, exercising, improving talents. Of everyone, it was the clowns who had the most work to do.

After a long day of rehearsals I watched them practice in the ring. Most of them were between eighteen and twenty-five years of age, and they had diverse talents.

During a break, one fellow shuffled over and fell into the chair beside me. He wore loose-fitting clothes and, of course, no makeup. His eyes were brown, deep and watery, very sad-looking, and his eyebrows had a downcast bent to them. He looked as much like a clown without paint as with it. He was sweating and breathless.

"I'm Dave," he said.

"Glad to meet you," I said. "How do you learn all this stuff? All those pratfalls, the stilt walking, the juggling aren't everyday skills!"

He laughed and wiped some sweat from his brow, shaking his hand free of it onto the floor. "We all went to college for it," he said.

I chuckled and smiled. Here was another circus person taking advantage of my naivete. "That's some degree. What was your major—falling on your behind?"

"No, really, we all went to Clown College. It's the only way you can get into Ringling these days. It's something Mr. Feld's father, Irvin, set up about twenty years ago. It's a ten-week course, and when you graduate you can audition for a spot in the circus— if there are any openings."

"Really?" I thought this was amazing.

"That's right."

I found out they studied everything, including juggling, walking on stilts, mime, acting, makeup, and pratfalls. They had to develop skits and "bits" to show to Mr. Feld and—as in any college—were required to study the masters. Only, instead of reading Shakespeare and Tolstoy, they watched old movies of Laurel and Hardy, the Three Stooges, Abbott and Costello, and of course Charlie Chaplin and Buster Keaton, along with other great physical comedians. They were taught by famous clowns passing down their knowledge to the next generations.

Not all of those performing were young, however. The most senior of our current Red Unit was Duane Thorpe, known in makeup as "Uncle Soapy." He had been with "The Big Show" since the 1950s and was immortalized in the movie *The Greatest Show on Earth*.

Through the rehearsal period, I had seen the clowns running back to their special area of the arena called "Clown Alley," and only clowns went inside. I did not know whether others weren't allowed or they just plain wouldn't go in.

"What do you do back there?" I asked Dave.

He moved his eyebrows up and down rapidly and spoke in a silly voice making odd clicking sounds. "All sorts of wild and crazzzy things. You wouldn't believe it! That's where we do all our brainstorming to figure out new gags and bits. We have to be in top form." He hunched forward and whispered, looking hastily around as if imparting a big secret. "The Nurembergs are tonight, you know."

"The what?"

He smiled crookedly, looking a little demented. "It's the Nurembergs. The trials. We all go in front of Mr. Feld and strut our stuff, show him our acts. He handpicked us out of the graduating class, and now we show him our bits and gags, hoping we can use them in The Big Show."

That night I, along with many of the other performers, made my way into the arena. We sat in the stands and watched as the clowns entered in full costume. Each one was different, having invented his or her own style of face makeup and character. You couldn't decipher the sexes, let alone any individual characteristics. I only recognized Dave because he waved at me. I realized then that I would not only have to memorize every clown but every costume as well!

Mr. Feld sat behind a long table with an album containing photographs of each clown in and out of makeup. As the clowns walked up to Mr. Feld he studied their makeup and either okayed it or indicated some aspect he did not like. Some had changed their makeup from the previous seasons, and others who had just graduated from Clown College were having theirs critiqued for the first time.

The next three hours consisted of all the clowns' auditioning their gags and skits. Some were hilarious, and some weren't even funny, just like comedy teams writing acts and jokes and trying them out for the first time. You had to see what went over well with an audience, cut things down, and hone the parts that worked best.

One of the cleverest bits was "Door in the Floor." Two clowns pranced out and laid a door flat against the floor of the arena. Then one opened it, and the two stepped inside, disappearing somehow into its depths, as if they were descending into a cellar. There was no trapdoor or hole in the concrete floor. They mimed the action by bending their knees. But from our perspective it looked as if they were walking down stairs. Then they reappeared, carrying a bird cage on a pole. They brought that out and went back for more stuff. Soon they had emerged with an entire sofa. It looked amazing. In actuality it was simple: all this furniture was collapsible and attached underneath the door where it could not be seen. But simplicity can be best.

There were different terms used to describe the clown gags.

A "track gag" is performed in place along the track of the arena floor in front of the rings, creating a diversion while Gunther readied his tigers or when another act had to be positioned.

A "walk around" is a single sight gag, a sort of pun. One clown was dressed as a big kite flying a Cabbage Patch doll. Another clown carried around a basket with a sign that read TEST TUBE BABY. He'd pull out a giant test tube with eyes, nose, and a pacifier stuck in its mouth, wearing a bonnet. Walk arounds were also used as diversions but weren't stationary like track gags. Each walk around gag would circle the track at least once, while nets were being set up for the flying trapeze act.

All through the evening Mr. Feld jotted notes, snickered, or looked stoic. At the end, he thanked them all and gathered up what he had written. He would let them know the next day. I know a lot of clowns spent a sleepless night. We all made bets on which bits would stay.

The next day, I was glad to find out that Dave's act had been approved. It was a walk around he had created by converting a hound-dog costume. He traipsed around the arena as a huge dog

carrying a poor dogcatcher in a net. His energy and lunacy added
to the madcap presentation.

I was sitting on the steps of my motor home, eating a peanut
butter sandwich during the afternoon break, when Robin Frye
came loping up, dust kicking from the heels of his shoes. "Are
you still figuring on traveling in your motor home?" he asked.
    "There hasn't been time to give it much thought," I said with
my mouth full, as I chewed.
    "Well, when you're finished, I thought I'd take you over to
the train and show you my old room. It's not much, but there's
a lot of people salivating over it, if you don't want it. I'm lucky.
Mr. Feld is having them build me a custom cabin, nearly half a
train car!"
    I finished my sandwich and we made for the train, going
behind the big arena. There were cages with tigers lounging inside, their hefty bodies spread across vast amounts of floor space.
They had a lazy way of shifting their heads to watch you pass,
but you could see an intense interest in their eyes. Suddenly I
wondered about the sanity of a man who would actually enter
a cage full of these beasts, whip or no whip.
    To tell the truth, I had never really cared for animals, so
landing a job where I was surrounded by them was a trifle scary.
I can't really point to any particular childhood incident that
might have traumatized me, but I've always had this sort of vis-
ceral distrust for anything that could not be reasoned with. Not
surprisingly, tigers magnified my paranoia to new heights. In
their gazes you could see a primal urge that even a well-fed belly
might not hamper under the right circumstances.
    In the history of the circus, there have been several famous
animal trainers who have been fatally mauled by their beasts.
There is no such thing as a tame tiger.
    "Watch out for when the tails go up," Robin told me. "That
means they're about to spray, and if it hits you, you'll stink for
a week!"
    This area was the most circusy of any place around. The
smell of hay and elephants wafted through the air, along with
the odor of dung and feed. The trumpeting of the big-eared animals mixed with the neighs of horses, the grunts of camels, and

the throaty growl of tigers. Human voices rounded out the atmosphere, with sweaty bodies engaged in a multitude of chores, hoisting bags of feed, hosing down animals, and cleaning up their messes. The riggers squatted down, measuring, cutting, and splicing cable.

Behind this maze was a wide open field. We crossed it, traversed a bridge over a narrow stream, and walked down a short, dead-end road with tall weeds growing at the sides. Parked in this desolate area was the Ringling train, which had its own track that eventually led into the main line. Hooked together, the train would be about a mile long, with forty-six separate cars. It was so long and heavy, carrying every single piece of circus equipment and supplies, that sometimes three engines were needed to pull it up hills.

Not surprisingly, the train cars were in worse shape than I had imagined. The dirty cars looked like they had been manufactured in the early days of rail, and never maintained since then.

These, however, were the animal carriers, and we did at least step into the latter half of the twentieth century when we arrived at the passenger cars. They had the dull shine of the wrong side of tinfoil, with a broad red stripe down the side with circusy white lettering that proclaimed RINGLING BROS. AND BARNUM & BAILEY CIRCUS.

I had seen the train in New York, when I had passed over it on the elevated subway. But from that distance it had looked exciting. Now it looked rusty and unsafe. The edges of the big steel wheels were the only part that looked clean, as they had been polished by the rails during untold thousands of miles of travel.

Robin looked at my face and laughed. "I know it doesn't look like much, but it's better inside."

I lifted my eyebrows and gave him what I hoped was a disbelieving look. I did not need to say anything else.

We shuffled down the line of passenger cars until we arrived at one that looked no better than the others.

"Here it is!" he said with an enthusiastic tone.

"Great!" I answered.

"Come on up."

He jumped onto a metal stair that descended from the space between cars. The first step was over three feet high, probably to clear any obstruction that might be on the ground, I guessed. He reached down a hand and helped me aboard. He motioned toward a covered space between cars, which provided access from one to another with a waist-high rail with a half-door cut into it.

"This is the vestibule," he said. "When you're traveling, you end up spending a lot of time out here."

He opened the door into the car. There was a hallway that ran down one side. We walked past three doors until we arrived at the end of the passageway about halfway down the length. This door had a decal of a roaring tiger stuck to it.

I thought it wouldn't be too bad if I had a whole half-car.

"Here you are," he said and opened the door theatrically.

I stepped inside and found a much smaller room than I had expected. It was the full width of the train, but only about eight feet long. It had dark wood paneling, a small kitchen area to the left (with two hot plates and a pint-sized fridge), a table between two booths like a cafeteria's and a window on either end. The carpeting was gray. It was obvious that it had once been white.

"Where's the rest of it?" I asked.

He pointed toward an accordionlike door across from us, built into a small square closet that jutted into the corner of the room. "There's the bathroom."

I shook my head. "I don't understand. Where's the rest of the train car?"

He smiled, his brow wrinkling in amusement. "On the other side of that wall, is where. There's another room on the other side; you can't get to it from here. That's Richard Slayton's room; he's head of concessions, so he's pretty well taken care of."

I moved into the room, followed by Robin.

"There's no bed," I said.

He strode over to the booths, reached under the table, and lifted it out of its brackets in the wall. The table lowered until it was flush with the booths. "There it is. The seat cushions go over it, like a motor home or a boat."

One step took me over to the bathroom. I found a tiny toilet and a narrow shower. There was no sink.

"That's your donniker," he said.

"What's that?"

He smiled. "It's an old circus word for a portable toilet. You have to shave over here," Robin said, indicating the sink in the kitchen. "It's a little inconvenient, but you'll get used to it."

Next he opened a small closet. "This is bigger than it looks," he told me. "There are shelves in here. Interesting story about this, you know. Before I had this place one of the act people lived here. Had a monkey he kept in this space. You can still smell him in here! When I moved in, I had one of the midget clowns get inside and construct the shelves."

"Only in the circus," I said and laughed. "I think I'll keep the motor home. No offense."

He nodded his head. "You can if you want. But I've looked at your vehicle. It costs an average of five thousand dollars a year for the maintenance, gas, and oil on one of those suckers."

"Five thousand dollars!" My voice echoed in the small room.

"Maybe more. Depends on whether anything major should go wrong. You're traveling a lot of miles, remember."

I took a look around the cabin. It was dingy and old and claustrophobic. "Well," I said, "I guess this is my new home."

As the week progressed, I became more polished and more satisfied with my work. Eventually, we started run-throughs in costume. Or rather, everyone did but me. My costumes had not yet arrived from New York City.

Everything was lavish, and it was a thrill to be in the center of so much glitz. Rhinestones sparkled, gold thread shone, and mirrors reflected the lights. Millions of dollars were spent on these costumes, which had to be replaced with each new edition.

The day came when one of the directors shouted, "Okay, we're going to bring in the elephants!"

I hadn't rehearsed with the animals yet, and the idea scared me. I hightailed it up to the top row of the arena seats, where I could see everything from a safe vantage.

Robin looked up, saw me, and started laughing. He loved animals, especially elephants, and each pachyderm knew his personalized whistle intimately.

"Look who's scared!" he teased loudly. "How can we have a ringmaster who *doesn't like animals?*"

"Oh, I like them," I yelled back. "I like them as far away from me as possible! I'm just going to sit up here and watch until I figure out the best place to stand down there!"

He was right though. I kept thinking: "How am I ever going to handle being up close to these critters for a full year?" But eventually, they cajoled me down, and I found the animals to be only a little less friendly than the performers.

On January 17, the unicorn was brought in for the first time. Up close, there was no mistaking him for anything else but a goat with one horn. Realizing I would have to protect the intrigue of the animal by actually believing it to be what it was supposed to be, I figured I ought to have a talk with Heather Harris, the unicorn keeper.

Heather had been a showgirl with the circus for a few years and had groomed poodles in her spare time to make extra money. The circus may look a little like a Las Vegas show, but the pay is much lower. Many performers take on extra tasks to improve their pitiful earnings. Gunther Gebel Williams and Mr. Feld had spotted her grooming talents and had chosen her to take care of the unicorn.

I was sitting on a wooden stool outside the arena, with the cages all around, while she brushed the long, fleecy hair of the one-horned animal. It was getting toward sunset, and the animal's shiny coat reflected the orange rays of the sun. Heather was a small-boned, platinum-blond beauty.

"I call him Sweetheart," she said. "He's really the nicest creature I've ever seen. When I was a girl, I always knew a unicorn would look like this."

I cleared my throat and tried to be tactful. "Did you ever think a unicorn might look more . . . ah . . . horselike?"

Her hand stopped. She leveled a cold, blue-eyed stare at me. "What exactly do you mean by that?"

My voice froze in my throat. "Nothing," I finally managed to say.

Her gaze remained steady; her words became hard-edged. "I know what you're trying to say. I've heard it often enough before. Those newspapers in New York just wouldn't quit!" Here her voice became mocking. " 'It's a goat! It's a goat,' they said, 'a goat that's had a horn surgically implanted in its forehead.' Well, the ASPCA X-rayed him endlessly and they didn't find any evidence of the kind."

"It grew like that?" I asked.

"It sure did. I mean, there might have been some laser grafting or something to fuse the horns together when he was a kid—" Her voice cut off and she looked around nervously. "But don't tell anyone I ever told you that. The circus veterinarian told me in confidence. But since you're ringmaster, you should know the secret."

"Thanks," I said.

"And as far as looking like a goat is concerned?" she continued. "Well, there's a tapestry of a unicorn hanging in the Metropolitan Museum of Art, given to them by John D. Rockefeller, Jr., in something like 1937. The tapestry itself, though, was made sometime in the 1500s and the unicorn in it looks *exactly* like Sweetheart here. So who's to say a unicorn doesn't have some goatlike characteristics?"

I put my hand up and laughed. "Okay, I give up already!"

Her expression softened. "I'm sorry. It's just that I've heard so much about it. I just gave you the same speech I give all the newspapers."

"It's all right. I'm glad you believe in him so much. Where did Feld get him?"

Again she looked around to make sure we were alone. "It was in 1985 when the circus was in Texas. An animal breeder brought him and a couple of his brothers over. He'd had them on display in a petting zoo, and a few mud shows and carnivals. So they'd been around a while before Kenneth found them and manufactured all the publicity!"

"That Feld's amazing," I said. "Well, I for one am a believer, as far as the unicorn is concerned. I have to be, if I'm going to bring it across to the audience. As you say, who's to know what's real in this world and what's not? You gottta believe what you see with your own eyes."

She nodded her head and went back to brushing. "Thanks," she said.

"I remember seeing him in New York," I told her. "The Spec is really beautiful: you wearing that metallic purple and gold dress, up there on that gold float, with the unicorn poised beside you. It's really a sight! How do you get that pearly cloud to hover above him like that?"

She laughed. "I coat him with baby powder before the show. It doesn't stick to him because I shampoo him in Woolite." She smiled mischievously. "I'm like any smart American girl. I trust all my fine washables to Woolite."

My costumes finally arrived during the second week of rehearsals. Custom-designed and fitted for me by the New York costume designer, there were three different sets gleaming as they hung on a rack in the wardrobe department, each one in a different color scheme: one red, another green, and the third magenta. The jackets were embroidered with millions of stitches, making big and small swirls. Inside the larger curves were metallic sequins. Each outfit was coordinated down to the top hat and had cost over twenty-five hundred dollars. The only things similar in all three were a black bow tie, a white tuxedo shirt, and white gloves. Each outfit also had black tux pants and shiny black shoes.

As I donned my costume for the first time I thought to myself, "Now I feel like the ringmaster!" My posture straightened, and the role finally came to life.

My only problem was that I couldn't find any black socks to wear with the outfit.

Walking stiffly in the new material of the magenta ensemble, I appeared in the arena, where everyone was waiting for a full dress rehearsal. I saw the hundreds of eyes perk up as I entered. Finally their new ringmaster actually looked the part. People whistled and applauded. I strode to the center bull tub, bent down, and pulled up my pants cuff, revealing my old white, multistriped athletic socks. The entire cast exploded into laughter.

Actually feeling like a ringmaster was so exciting that that evening I phoned everyone I knew who could possibly come to see me. I had friends in Clearwater who would come to a dress rehearsal in a week, and my mother told me she was flying all the way from Seattle, where she was living, and would be at opening day with my sister and my niece.

That evening I was requested to attend a production meeting in Mr. Feld's office. The only reference he made about me was directed to the wardrobe supervisor.

"Kristopher's opening costume isn't hanging right in the back. Tack the tails together."

I couldn't believe the man's eye for detail!

It was dawn on January 23, a Thursday. I rolled over in my bunk in the motor home and groaned when I saw the orange light filtering through the slats of blinds. As tired as I was, I had not slept much that night. The dogs next door conspired to keep me awake, but it was the thoughts in my head that were the real culprits. The show was officially opening today—and I was not ready.

All night, my various announcements had whispered through my head. They were all there, but they were not filed correctly. Some always wanted to come out before their time; others seemed to be buried under the wrong headings further back and did not show up for their cues. The main announcements were all there, yet there were dozens of shorter pieces that had to be perfectly timed as, for instance, just before a trapeze artist did a triple somersault. Even the slightest distraction could throw off your timing.

I had finally come to realize that the responsibility of the job was enormous. It was possible that an announcement uttered at the wrong time could hurl the entire show into disarray. Someone could even be injured. What if I said it was time for the triple somersault, and it was supposed to be a full twisting double layout? An instant of confusion might cause a performer to miss a hold and fall to his death.

I had also not gotten used to the animals, as we had been performing with them for just three days. The size and force of two dozen elephants dancing a few feet away, horses galloping in a dizzying frenzy around me as tigers leaped and growled menacingly was very disconcerting.

All this plagued my dreams that night, and my mind was hazy in the morning.

I tried to console myself, remembering that the dress rehearsals and the "preview" performances had not gone badly. But, on the other hand, none had gone exactly right. Something had messed up in every show. Not that an elephant getting out of line was my fault, not that I could do anything about a cranky tiger, or a fallen teeterboardist, but neither was I skilled enough at this point to cover it all up, to ad-lib, stall for time, or speed things up precisely as the situation demanded.

So now, in a few hours, I would be in the spotlight and on the spot. The critics would be there. The reporters would be there. And most nerve-racking of all, my grandparents, my mother, my brother, my sister, and my five-year-old niece would be sitting in one of the front center rows.

There was no use trying to trick myself into sleeping. I got up and made some hot chocolate. At least I could do this, because Heather, who had traveled in a motor home for a year, had come over and shown me how to hook up everything. After Lakeland, I wouldn't have to worry about it, because my father was picking up the trailer there and I would then move into my room on the train.

It was a haggard ringmaster who reported for duty at ten o'clock. I sat there in my bare, makeshift, dingy blue dressing room looking in a hand mirror, considering the use of makeup to hide the bags under my eyes. I decided my tan would have to do.

"Hey there, Kristopher?" someone said. I was expecting Mr. Feld to come give me a pep talk.

"Come in," I said.

Robin Frye stuck his head between the curtains, flashing me a harried smile.

"Break a leg!" he told me.

"Thanks." My voice was not lively.

He narrowed his eyebrows. "Don't worry, you'll be great." Somebody tapped him on the shoulder. He looked away, said something real fast, and turned back to me. "All right, I gotta go. See you in the ring!"

Tim Holst came by a minute later to give me an even briefer message of assurance. Mr. Feld was apparently busy elsewhere. My only other visitor was Tina Gebel.

She stood in the center of the room with her hands on her hips, looking annoyed, as she demanded to borrow some hair spray.

I shook my head.

She looked puzzled. "You don't use hair spray? Dinny always had hair spray!"

"I'm sorry, Tina. I never use the stuff."

She shook her head. "I don't believe you. How do you keep that perfect hair in place?"

I smiled. "It's like this naturally. Really!"

"Hmmh!" she said, then turned her back and left, uttering not a single word of confidence.

I took my opening costume from its hanger, holding it to the naked light bulb, seeing the magenta sequins flash. I pulled on the pants, then the white shirt and bow tie, and bent down and tied my shoes. A glimmer of energy tingled in my fingers. I stood up, put on my orange vest, feeling it close around my chest. I then took the magenta jacket with an orange and yellow lapel and slipped it on. For the first time I realized the great weight of the costume, which I had to carry for an energetic two-hour show. It probably added twenty pounds to my frame.

I stepped into the hallway and was dazzled by the commotion. People seemed to be in "fast forward," their movements quick and jerky, as they got ready for the show. Somehow, this atmosphere made something in me click.

I looked down at my glittering costume, realizing my position in the show, and the tiny bud of energy I had felt now blossomed. I could feel a surge in my chest, rushes of energy sweeping through my body, my heart beating in my chest so hard I could almost sense the way it made the blood rush through my arteries.

This was why I was in show business.

It was not just the adulation from the audience, but these

sudden feelings of pure unadulterated life force that made my brain work at high speed and my body seem strong enough to lift an elephant. Each performance was a unique experience with its own natural highs.

I could never understand why people took drugs. I had never had an urge for them, knowing that there was no artificial feeling that could rival what I felt now.

The fatigue fell from my bones; my muscles limbered up; the fog was expelled from my mind.

I heard the band strike up the overture for the show. Instantly the commotion around me grew into a flurry. Robin Frye came running past and snapped his fingers.

"You're on!" he said and then was gone.

I jumped into gear and walked briskly to the curtains, drew them back, and stepped through. In front of me was a wall of people. On both sides, that wall continued in a circle around the arena. I had never seen such a crowd from this vantage point before. Being a part of a crowd just *wasn't* the same. No performance in the past had prepared me for the scrutiny of four thousand excited people, eight thousand eyes. Suddenly the audience broke into applause. The noise was deafening down in the center ring.

I smiled and raised my hand. The noise became immense. Shouts and whistles added to the din.

The house went dark, the band stopped, and there was a drum roll to build excitement. The power of ten spotlights fell on me, setting my tux ablaze, the rhinestones flashing as my body moved. I stood on the little stage in the middle ring and looked around at the darkness. The light in my eyes was so intense I could not see beyond it. Yet I knew the crowd was there. I could hear them and I could smell them. I knew my family was out there, only a few feet away, their eyes focused keenly on my every move, hanging on every word I spoke.

I took my microphone and propelled my voice into it like a javelin. It was amplified a thousand times and vibrated through the air.

"Ladies and gentlemen! Children of all ages! Producer Kenneth Feld proudly presents the One Hundred and Fifteenth Edition of Ringling Brothers and Barnum & Bailey Circus, The Greatest Show on Earth!"

The crowd went wild. These were local people, and the Venice and Sarasota population was as proud of their circus as any town with a winning Super Bowl team. And I was their quarterback.

I went through my opening lines, wanting to make the entire event the most magical and special moment in anyone's life.

"And now, the eternal clowns," I said. "A mountain of mirth to entertain you!"

A wide spotlight lighted ring one and showed a pyramid of clowns who were standing on steps of a platform so they resembled a hill. As I said this, they jumped up like a flower blossoming and then spread across the ring, making faces, doing flips, and acting crazy.

A ripple of laughter drifted down to my ears. I turned and gestured at the other ring. "We have girls, girls, girls to delight us, excite us, and invite us to discover that the circus has it all!"

That ring lighted as I said this, and the showgirls, dressed in dazzling costumes that matched the colors of my tux, with high ostrich plumes waving above them, sprang out and stepped lively around the circle as the band started a rollicking tune. Then they crossed to the runway, merging with the clowns, and paraded down the front and back tracks. In moments the entire arena was lighted, and horses, elephants, and other performers joined the melee. I sang a song praising the circus and extolling the virtues of the unicorn they would see.

When I finished I introduced the first act. "And now three rings of circus Liberty horses, presented by the Gebel family!"

The entire Gebel clan ran out, arms raised. Gunther, dressed in red with gold embroidery, bowed, and the crowd became ecstatic. The Liberty horses pranced out behind him, their hooves striking the ground in perfect unison. Untethered, they performed an energetic dance in which they became special formations of twos, threes, and fours. The height of the act was when he ordered a beautiful bay to stand on its hind legs and walk around the ring. While he did this, Sigrid and Tina directed their own horses to gallop around in the other rings. All was awhirl. It was a universe of movement underneath the vaulted tin roof.

When the acts were finished, the family dramatically took their bows in the spotlights while the audience voiced their enthusiasm.

Then the "walk around" clowns jumped to their tasks: Uncle Soapy showing off his puppet monkey in a bunch of bananas, the test tube baby, the clown dressed as a kite flying a kid. The lights were bright now, and I could see the rows upon rows of adults and children.

The kids' eyes glistened, their faces rapt with wonder. It was wondrous being in the center of all this laughter and good feeling.

Meanwhile, the riggers had mounted the nets and it was time for the trapeze act.

I announced the Flying Españas with an awe-inspired voice, as I looked high into the air and saw these blue-suited figures in tights posing, "styling" for the audience, one group over ring one, another group over ring three. The Españas were a big family that included a few non-relatives, all from Mexico. Each troupe started with simple leaps and holds and various pairings, the moves becoming more complicated as the music built.

"And now," I announced when the music stopped, "the most difficult trick on the flying trapeze! The legendary triple somersault above rings one and three!" I gestured magnificently at the rings on either side of the center. The drums rolled with drama. I stood there and watched with the same attention as the audience, my eyes glued to the performers.

We had only done two full run-throughs of the show before this opening, and I was as truly amazed at the acts as even the most attentive child in the seats. The only thing to hamper my total involvement was the next lines running through my head. Of course, I also knew that not only was this not the first time this triple somersault had been attempted, but that these seasoned performers could almost do it in their sleep and, after a three-show day during the previous year, probably had.

The performers took their bows and I continued. "Our celebrated collection of crazy clowns bring back those glamorous days of Hollywood!"

Two comical characters pose with me in Knoxville, Tennessee.
That's Dave on the right, just before he left the show.

The inside label of one of my exquisite, tailor-made costumes.
(Brian Masck/*The Muskegon Chronicle*)

Honorary
ringmasters Pat Sajak
and Vanna White.
(Vanna wasn't about
to be out-sequinned
by me!)

The Kenneth Feld
eating popcorn with
the Russian girl in
Washington, D.C.
(AP/Wide World Photos)

Gunther took the time for a photo with me just before I entered the ring for the last time.

The unicorn is taken into custody by the police in Daytona Beach! Keeper Heather is distressed, as Sweetheart, wearing his protective cardboard horn cylinder, wonders what all the hubbub is about. (Michael Takash/*Daytona Beach News-Journal*)

The many uses of a train yard.
Left: A makeshift clothesline
put up between cars was a
familiar sight. (Ron Otis)
Below: Two workingmen grill
a steak over railroad ties.
(Ron Otis)

Mr. Feld's right-hand man, former ringmaster Tim Holst, and me.

Susie Turcot and I posing (*not* eating!) in the pie car. It never looked this good in real life.

Robin and Sarahjane,
performance directors.
(No, SJ never wore a
plume; it belongs to the
horse behind her.)

Marc Lafontant and Susie
in my room.

Here I am in my train room. Not bad, eh? I was never without a jar
of JIF Creamy Peanut Butter.

A small replica of a Model-T Ford, painted in preposterous colors, rolled into the arena and came to rest in ring three. Uncle Soapy, dressed in a chauffeur's uniform, rolled out a red carpet and opened the door. One after another, clowns sprang forth dressed as famous comedians and stars. As I announced them, out came bizarre caricatures of Chaplin, Buster Keaton, Laurel and Hardy, W. C. Fields, Rudolf Valentino, Carmen Miranda, Tarzan, Will Rogers, Mae West, King Kong, Shirley Temple, Sherlock Holmes, and finally Frankenstein, towering above them all. These clowns did not come from a hole in the floor. They all rode out inside the gutted car and had to shove themselves inside, back to back and belly to belly, every show to achieve the effect.

After this came the animal antics of the Eric Braun dogs in the center ring, the Reinand chimpanzees in ring one, and Tina Gebel's trained Russian wolfhounds in ring three—all going on at the same time. The chimps clowned on a tightrope, the Braun dogs jumped through hoops and pretended to need enticing to do so, and the wolfhounds jumped over a high bar and ended up twirling one of their number around on a swiveling stage.

Next Eric Braun balanced a poodle on his forehead, as the poodle stood upside down on his forepaws and nose, and then catapulted the dog from a seesaw into the air, to land perfectly in that same handstand position on Eric's hand. After that, he took a small stage and put it on top of a high pole, and the dog posed on that as Eric balanced the whole contraption on his forehead, the dog twenty feet in the air.

The chimps rode tiny two-wheeled bikes and unicycles. Later, a chimp stood on a seesawing board on top of a rolling pin while balancing two plates on sticks. Meanwhile, all the boring wolfhounds did was run in circles.

At the climax of Braun's act he took the five-year-old poodle and sent it forty feet high, riding in a basket dangling from a helium balloon. The brave animal then had to jump through the air into Braun's waiting arms.

Eric, his wife, and their children—who were all involved in the act—took their bows, as did the Reinands and Miss Tina, all simultaneously.

Next came the teeterboard troupes doing an age-old act called *Charivari*, in which the special acrobatic stunts are comical. These men and women came from all over the world. Some were famous gymnasts in their respective countries.

Next came Sabu. His was a dangerous aerial act performed without a net. He was a short, Aztec-looking Indian from Mexico, with a body formed of muscle. Without touching the wires, he made the trapeze bar turn in circles until the two suspending ropes were twisted around each other. He balanced on a chair, sitting with only the back legs touching the bar, the front ones in the air. Then he switched the legs so that two diagonal ones took the weight as he did handstands.

The crowd loved this one and oohed and aahhed.

At the climax of his act, Sabu stood on the bar and, without touching the ropes, made it swing in a wide arc. He then sat down, balanced in a peculiar pose, and snatched a handkerchief with his teeth from where it was draped over the trapeze bar near his feet.

Now it was time for the Spectacle. My heart pounded and my palms sweated rivers.

Some of the music was appropriated from a Broadway show called *Baby*, with very catchy tunes. Our words were different, though. I stood in the middle of a circular stage painted a pastel purple, a short, fake stone rail around it, which was supposed to look Elizabethan or Renaissance.

Clowns towed out four big floats in the shapes of winged horses and cajoled kids from the audience to take a ride. Each kid was fitted with a paper unicorn hat.

The showgirls wore incredible costumes with wide colorful capes and high, coned hats trailing long diaphanous veils.

I incorporated some funny steps—à la Dick Van Dyke—and funny arm and hand movements while singing about our "genuine, superfine, one-of-a-kind" unicorn.

Every second the extravaganza multiplied in force. And as it did so, a thousand flashbulbs exploded in the audience as people snapped pictures. I felt like a tiny speck in the middle of it all. Out came elephants draped with giant tapestries of shining gold thread with unicorns embossed on them. Following the elephants were dozens of horses ridden by fellows dressed as noblemen. There were showgirls dressed as belly dancers and more elephants draped in Arabian tapestries. Clowns, harlequins, jugglers, and acrobats; hundreds of people, elephants, and horses on the floor. Another troupe came out carrying a giant inflated balloon in the shape of a bird. The lights played on an awe-inspiring mass of rhinestones, a million dollars in costumes parading in front of everybody, a hundred Las Vegas shows put together, the music and my voice above it all!

Then, while girls twirled, skirts whirled, white horses danced, and elephants pranced, a drum roll rattled through the air.

I stood straight and gestured with my high top hat in my hand. My voice was as mellifluous and rich as I could make it, tinged with promises of great things to come. "The frontier of reality is left behind as we cross into a time and place filled with awesome splendor, a world where comical creatures and beastly buffoons frolic in the spotlight of your mind! Find the limits of your imagination and behold the sensation of the ages, the living unicorn!" I held up my hands triumphantly.

A float appeared, spotlights glowing on it. It was colored a light purple, with a base fashioned like clouds holding up a giant, golden shell. In the shell was the beautiful Heather wearing her gown of purple and gold. She stroked the unicorn, that well-fed beast, that fleecy animal which stood with its front feet propped up on a platform, exhibiting his horn. The music changed to a minor key, with booming drums behind it.

As the float glided out to the runway, six girls with butterfly wings dropped from above and flew in circles over each ring. The music broke back into the *Baby* tune, and I sang again, my voice filled with enthusiasm.

All this time, I was having fun with my "isms" (my own word for physical performing traits unique to any particular individual). I did crazy steps and funny shoulder movements all integrated into an energetic, loose-jointed dance a little like the scarecrow in *The Wizard of Oz*. I also loved to gesture grandly with my hat. Finally, I ended the song on an uplifting note.

And all this was just the end of the first act!

It was a breathless intermission. I changed costumes and

drank a glass of juice, even though I was thirsty enough to drink a river, but that could pose a danger during the show.

Before I knew what was happening, a circus publicist grabbed me and whisked me off to a phone.

"What's happening?" I asked.

"It's an interview," he told me in a nonchalant voice.

"Now? Now?! I've only got minutes to get ready for the second half!"

"That's why they want to do it now. While you're all pumped up."

I shook my head, let out a breath, and got on the phone.

"Hi," I said.

"Hello," came a vivacious female voice. "I'm calling from Cincinnati for *USA Today*. We're doing a follow-up on your story from when you got the job. How do you feel?"

"I feel great," I told her, "like I'm on the peak of a roller-coaster ride, or on a cloud that will never come down. It's like playing in the biggest production of *Barnum* ever conceived!"

"Thanks," the voice said, exuberantly. "That's all I need."

When I came out of the office, performers were in a frenzy preparing for the next act. Though I was hyped up, I could not believe I had to go out there and do a whole next half. It seemed the show should be over. Then a thought hit me. Not only did I have another half, but after that—a whole other show.

The second half was as energetic as the first. Of course, there were more clowns. Then Gunther performed a complicated tiger act in which he made them dance and jump through hoops. There was more aerial artistry, this time from the female sex. The teeterboardists performed: Attila and the Kis Faludi troupe performing in ring one, the Romanians in ring two, and the Bulgarians in ring three—their acts climaxing with a member of each troupe doing the double backward somersault to a five-man high.

More comical dog shenanigans from Eric Braun. Then a tightrope act from the Posso Brothers from Colombia. This was all topped off by the Globe of Death, executed by the Urias Troupe from Brazil. In it, three men drive motorcycles at high speed in circles around the inside of a big steel-mesh globe. Their mother stands in the middle of it all, as the loud machines buzz threateningly around her, passing within inches of killing her and nearly crashing into each other on every spin.

The finale was great. The opening song was reprised, and I sang and danced until my body quivered inside, as if a motor were vibrating in my body. As the performers marched around the rings and took their bows, I wondered whether all the sequins would eventually blind me. The thundering applause from a standing ovation threatened to be permanently deafening. As I stood in the middle of all those performers, with four thousand human beings yelling their appreciation, my mother and family on their feet seeing one of their own in the midst of such pomp, I knew I would have the energy for the next show.

3

EMBARKING ON ESEMPLASTIC ESCAPADES

Hitting the Road

BRIAN MASCK: THE MUSKEGON CHRONICLE

Venice is known as a real circus town, and the audiences that opening day were rousing. To top it off, Kenneth Feld hosted an elaborate party for the cast, which took place in the arena. There, I talked to many performers I had not yet met and was gratified with a great number of positive comments about my work. People said that although the shabby old winter quarters arena had terrible acoustical problems, my voice had rung clear.

The entire week was one good performance after another, playing to packed houses. There were circuses, and there were circuses. This was "The Big Show," and the crowd appreciated it.

During the week, friends of my parents from Muskegon, who were visiting Florida for the winter, saw the shows and came back to congratulate me. My experiences in that first city were so good I was sorry to leave. Yet, the circus was scheduled to open in Lakeland in a few days.

My father arranged to meet me in Lakeland to pick up the motor home. Then I would move onto the train. I found I was looking forward to that, because I had begun to feel that I would not really know circus life until I had lived on the train.

In the early 1800s, when the circus was the most popular form of entertainment in America, the roads were not yet paved. For decades the workers, animals, and performers trekked across muddy tracks in the rain, and stony, potholed roads under the sun. It was almost always treacherous going, often hampered by rival companies who might fell trees across the path or otherwise delay the competition.

In the beginning of the 1860s a few intrepid circus owners tried moving their shows by rail. However, they soon became discouraged by a simple problem. There was no uniform rail gauge, so cars from one railroad were unable to travel on another. The circus would have to move animals, performers, and all their gear from old cars to new, not once or twice, but occasionally three or four times a night! Clearly, it became unfeasible for them to continue.

Then, in the latter portion of the 1860s, uniform rail was established, and among the first to realize its opportunities were P. T. Barnum and his partner William Cameron Coup. It was Coup who engineered several developments to facilitate moving circus wagons on and off the trains. Circus wagons were the colorfully painted coaches that were used to travel overland between towns. When trains first came into use for transport, the wagons were still needed to facilitate hauling all the equipment, supplies, performers, and dangerous animals between the train stop and the site of the circus performance, which could be miles away. The wagon wheels were painted wih spirals and interesting designs, and the sides often depicted ferocious animals or scenes of tropical paradises. These colorful wagons attracted the attention of locals in each town where the circus stopped and were the best method of advertisement.

The importance of the wagons was self-evident, but a logistics problem arose trying to roll them over a long line of flatcars, which had wide gaps between them.

So it was Coup who invented the "fishplate," a special plank machined to fit over the space between flatcars, so wagons could be run onto and off of a string of cars. Other devices included snubbers and hook ropes to aid in keeping the wagons in control during the loading and unloading. All these inventions are still used today, over a hundred years later.

Other traditions still exist as well. To fully know the circus, and feel a part of circus history, I would have to live aboard the train. In fact, Ringling Brothers is the only circus in the United States still traveling by train. Smaller "mud shows," circuses still performed under tents, travel by semitruck and trailer.

"Load in" and "load out" had become a true art over the years. The night before we left for Lakeland, while I was asleep in the motor home, the entire circus was broken down, hauled aboard the train, and moved out.

I awoke late, the sound of rain battering the metal roof loud and steady. Pushing aside the curtains, I saw a deserted, rain-swept parking lot with a low gray sky above it. Only one other trailer remained, parked several spaces away from me, another late riser inside. It would be another year before callused hands hoisted cables, calliope music played, horses' hooves pounded a staccato beat, elephants trumpeted, clowns frolicked, and performers opened a new edition of "The Greatest Show on Earth."

A half-hour later, I motored out through the gate. Looking to the side, I noticed the guard's booth shut up, no sign of the old man whose shriveled frame was usually to be seen. I imagined he would come later to lock the gate for the season. Next year he would again greet the new acts with a sly smile and throaty growl. For a second I wondered what he did the rest of the year, as he was not part of the traveling company.

As I accelerated onto the main road, I could see the empty

arena in the downpour, sitting in the middle of a muddy field, and wondered whether I would be one of the ones returning, or whether the year I was embarking upon would burn me out as it had so many others.

It was a two-hour drive to Lakeland on a smooth highway running through the flat country of Florida—open plains with high grasses and rounded tree outlines in the distance. Grazing cows spotted the fields underneath giant power lines that sloped between tall steel-webbed towers probably going to Orlando, a city that I imagined used more electricity per capita than any other in the world, except maybe Las Vegas.

I sang show tunes all the way—my favorite pastime while driving—and reached my destination before noon. I drove directly to the Lakeland Civic Center and parked next to an unfamiliar trailer.

Here it was cooler than Venice, but just as sunny. As I jumped out onto the parking lot, the door to the other trailer flew open, banging against the side of the corrugated aluminum. Framed in the doorway was a short man with powerful shoulders and a beer belly bulging underneath a T-shirt. It was Setso Dukovi, the leader of the Bulgarian teeterboard troupe.

He stepped out and shouted in a thick accent like the Swedish chef character on "The Muppet Show," "Hello dere a neighborrr! How vas yourr a drrrive?"

"It was great," I said. "I love to travel."

He thumped himself on the chest so hard it would have felled a small tree. "Bulgarians a too! From Gypsy blod, you know? Ve travel for a tousand a years."

"I can well imagine," I told him. "Is there anything in your blood that can show me how to hook up my trailer to the electricity?"

He laughed loudly. "It take anoddera Gypsy. Let me showa you."

He led the way to a rectangular plywood box sitting on two legs with wheels. It had been painted black years before, but was now scratched, gashed, and lopsided. Running under the lid were several cables that connected to the motor homes.

Dukovi slammed it with a palm, making a wallop sound. "Ve call dis de a gypsy box."

He opened the lid to show me a rusted breaker box and outlets into which were plugged the incoming cables.

"Is it safe?" I asked.

Smiling widely, he shrugged. "It isa today. Tomorrow, who a knows?"

I thanked him and plugged in, hoping for the best.

This was my first "load in." The circus wasted no time. The train had pulled out of Venice at 2:00 A.M. when I was sleeping and had parked about a mile from the Lakeland arena. Already, men driving small tractors, about the size of large riding mowers, were pulling colorful circus wagons. These had been hauled over in the train cars and were filled with equipment and costumes and cages of animals.

Inside, wardrobe folks were erecting makeshift dressing rooms out of aluminum frames and dingy blue curtains. Working men, sweating hard under the keen-eyed supervision of Joe Burt, the rigging foreman, were constructing a huge steel frame on the floor to which all the wires and cables for the acts would be anchored. In the afternoon I went by again and saw them hoisting it up through pulleys in the ceiling. Below and to the side was old Joe, red-faced and swearing between orders. "Pull a hair on the left! That's enough, damn it! I said a hair, not a yard!"

I would have stayed through it all, but the ringmaster of "The Greatest Show on Earth" had to do his laundry, so I hustled out to find the nearest place to do so. I promised myself I would watch the complete load in at a later date.

Though the sky was clear and the sun shining, the breeze was a cold one. Lakeland is far enough north to get ice and frost, and the temperature seemed to be dropping.

I drove the mile to the train through this picturesque town, which had once been quite rural but was now in a boom period of building retirement communities and strip malls. The old orange growers and cattle farmers seemed a little ill at ease with this influx of wrinkled northerners. The Lakeland Civic Center was a large, futuristic building built among the older downtown buildings, to draw crowds from Orlando and Tampa, which were a fairly short drive east and west.

I found the train, silver cars at rest under an overpass in a fairly desolate area. I looked at it a moment, picturing myself at the window of my room staring out at passing countryside as the train hustled from city to city. It wouldn't be bad stopping in places like this, better perhaps than living in the parking lot behind arenas, with the smell of elephants always in your nostrils.

A clown without his makeup, wearing jeans and a T-shirt, was juggling outside in an open patch of dirt. Beside him was a small portable barbecue tilting to one side. Smoke was rising from under the blackened lid. The smell of cooking hamburgers was in the air. I stepped out from the motor home and waved a hand. "Hey there. This area is pretty nice!"

He smiled. There was something knowing in his smile. Still juggling five plastic bowling pins, he said, "Yeah, this is great! Just wait for the rest of the year."

I shoved my hands into my pockets and shivered as a cold blast of wind hit me. "Not usually this good?"

He snickered. "Man, you haven't seen nothing yet! I mean, they stop this train in the most godforsaken, dismal, ugly armpits they can find. Anywhere out of the way enough to cost the least amount of money. It's expensive to park a train, and you know old Kenneth Feld!"

"He hasn't seemed that bad to me so far."

"Just you wait," said the clown, grinning. "He'll get you yet."

I unpacked the trailer, then drove back to the arena, figuring to spend one last night in the motor home. When I tried to plug back into the gypsy box, all the outlets were taken, as more people had come in. I cranked up the gas generator to warm up the place and drifted off to sleep.

The next morning would be Tuesday, January 28, 1986, a terrible day I will remember for the rest of my life.

The day started out beautifully. It was again clear and cold. The sky was an ultramarine, luminescent blue unbroken by any clouds.

I realized I had unpacked from the trailer into the train the pair of shoes I would need for the show. The parking lot was bustling with activity, and I nosed the motor home out slowly through the people and animals. After I picked up the shoes from the train, I drove up over the overpass on my way to shop for some necessities and clicked on the radio.

A man's voice came from the speakers. It was a voice filled with tension and awe.

"All is clear for the space shuttle *Challenger* to launch. It is the final countdown. Ten . . . nine . . . eight. . . ."

I was just coming off the overpass and realized I was facing toward Cape Canaveral seventy miles away. The land was flat between here and the coast, and I knew from living in Orlando that you could see a takeoff clearly.

I pulled over to the side of the road. The countdown continued until "Zero!" and far in the east I saw an orange-yellow flare. As it rose above the horizon, lighting the sky around it, I pictured those people who would soon be floating above the earth. I could imagine the force of the rockets pressing them against their seats, imagine the thrill in their hearts and the pulse in their throats. It was amazing to me that for the first time a schoolteacher was blasting into space, an ordinary citizen fulfilling outlandish dreams.

The commentator continued to prattle on about something as I watched the capsule curve to the right with a more dazzling light as the boosters squeezed out more power.

Then my stomach dropped as I watched it explode.

There was a flash so bright it seared my eyes seventy miles away from the source. It split into two sparking, flaming parts, which curved away from each other and fell back toward the earth, trailing two lines of smoke.

The commentator was silent. I held my breath, waiting for him to say something, explain that this was not a catastrophe, that I was seeing it wrong.

"There has been an accident!" the man said. "It appears that the space shuttle *Challenger* has blown up! More details as we get them." He started to describe what he had seen, which was exactly what I had seen.

I sat there numbly as the fiery pieces floated slowly to the horizon. One of them was the capsule in which five human bodies were trapped. Bodies I had seen on TV over the past several days in animated discussion of their coming adventure. People with expressive faces filled with a brave, optimistic glow. Now they were cinders.

Sitting there, I realized that this was an event like Kennedy's assassination had been for my parents' generation, and what the attack on Pearl Harbor had been for the generation before them: an event of such proportions that most people would later remember exactly where they were and what they were doing when they heard the news for the first time.

In a daze, I started the car, its engine's ignition startling me, as if it were somehow signifying its status of younger brother to that massive explosion. I drove to a Sears and ran up to the electronics department.

There were crowds in front of all the TV sets, which were blaring out the news, replaying the fateful event. Everyone was silent, solemn, unbelieving. I watched it through a watery haze in my eyes, as I think everyone else did too.

That night we had two shows. I had to sing and dance, I had to win over an audience with my shining charisma, and I mustered up as much energy as I could, considering the day's tragedy. The crowds were not in the mood for it either. The applause was as scattered and weak as the performances.

My father and grandparents were at the second show to see me as ringmaster for their first and only time. It was especially difficult to sing out the final number, "Always Leave 'em Laughing." As performers we are supposed to put the real world out of our minds, give as good a show as if it were always the most splendid day of our lives. Yet even the horses seemed affected by the atmosphere and clomped around without energy.

My relatives said they enjoyed the show as best they could, and they seemed proud of me. I was sad, a little excited, and a little anxious seeing my father motor away in the trailer. Now circus life would truly begin.

Robin Frye gave me a lift to the train that night in a staff car provided by the circus, which hauled them in a special train car.

"Well," I said, as we drove through the night, "that was one heck of a day."

He nodded his head, speaking slowly in his down-home accent. "A lot easier on us than some others."

"That's the truth," I agreed.

We pulled up to the train and parked.

"I guess I'm really one of you now," I said. "What's it like living on the train for a year?"

We sat in the warm car for a minute, and I thought of the cold outside, which the news reports said might be somehow responsible for the *Challenger* explosion.

"It has its ups and downs," Robin muttered. "Some days you just love it, and others it's almost unbearable. It's really an unnatural life-style."

I nodded my head. "It's probably like when I lived on the cruise ship. People don't have true day-to-day struggles like the rest of society. No bills to pay or anything."

He blew on his hands and smiled. "Yep! That's the good part about it, for sure. That's why so many of the showgirls and clowns are so young. It's a chance for them to travel and live on their own with no worries."

"Uncle Soapy's been here for thirty-eight years now," I said.

Robin nodded his head. "I wonder what he would have done if he weren't in the circus?"

The second day in Lakeland was better. The weather was warmer, and the shock of the accident had worn off of the performers and the crowds. Now we were able to do what we were supposed to do—entertain. Friends from Clearwater drove over to see me, and we had a nice reunion. That night, just as I was beginning to feel lonely in my room on the train, a few clowns dropped by with a pizza. They were high-energy performers, always funny, always "on," the closest to the breed of entertainers I was accustomed to.

The week whizzed past, blurring into one long performance, and "Moveout Day" from Lakeland came before I knew it. I was asleep in my room when I felt a hard jolt wake me up. I looked over to the clock. It was 5:00 A.M. Apparently we were starting late. I had been told to expect this sudden start a few hours earlier, as the train's normal pullout was 2:00 A.M.

I lay in my bunk and did a few figures in my head as I watched the flash of street lamps pass across the room. It was 130 miles to Daytona Beach, our next stop. We would be there in a few hours, early afternoon at the latest if there were delays. If I were lucky, I could be on the beach working on my tan long before the sun went down.

Wrong!

I had been figuring time by road distance and highway speed limits. In the train we had to detour north to Jacksonville before switching to a track down the coast. In addition to the extra mileage, it became apparent that the circus train had low priority. Every sort of passenger and freight train imaginable was allowed to go before us.

As we headed back south with the sun already setting, I began to wonder whether I could handle this for a year without going crazy. Though the clowns, showgirls, and workers could all pass from one car to another and meet in the "pie car" (the dining area), mine was a "private car," with restricted access, meaning I was physically cut off from the rest of the train and there was no place for me to go.

It turned out that most of the other people who lived in the same car in the smaller rooms all drove overland in their automobiles, so I was alone.

Finally, just as night darkened the view outside my window, the brakes squealed and the train slowed down. After a considerable amount of maneuvering we came to rest. The clowns who had brought the pizza the night before dropped by again. We walked to the store and bought tacos, and I fixed some guacamole. Then we played a board game called Racko. I have a particular zeal for such games and had brought an assortment with me.

We had the next day free while they set up for the first show, which would be in the evening. The weather was beautiful again, and I took the opportunity to go to the beach and lie in the sun. I walked to a pay phone and called for a taxi, then found my old spot on the beach, a place I had often come to when I used to work nights at Disney World in Orlando.

Interestingly, the new Ocean Center, the auditorium where we would be performing, was right across the street, a small coincidence, because I used to look at that lot and wonder what would eventually be built there. I had always pictured some sort of resort. Now, not only did I know, but I'd be performing there.

Later I caught a ride back to the train and rested for a while before we started our first show. As the time drew near, the circus bus, which shuttled performers back and forth between train and arena, started boarding. In Lakeland I had been lucky enough to hitch a ride with Robin Frye. This time I got in line behind the clown I had first seen in Lakeland juggling outside the train while he barbecued.

"How you doing?" he said, as we climbed the stairs. "I meant to tell you, you did a good job back there in Lakeland. As good as possible, anyway."

"Thanks."

"Don't mention it." He clambered up, drew a quarter from his pocket, and dropped it into the palm of the driver.

Puzzled, I started to move up the aisle.

"Hey! Ringmaster!" the driver yelled. "You didn't pay."

I looked behind me and saw other performers, some of the Dukovis and other Iron Curtain teeterboardists. All had quarters prepared.

"You mean you have to pay?" I asked.

"Yep."

"A quarter? Twenty-five cents?"

"Yep!" The driver was starting to become a little flustered now. His face became red, and a vein in his forehead started to pulse. "Now hurry up. We have a schedule."

The line of Europeans was starting to grumble menacingly.

I fumbled for some change in my pocket.

"I don't understand," I said. "Who's the quarter for?"

The clown in front of me had stood watching the situation. "It's for Mr. Feld, Kristopher. I told you he'd get you sooner or later!"

I was beginning to realize why Mr. Feld was such a great scapegoat for those who were unhappy.

We sat next to each other for the seven-mile ride. We spoke

as the old, white-painted school bus, with the Ringling Brothers logo on the side, rumbled lurchingly to its destination.

"Why does he make us pay? I don't understand."

He shook his head. "He's cheap. What can I say? He pays us a whole $180 a week and then takes it back wherever he can. I mean we've got thirteen shows a week. You don't always go back after every show, but it usually ends up taking five bucks out of your pocket. On top of that he takes another ten bucks a week for our rooms. Calls it a porter fee! Can you imagine that? Then, have you seen the prices in the pie car and pie car junior?"

I shook my head. I had only ducked into "pie car jr." once, a small wagon selling snacks that was always parked behind the arena.

"You ever been there?"

I cleared my throat. "I have my own cooking facilities in my room."

He laughed. "Yeah, I know. Well, you just got a dose of how he treats most of us. Have you seen the rooms he makes us live in?"

Again, I shook my head.

He rolled his eyes. "Tomorrow I'll show you. You won't believe it. I mean you really won't!"

I found my dressing room at the arena. I was one of the privileged few who got a real room. Most had to make do with those aluminum framed stalls with curtains around them. Robin Frye had stuck a strip of masking tape on the door that said MR. RING-MASTER on it. I liked the sound of that, Mr. Ringmaster.

So, here we were in Daytona Beach. Certainly not the biggest city in the world, and the audience reflected it. Though we had six thousand seats available, only about half were filled. This was the "rodeo route" the 115th was traveling. The first year of the tour was called the "big route," and included major cities such as New York, Los Angeles, and Chicago. This second year took in the smaller cities, but the number was twice as many as the first year, which gave it a rodeo feeling.

It was strange, these new words popping into my head. I was starting to think in circus lingo. This route, that route, putting the train to bed, calling the toilet a "donniker." One day a musical theater actor, the next a carnie. Or at least an actor playing a ringmaster among carnies!

It turned out to be best that the audience was small that night. The sound technician was new and just learning his job. He kept forgetting to turn on my microphone and couldn't balance my voice with the band. He was also responsible for the light cues and often drowned me or an act in darkness. It made the entire circus look amateur. I couldn't imagine why they hadn't fired him already. But then I realized an experienced technician wouldn't work for the lousy $225 a week they were paying him.

Things did not improve after opening night, and to top it off, on Saturday the police raided the circus.

Saturday was difficult anyway. It was to be a three-show day: three energetic, two-and-a-half-hour shows. In legitimate theater you only had eight in a week, which included two matinees. At the most, you had two shows a day. In the circus, however, we did up to three shows a day at different times depending on the city and the local promoters. We often had a ten-thirty morning performance, which we called the "kiddy show," with later curtains at one or two in the afternoon and seven or eight at night. So sometimes we had to do thirteen shows a week, though we usually did twelve. And working a "six-pack," those long weekends, where we did three shows per day, we were ready to collapse by Sunday night.

We performed our Saturday afternoon matinee, and just after the crowds had oozed out the doors and I was in my dressing room taking off my heavy tux, there were some shouts in the hallway.

I opened my door and looked out. People, half in and out of costumes, were running by. I stopped the Hungarian boy Attila. His face was charged with excitement, which seemed to light up his blue eyes.

"The police are here!" he chirped gladly. "Lots of cars outside!"

Everyone was hustling in the same direction, so I joined the stream, with only my pants and tennis shoes on. When we got to the arena, it was a sight to see. Two news teams, cameras rolling, bright lights blaring, were bringing up the rear of a phalanx of uniformed cops and casually dressed but official-looking people who were flipping out wallets showing badges to a flustered Tim Holst and Robin Frye.

"We're here for the unicorn!" I heard a man tell Mr. Holst.

"What do you mean?" Holst asked, his round, gnomish-looking face turning red.

The official-looking man waved a hand at another official-looking fellow at his side. "This man represents the ASPCA, and you're breaking a Florida law, bub!"

Holst looked at Robin Frye, who shrugged a "don't ask me" shrug.

"So what law is this?" Holst questioned the man.

"There's a Florida statute," the ASPCA man said, "which states that the display of freaks is unlawful." The man had a very strident, righteous ring to his voice.

Robin Frye laughed. "That's no freak; it's a unicorn!"

The man narrowed his eyes. "Well, it cannot be shown until we determine whether any surgery has been done to alter the animal, and whether it is in pain. We have a court order here. Now bring it out!" He flailed a few papers in Robin's face.

There was nothing to do but bring out the unicorn. Heather reluctantly delivered Sweetheart into the man's hands, who hustled the animal out and whisked him away in a van, while the reporters snapped pictures and videotaped his departure.

I walked over to Robin Frye, who was talking with Tim Holst.

"What do we do now?" I asked. "We can't do a show without the unicorn!"

He looked at me with a mischievous expression on his face. "We have another one, Kristopher. Didn't you know that?"

I searched through my mind and remembered that Heather, the groomer, had mentioned something about the unicorn's brothers.

And suddenly I was mildly outraged. "You mean the unicorn has an understudy? The ringmaster doesn't, and the unicorn does?"

Tim Holst grinned sheepishly. "Guess what?" he said. "They eat better than you do, too!"

I laughed. "Well, I suppose they are, after all, the stars of
the show."

I walked over to where a group of clowns were standing.

"Can you believe that?" said my clown friend Dave.

I shook my head. "No. Wasn't the unicorn cleared last year?
I thought the ASPCA already tested it."

He laughed, and so did the others. "That's not what I mean.
Of course they cleared it! We were just thinking this is probably
all a plan of Kenneth Feld's. I bet he called them himself and
reported us!"

I felt stupid. "What do you mean?"

"What I'm saying is the crowds here haven't been too good.
One little phone call and pow! Look at all this free publicity.
This sucker's going to be all over the local news, and everyone's
going to come and see for himself. And the beauty of it is it didn't
cost Feld a dime!"

"I can't believe he'd do that," I said.

"Can you believe he makes you pay a quarter for the bus?"
said he.

I thought about it for a second and shook my head in wonder.
"I guess anything's possible," I told him.

The unicorn was returned amid a lot of fanfare before the
next show. Heather said he was much too flustered to go on, and
they put in his understudy, who was just as fleecy, but didn't
have as large a horn.

I had come to forget the unicorn's resemblance to a goat, its
definite genetic origins. I had to believe in its authenticity to give
my performance the flair and truthfulness I needed to win over
the crowd. I mean I had to bow to that thing over five hundred
times during the year. I certainly couldn't bow to a goat! So, in
my mind, Sweetheart was a unicorn, whether or not its horn was
really the result of laser fusing performed on it as a kid.

The unicorn, I thought, was an idea old P. T. Barnum would
have been proud of.

One morning in Daytona there was a knock on my door. I was
just preparing to get over to the beach for some sun before the
afternoon show.

I opened the door. It was Don the clown.

"Well, good morning, Ringmaster. How are you?"

"Fine, fine. Come on in."

He stepped inside and noticed my beach bag, suntan lotion, and Sony Walkman sitting on the counter.

"I see you're getting out of here," he said.

"That's all right. Sit down. What can I do for you?"

He was a very tall, delicate-looking fellow with light skin. His eyes always looked a shade disturbed, and his brown hair had a lopsided tilt to it, sort of like a wig that had slid to one side of his head.

"Well, you said you wanted to see the rest of the train. You know, the clown car and all. I thought I'd take you for a little tour if you wanted."

"Sounds good to me," I said. "There'll be another time to get sun."

"You look pretty tan already," he said. "A real sun worshiper, eh?"

"You bet! Have been all my life. I'm in my element on a beach, if not in front of an audience."

The clown car was up about a hundred feet from my private car. We walked along the dirt path next to the tracks. Some people had parked their cars there. A few bicycles were chained to struts and iron pieces descending from the undercarriage of the train cars. A group of teeterboardists were cooking on two barbecues in a small clearing. A few showgirls had various pieces of clothing hanging out to dry on strings tied between branches of small springy bushes. It really was like a Gypsy caravan. There were radios playing; and the hubbub of a dozen different languages being spoken, or being yelled, or being boasted, or being cursed; and of course the international language of laughter.

We greeted various performers we passed; they all looked at home and unpretentious in this atmosphere.

As we walked, I looked at the train in more detail than I had before, realizing all it had seen, all the people from different parts of the world who had called it home over the years. Underneath each car were myriad mysterious pipes and fittings. It was easier to guess the function of some than of others. Big holding tanks, for instance, were for sewage. In each city a crew of workers from a local sanitation company came out with a truck and stuck big hoses into these tanks and pumped them dry. That was a time to find something to do far from the train. The stink was amazing.

Another train car, without sidewalls, held two generators, each about twenty feet long, situated on each side of a walkway up the middle of the car with steel mesh separating them. They were painted yellow and made an ear-numbing racket.

Don jerked a thumb toward them as we passed. "When the heat gives out in the cars up north, I go stand between those suckers for a while. They get so hot you could toast bread against them!"

We got to car 54. From the outside, it had that same gleaming metal Airstream look to it, with the Ringling Brothers logo in the red stripe down the side. We stepped up into the vestibule.

Don gestured grandiosely and spoke in a Transylvanian accent. "Velcome to ourrr humble abode!"

This car differed from my own by having a hall running down the middle, instead of along one side. Immediately inside was a widened area containing a small stove with a door that couldn't shut tight over the oven, rust spots all over it, and a layer of grease pooled around the gas burners. Four small refrigerators were placed two beside each other and two more standing on top of them. Hanging above a few narrow shelves with rusting canned goods and peeling labels were net hammocks with onions and potatoes. A clown, in regular clothes, was boiling water in a dented aluminum pot.

He turned to us. "Hey there, Mr. Ringmaster. Come to see how the peons live?"

I gritted my teeth, feeling sympathetic, yet aware I was being confronted. "I'm getting the tour."

"Have fun," he said.

Don pointed at the refrigerators. "We each have a shelf assigned to us. Now going on to other features of interest . . ." He walked in front of me, lanky frame filling the narrow hall as he gestured to sides all painted a dismal battleship gray. "These are called roomettes."

Most of the clowns were outside somewhere, so their doors

were closed. However, these people would never fully know privacy, as the sliding, plywood doors were invariably a few inches too narrow for the openings. There were cracks on each side that afforded a good view of each roomette we passed. You could see each was personalized, some with wallpaper, mobiles, and other hangings. Each door had a poster or sticker of some kind on it: one sported a maddened, teeth-clenched Rambo brandishing a machine gun over a NO TRESPASSING sign. Some others were less violent.

"Pretty tiny, eh?" Don asked as he saw me peering through the cracks into the rooms we passed.

I nodded incredulously, amazed they could live like this.

"Well, this is mine," Don said, sliding a door open.

Neither *room* nor *roomette* adequately described the size. *Closet* was a more accurate word. There was scarcely a twelve-inch space to squeeze into between the door and the rumpled bunk. There was no other floor space. A few shelves were attached to one wall above the head of the bed facing a poster on the opposite side. Everything but the dirty window was painted a flat blue.

"We have to paint them ourselves," Don said. "So we use whatever we can find to make them livable and homey."

"This is all you have?" I asked. "Just how long is the bunk?"

"Six feet," he answered.

I looked him up and down and cleared my throat. "But, Don, you're way over six feet!"

He nodded sadly, but smiled. "I have to sleep with my knees bent clear up to my chin!"

It might have been a slight overstatement, but not by much.

"If you have a hot date or something," he said, "you can lift up the mattress and fold up a table from beneath it. It makes a tiny little booth, just like in your room. But we don't do that often; it's tough to cram two people in here. Plus, the girls don't like the smell."

Now that he mentioned it, there was a peculiar odor to the whole railroad car. It smelled as if we were breathing the original air that had been trapped inside when the thing was welded together, air that had been breathed and rebreathed for fifty years now.

I wrinkled my nose. "It is a little close."

He chuckled. No. It was more derisive than a chuckle. "The windows don't open. You're smelling what twenty people crammed into sixty feet of space smells like. There's no showers we're allowed to use aboard the train. We always have to wait until we get to our next arena and wash up there. On long runs we go three, four days without washing. Imagine how rank that gets!"

I could only shake my head. "That must be miserable." I noticed that the thick air was completely still. "What about the air-conditioning?" I asked.

He held his hand up to a vent. "You feel anything coming out of there?"

I reached my fingers up near his. Not a breath touched my skin.

"We're a very low priority here. As ringmaster, if your air gets gummed up, all you have to say is boo and it gets fixed. Us? We'll wait forever."

He showed me the only other point of interest in the car.

"This is our wash area."

It was a widened area in the center of the car. Three sinks were set in counters on each side of the passageway, with three stools in front of them. On the walls were misty mirrors with thousands of nonreflecting spots where the aluminum backing had been eaten away.

"Well, it's better than nothing," I said.

He shook his head. "Not really. Remember there's twenty of us! We have to do most of our makeup in the arenas. Let's blow this joint, eh? Let's go look at the bunk car."

It was too hard walking down the passageway inside the cars. In places it was so narrow that if someone were coming the other way you virtually had to climb over each other to pass. We went back outside, down a few cars, and stepped up into another vestibule. In front of every stairway was a short, red metal stool placed there so you could step onto it and get to the first stair, which was three feet off the ground. It was some workman's job to haul a tractor pulling a cart full of stools and place each one just so after the train was fully parked.

Don and I stood in the vestibule in front of a wooden door that led into the next car.

He pinched his nose with his fingers and rolled his eyes. "You think the clown car was bad? Wait till we walk through here. This is the workingmen's car."

He opened the door, and a fetid odor rolled out at us. Taking a deep breath, I stepped inside. It took a minute for my eyes to adjust to the dim light. A couple of fellows were standing in the hall smoking cigarettes and talking.

"Hey," said one, tipping his baseball cap.

"Yeah," said the other.

Both had several days of graying stubble shadowing their cheeks. They wore similar T-shirts with cigarette packs rolled in the sleeves and wide ovals of sweat staining the underarms. Their dungarees were dirty enough to have been worn while slopping hogs. Neither of them had a full set of teeth.

"How you doing?" I said. "I'm getting a tour of the train."

The man with the cap snorted and spoke in a southern accent. "Ain't nothing much to see hereabouts. Just a few old guys talkin'. This here's Ed, and I'm Hank."

We shook hands. Their palms were oily and gritty.

"Pleased to meet you. Are you riggers?"

"Yep."

I nodded. "Been with the circus long?"

He nodded back. "Two, three years, I reckon. How 'bout you, Ed. A year, right?"

Ed blew out a breath of smoke. "We're old-timers here. Most don't last but a couple months."

"Why's that?" I asked.

The two of them looked sideways at each other, a silent communication going between them about how ignorant I was.

"Well," said Hank. "They're mostly bums, you know. We pick 'em up outside the arenas. As soon as they got a few weeks' pay in their pocket and a new town, they disappear. Pay's pure and total crap, and there's not much else to keep 'em here, is there?" He made a quick gesture with his hand, indicating the cabin.

I could see his point. This was what they called the bunk

car. At least the clowns had those little roomettes; this was worse. Here, there were merely narrow bunks, one row over a lower one, on both sides of the car. Each had a discolored canvas flap that hung down for some small attempt at privacy. It was very dark in the passageway, but I could see that each bunk had a scratched, dirty porthole that let in some light. I couldn't see any place anybody could keep personal belongings.

Their kitchen facilities at the end of the car from where we were standing were even more primitive than the clowns', just a couple of hot plates sitting on a counter and one small refrigerator that was making gasping noises and rattling alarmingly.

"Why do you stay?" I asked the workingmen.

Hank laughed. "Ain't got nothin' better to do, I guess."

Again I looked around the car and shook my head in amazement at the poverty. It looked like a coal miners' bunkhouse from the 1800s.

"You can see that Kenneth Feld provides a real palace for his workers," Don said in a disgusted voice.

"Well," I said, my voice a little weak. "I sure won't ever complain about my quarters after seeing these other cars!"

He looked at me levelly, knowing the comparative splendor in which I lived. "I bet you won't."

I cringed inside. There was a bitter flavor to his voice that scared me a bit. But I realized it wasn't directed at me. It was Kenneth Feld he despised.

I could see the circus producer made no accommodations to the twentieth century. Here there were no unions to protest living conditions or low pay. The Actors' Equity Association (AEA), which I belong to, had no jurisdiction here. Some people say the unions are strangling the automobile factories and the airline industry, but I guess there are still plenty of places where they're needed. You sure couldn't count on a benevolent dictatorship in show business!

For decades of American history, the theater actor had been forced to do so many shows a week he or she sometimes dropped from exhaustion. Vaudeville days were the worst; hardly anybody made money. Now, though most theaters and producers still don't pay much, there are fair regulations about working conditions and a minimum pay scale that theater owners must adhere to if they want to use Equity members, who constitute most professional actors.

The circus performers, however, had never been a part of AEA, I guess because of the great influx of foreign talent that's used and without which the circus could never operate. I did find out that the show had been under the American Guild of Variety Artists for a time, but the performers themselves voted out of the union because it wasn't doing anything to protect them.

Now I knew why Mr. Feld had never allowed a newspaper reporter aboard the train. He certainly didn't want the living conditions publicized! It might prejudice the circus-going public, who only saw the glitzy show and would never know the dirt behind the scenes.

4

STEP RIGHT UP, FOLKS

The Great Hat Caper

At 2:00 A.M. of February 3 I was awakened as the train headed out. We had done our last show that evening to standing-room-only crowds, as all houses had been jampacked after the unicorn incident. I would probably never find out whether Kenneth Feld had really had his hand in the raid or not. But whatever the case, it certainly changed the density of the crowds. The story even ran nationally in the newspapers.

Immediately after the show, the workmen had brought in the tractors as the performers and stagehands packed up the costumes, portable dressing rooms, and props. Within a few short hours, the arena was bare, only the smell of elephants remaining, which would probably hover for weeks. I could imagine some singer like Johnny Mathis booked in the auditorium the next weekend wondering about that lingering smell as he performed.

As the train shifted and was put in gear, a long shaft of light strobing through the room as we passed a sign, I thought about our journey. We were finally leaving the state, headed for Atlanta, Georgia. In my mind the journey was really beginning now. It was like traveling when you're a kid. Things don't really seem exotic until you actually cross those state lines. I closed my eyes and rolled over. There would be plenty of traveling time to think.

"Hello, there. I'm Bob Grote, but they call me Teach," the man said, holding out his hand to shake.

We were standing in the vestibule watching the countryside rush by somewhere in the piney stretches of Georgia. The trees we glimpsed had shaggy strands of Spanish moss hanging from them now. Once in a while we would pass a field of brown grass with sleepy-looking cows munching their cud, dumb, half-lidded eyes gazing in our direction. Rolls of hay lying nearby completed the picture.

Teach was a hefty guy, with a disarming smile and silver hair, whose train room was situated at the end of my hall.

"I guess you're the tutor?" I said.

"That's right, Mr. Ringmaster. Someone's got to learn these kids a thing or two besides a double backward somersault!"

I leaned on my elbow against the rail. "You teach all the kids?"

To the side of me, I could see him nod his head. "I was specifically hired to teach the Gebel kids, but I end up doing class with the others too. I love children, so I don't mind. They're not all good students, to be sure, but most of them are pretty smart all the same. Definitely more outgoing than kids who don't get to travel much."

"So how did you come to join up?" I asked.

He got a slightly perplexed look on his face. "It was so long ago it's hard to remember! Let me see . . ."

He had been a substitute teacher in Maryland, and decided to attend graduate school in Florida. He put in an application for a teaching job in Sarasota at a time when that school system had just gotten a request from Sigrid Gebel for an unmarried male teacher. He interviewed for the job and was hired. The Gebels had wanted a tutor primarily for Buffy (Mark Oliver), who was then five years old, but Teach ended up taking on the duties of teaching all the kids traveling with the circus.

Teach had been with the show for over eight years now. "I've seen 'em grow up, been their only teacher during all their formative years. It's really a great responsibility, and it's tough at times. The hectic schedule, the late night performing, that always gives the kids a great excuse for not doing their homework. Sometimes keeping their attention is very difficult. As far as the kids are concerned, the show is always number one. That goes double for the Braun children. School is definitely secondary. And sometimes, the parents are really no help. The Gebels, for instance, thrive on their celebrity status, and they're always whisking Buffy and Tina off to some opening gala or TV show."

He gritted his teeth, and I could see him remembering some past arguments. "Yep," he continued, "it gets very frustrating at times! But I'm proud to say that when a kid leaves this show they go straight into the grade they're supposed to be in, or, in some cases, a grade or two above. It's because I give each kid the individual attention they need."

Many of his favorite students were the foreign kids who saw this country very differently from the Americans who had grown up here. He saved their compositions about backstage circus life and traveling. "Great thoughts," he said, "can come from innocent minds."

"So I guess you must really like the circus people," I commented.

He chuckled. "I love the characters," he said. "I guess that's it. The people in the circus are the greatest bunch of characters I've ever met. They keep me interested. The kids keep me interested."

"I can see that," I agreed. "But on the other hand, the thing I've noticed is that the kids don't know what they have here.

They're so used to it all, it's boring to them. Like the Braun kids. They're so bored with the show I can't stop them from talking when we're out in the ring. I bet they'd give anything to be normal kids going to school every day."

He took a deep breath and smiled knowingly at me. "You never know what you've got till it's gone, do you?" he said.

I leaned out and sucked in a lungful of air. "I guess you're right," I replied.

Our stint in Atlanta was at the Omni. It was a large, well-designed arena, capable of holding a sizable crowd, and we filled it to capacity. The people were real fans, always cheering with abandon, and their enthusiasm was very satisfying for us. After Atlanta we hit Chattanooga, Tennessee, and then were off to Columbia, South Carolina.

I had begun to "click" with a few people now. Besides Teach, I had become friends with Sarahjane Allison. She had been introduced to me last year as the sound technician when I had met her briefly at the Meadowlands, but she had now been promoted to assistant performance director under Robin Frye (who had himself been recently promoted to performance director after Tim Holst had been moved from the job to that of Kenneth Feld's right-hand man).

A gravel-voiced woman who smoked too many cigarettes, she was very pretty and had luxuriant, long thick hair. With a degree in technical theater, she was initially recommended for the job by Dinny McGuire, who had worked with her in a campy vaudeville/melodrama show in Bakersfield, California. She had recently been offered the opportunity to travel with Ben Vereen as one of his technicians and had been about to leave the circus when we left Venice. But Kenneth Feld had appealed to her to stay and offered her the promotion and she had accepted. She had a car, which she asked me to drive "overland" to Columbia, thus allowing her to relax aboard the train instead. I found it amusing that they called driving between destinations "going overland" when the train couldn't help but do so as well.

Although there was room for automobiles to be carried aboard one of the train cars, it was for the use of "higher ups" only. So exhausted performers, who had been driving between cities, were always looking for willing people to handle that chore for them.

Sarahjane, whom we usually just called SJ, didn't mind that I'd invited the clowns Quay and David along to liven my journey. Both were thrilled to get out of the hated clown car and joined me happily. We traveled down an old highway, through deteriorating southern towns. I was at the wheel, Quay by my side, and David in the rear.

David was the clown I had first met in Venice, whose dog-catcher walk around was so clever. He had a mind that never quit, and energy like Robin Williams's. But today he was not happy.

"I have to get out of the circus," he griped. "It's driving me crazy. I just can't live like this anymore. I'm a talker, you know. I should be doing stand-up or something. I like a smaller audience, and some of the antagonistic comments from the guys in clown alley get to me!"

"Your bits are great," I told him. "You're one of the funniest clowns in the show."

I watched him in the rearview mirror. He was shaking his head. "It's stifling me. I just can't be myself. I have to be Kenneth Feld's version of funny, and that's like doing a sitcom if you should be acting Shakespeare. It just isn't the same." He leaned over the seat to speak more directly. "I just don't feel like I'm giving my best to the audience, so I think I'm going to quit. If I don't show up one night, you'll know I'm gone. I don't know what it is, really. When I'm in the ring, and everyone's laughing, I feel good, but as soon as I get back to that clown car I feel like committing suicide, and it's only been a month on the tour. I can't imagine how bad it's going to get."

He pushed himself back to slump in the seat and stared through the window at the gloomy weather outside. I remembered that part of his clown makeup was a tear he painted underneath an eye.

We arrived at Columbia, South Carolina. After eating breakfast at a local IHOP, we lounged around the big fountain at the university's campus, dangling our feet in the water as we soaked up the sun's rays on a summerlike day in February.

"Well, maybe the circus just isn't your vehicle," I said to David, continuing our conversation from the car. "I remember a story someone told me on a cruise ship once:

"A psychiatrist took on a new patient.

" 'I don't know what it is, Doc. I've tried everything but I can't shake this depression. Nothing makes me happy anymore. You're my last resort. You gotta help me!'

" 'I have a surefire remedy,' the doctor replied. 'I haven't been so happy myself lately. But the other night I went to the circus and have to say I'm now a happy man. The star attraction is a clown who shows you just how small your problems are. His name is Lo-Jo, and he's billed as the funniest man in the world. After seeing him, I promise you you won't have a care in the world.'

" 'But, Doctor,' the patient replied, 'I *am* Lo-Jo the clown!' "

"Oh, that makes me feel great," Dave said.

I smiled. "I'm not saying I know the moral to the story. But maybe if Lo-Jo realized how happy he truly made people feel, he would have felt better himself. Or, if not, he should find another line of work."

He looked at me quizzically. "Are you happy, Kristopher?"

I didn't answer right away. I wanted to give him a real answer. Finally I had to shake my head without having come to a decision. "I don't know. But at least it seems right to me to be doing this now. So I'll flow along with it for the time being. I live for today, and if I'm not happy with my life, I make it a point to change it."

It was always entertaining to read what reviewers and reporters in each city had to say about me. In Columbia, for instance, the writer interviewed me over the phone and did not actually visit the circus. When the article was published in the paper, I found the reporter had tried to describe me from the publicity photo Ringling had sent him, comparing my appearance to Jamie Farr, from "M*A*S*H," whom I do not resemble in the slightest.

An old acquaintance sent a telegram to the arena in Columbia saying she'd be at the show with her sister. We went out for dinner between shows and found that the nearest good restaurant was full and had a long line in front of it. My friend went up to the hostess and politely told her I was the ringmaster of "The Greatest Show on Earth," and had to be back in a short time for my next show.

Such was the influence of the circus that we were seated immediately, while other hungry customers watched us hurry inside. I felt very uncomfortable and never abused my "fame" again.

From Columbia, we were off to Raleigh, North Carolina, the site of my next adventure, which I later billed as "The Great Hat Caper."

When we arrived, the sky was a dull gray, shedding a dandruffy snow. The weather depressed me, and I was already in a bad mood when I went to inspect the Dorton Arena, which I hated on sight. The major disappointment was huge picture windows that couldn't be covered, so our matinees would have to be done without the theatrical use of spotlights, blackouts, and other special effects. Worst of all was the floor—concrete.

Unfortunately, this problem wasn't by any means restricted to the Dorton facility. Almost all the arenas so far had concrete floors in their centers. I disliked the concrete for the same reasons that athletes do not like artificial turf—it's tough on the body.

It was only February 24 and I was already having trouble with my legs. This was the beginning of a year battling shin splints and knee problems. Marching, dancing, and running on concrete in thirteen shows a week jarred the bones so much that I had to tape my legs with Ace bandages between shows from that day on.

Here was another point where Actor's Equity requirements for safe working conditions would have made a difference. The union won't allow rehearsals or performances on cement floors because of the terrible damage they can cause to performers, especially dancers. Wooden floors have just enough "give" in them to lessen the risk of injury.

On top of that, the security of the Dorton Arena, located on the state fairgrounds, proved to be lax. For the first couple of days we were finding kids backstage, where they had come through the rear entrance.

On Sunday, the last day of our performances there, I walked over to the arena and opened the door to my dressing room. At first sight it was plainly evident that I'd had visitors during the night. Though my brightly colored tuxes were hanging placidly on their rack, the spot on my dressing room table, where I had lined up my three sequined top hats the previous evening, was completely bare.

I found Robin Frye bustling around and took him by the arm.

"I don't want you to panic," I said. "But I think my top hats were stolen last night."

He looked at me with widened eyes and arching eyebrows. "What???"

"They're gone, Robin. I left them on my dressing room table and they're not there."

"Darn!" he said. He was visibly alarmed, but "darn" was the strongest language he would ever use. "Let me see."

We ran up to my dressing room. Sure enough, they were still missing. I pointed to the counter. "I left them there. And they're not there now."

"I can see that, Kristopher. Have you asked anyone? Maybe one of the band members took them. A couple of those fellows think they're real jokers." I often shared dressing rooms with the band.

"I haven't asked."

Well, of course, no one had them. We assumed that the person in charge had forgotten to lock the doors that evening. I was forced to do the shows that day without the hats. This really threw me off, as I did a lot of "business" with them, making grand, dramatic gestures that just weren't right bare-handed. It felt tantamount to doing the show naked.

That was our last night, and we had no luck discovering the whereabouts of the expensive hats. Knowing Feld, I certainly couldn't plan on having others made. So I decided to write a letter to the *Raleigh News and Observer* reporter who had interviewed me over the phone. I asked him to print the letter in the paper asking for my three hats to be returned.

Little did I know how my little action would mushroom. It appeared that a ringmaster's missing hats was news!

The reporter called me up at the arena to get the facts and

printed an article in the paper. It was picked up by the UPI and AP wires, and the story ended up in newspapers all over the country.

I received letters from friends and fans all over the country with copies of articles with titles like RINGMASTER WANTS STOLEN HATS BACK. Most quoted the UPI article verbatim.

> RALEIGH, NORTH CAROLINA—The ringmaster of the Ringling Bros. and Barnum & Bailey Circus says he feels "naked" after a thief stole his $300-apiece sequined, red, pink, and green hats. Ringmaster Kristopher Antekeier wrote the News and Observer of Raleigh seeking the return of the top hats he said were stolen during a recent performance at the Dorton Arena while the circus was at the North Carolina State Fairgrounds in Raleigh for a six-day run that began February 25th. The hats were custom made for Antekeier as part of his $2,500-apiece costumes. "Not only are they a monetary loss for the circus, but are of incredible sentimental value to me," he said. "Each one was coordinated with my sequined tails." Antekeier says he doubts the circus will replace the hats because of the cost.

The best lead-in, however, was by a local television news show: "Ringmaster goes topless at the circus!"

I was right about the circus's not replacing the hats. I was forced to use a tattered black top hat I'd used in rehearsals, but it didn't look great out there and did not have the same feel. We were performing in Asheville, North Carolina, about two weeks later when we were told that the Raleigh police had caught two kids playing with the hats on the fairgrounds after we left.

My favorite one, the green and purple, was not returned. But the other two were sent to me with a letter from the boys apologizing for stealing them and telling me they had been instructed by the court to do community service work at a senior citizen's home to pay for the "injustice they had done to society."

So that was The Great Hat Caper. I could just imagine these youngsters pretending to be cat burglars, creeping into the darkened arena past the growling tigers and snorting elephants. Was the guard there? Had they waited for the precise moment when he turned away in order to make a dash for it? Watch out, folks! Guard your top hats carefully. Next time, it could be yours!

On the way from Fayetteville to Asheville I had had a revelation. We were chugging slowly up inclines blasted through the mountain range, mountain peaks around us, drifts of snow covering the shaded areas, green trees carpeting the parts bathed in sunlight. Drawing a breath of the clean air made your lungs ache. Standing in the vestibule balancing a mug of hot chocolate, my fingers gripping the warm mug, I suddenly knew that I was happy.

Traveling like this appealed to a wanderlust I had always known I had. The day I graduated from high school, I flew out of town to start my career and travels. Living aboard the train was satisfying that wanderlust without the usual hassles of living on the road, because home came with me. I always had my familiar room to return to. I never had to pack and unpack suitcases. To make my room more inviting, I had hung photographs of my loved ones on the wall and was adding new ones of me taken with people I had encountered along the way. If Kenneth Feld had offered me my second-year contract right there and then, I would have seriously considered signing on.

Luckily, he was not aboard.

Asheville—where my hats were returned—was a darn sight better than Fayetteville. There we had played in the smallest building I could imagine the circus being performed in. It was scarcely as big as a small high school's gymnasium. I mean, a half-dozen elephants seemed to fill the arena. The ceiling was so low that the flying act couldn't do its entire repertoire of tricks, and would never have attempted the legendary triple somersault that they usually ended with. They would have broken their necks on the ceiling.

But now we were in a real arena again.

At our first show there, before my hats had arrived, I stood in the spotlight and made my opening announcement. I couldn't believe it. There was no response!

Beside me was a guest ringmaster, a local DJ who had helped

with ticket promotions. We did this in various cities and were later to have a few celebrities. I would walk to the center ring just before the show started with the special guest, introduce the celebrity, and he or she would blow a whistle to start the overture by the circus band. I would usually open with a little ad-libbed patter of some sort, and I always started with, "Good evening"— whatever the name of the city was—"how are you?" The response was always enthusiastic. Sometimes people would cheer for several minutes.

This night there was nothing. Not a clap. Not a whistle. I stood there with the spotlight in my eyes, knowing the crowd was out there, but wondering whether I were in some dream. How could so many people be so quiet?

"Oh, geez," I thought. "This is a tough crowd!"

The band broke out of the overture, and I sang the opening song as the performers and animals paraded around, costumes glittering under the lights. Throughout the number, clowns and showgirls would look at me and yell, "Asheville! Asheville!"

I kept thinking, "What about Asheville?" I was so puzzled I almost messed up my lines trying to figure out what they meant.

Finally the opening was over, and while the first act was performing I hastened over to Robin Frye, who had a lopsided grin on his face.

"So you say you're the professional, is that right?"

I was out of breath. I could only think my fly was open or something but, after a stealthy check, found it was all right.

"What's wrong?" I asked.

He shook his head. "I love to see you goof."

"What? What?" I pleaded.

Robin kept me waiting, letting me come to a boil before speaking. "Do you know you just said 'Good evening, Fayetteville,' and we're in Asheville!"

My heart dropped. I slapped myself on the forehead.

"What an idiot!" I said. "How embarrassing." I could see into the stands now, and it made my face heat up. Thousands of people had heard my mistake and had been insulted, to boot. No wonder they hadn't applauded.

Robin patted me on the shoulder. "They won't forget it, either. The reviewers are out there, Kristopher."

I groaned.

The reviewers were fortunately more merciful than the audience, and I never repeated the error, though sometimes I really had to concentrate. I could just imagine those singers and bands who played a different city every night. Now I knew why they always had to be reminded of where they were.

Cities became a whirl in my mind, broken up by sections of train travel. I slowly became aware that many acts were nervous about their job futures. The month of April was approaching, when Kenneth Feld would be renewing or canceling the performers' contracts. He was known to cut people whom he had employed for years. The scuttlebutt was that Feld wanted a totally new show next season and would be shuffling pink slips like a Vegas blackjack dealer does cards.

But before we arrived in Washington, D.C.—Feld's seat of power and the location of Ringling's main offices—we had two major cities to play: Knoxville, Tennessee, and Charlotte, North Carolina.

Knoxville, as it turned out, ended up being one of my favorite stops on the tour. Although it was March, we hit a period of sunny skies and warm weather. Even our surroundings were nice. They parked the train in an abandoned station. It was one of those old ones you see in black-and-white movies, with wooden benches and ornate wooden detailing around the depot. It was easy to imagine the platform alive with people greeting their loved ones. Now it was empty and rotting, but its history seemed to call out to me. The train was split in two parts and lined up against the old boarding area, with an overhanging roof.

Our trip here had been almost totally devoid of entertainment. A frustrating fact of train life was watching TV. You could only read so much, and as I've mentioned, I was often alone aboard my car, with no way to get to the rest of the train. So TV became a pastime. The only problem was that reception would often die as we passed out of the broadcast range of a station. I'd be totally engrossed in a show and lose the final minutes when the murderer was about to be revealed or the final lightning round was about to start on a game show. Broadcasting stations in this part of the country were sparse, so I had been bored for hours when we finally pulled into town. I jumped off the train as soon as we were "spotted."

I'd always had a kid's love for great attractions and theme parks, so I wanted to see the site of the World's Fair that had taken place in Knoxville in 1982. I was disappointed, because all I found was a giant, empty expanse with little to show that anything of importance had ever happened there. Millions of people had traveled to this spot from all points of the globe, yet not much remained to tell of it.

Poured concrete with rusting fences lined a small waterway. An abandoned amphitheater, where some entertainers had performed a revue, still existed. Some empty glass buildings, probably used as designated pavilions of foreign countries, stood solemn in the wind. And the empty landmark tower where a restaurant once served customers, high atop downtown Knoxville, was rusting away.

While we were here, I realized how much I needed to get away. A few clowns felt the same as I did, so we went on an excursion intent on meeting some local people. We found them at a club, and had such a great time that I still keep in touch with some of the folks whom we met there. People in Knoxville were friendly all around, and the audiences were lively and responsive. Our mood here was extremely positive.

Unfortunately, however, not everyone was happy.

David the clown had come over to my room, where we sat with the television on but the sound off. I was drinking lemonade and he was emptying a bottle of beer.

He scowled and slammed the drink down on the table. "I can't believe it, Kristopher," he said. "We're right here in my hometown! I wish I could jump the train, jump the entire show!"

"So what are you waiting for?" I asked.

"Kenneth Feld wouldn't be happy," he said. "I can't imagine what he'd do, but he'd do something. I mean, what if every unhappy clown decided to walk?"

A smile spread across my mouth as I considered the question. "There'd be a lot fewer clowns!" I said.

He nodded. "So Feld would have to do something." Then he sighed. "I guess I'll stick it out as long as I can. But I tell you, there's nothing that I'd like to see better than the rear end of this train fade in the distance."

It was in Knoxville where I got to know Attila and his cohort Little Laci (Lahtzee).

Attila was the little blond teeterboardist who had befriended me during rehearsals in winter quarters. At that time I had figured his age as somewhere around fourteen and was surprised to find out he and his buddy, who looked no older, were both seventeen. Laci was dark and swarthy, almost Latin looking. They were the small fellows who made the daring double backward somersault leaps to the five-man high. Their small stature was their greatest asset.

Actually, both fellows were referred to as "little" because older men in the Kis Faludi troupe had the same names. Hence they had a Big and a Little Attila, and a Big and a Little Laci.

Hungarians who had only been in the U.S.A. for a couple of years, they were fascinated by everything American. Board games and cards were very high on their list of priorities, so when they found out I had several games, they started visiting fairly often.

The three of us sat at my table with a Monopoly board between us. I had the bank far away from the reach of either boy, as their fingers had a tendency to fondle the $500 notes. Then, with great flair, when you thought they were broke, they would pull out a lifesaving bill from some hiding place.

Attila was blowing on the dice in his hand. "Boxcar's 'll lan' me on Boar'walk!" he said.

He let the dice spin through the air and plunk hard on the board, making everything jump. Miraculously, they landed on double sixes. "Aaeeah!" Attila cried, bolting to his feet and raising his arms in the air.

I shook my head. He always did have amazing luck.

He saw something through the window and suddenly sat down.

"What's wrong?" I asked.

"Ees George," he whispered.

"So?"

He looked at Laci, who shrugged.

"George no like us come 'ere too much." He cringed as he spoke.

"I don't think I understand. What's the problem?"

Laci sighed and answered for them both, though his English wasn't quite as good as his friend's. "He say you 'staff,' and we shu'nt bother you. Maybe if we get you mad you make trouble for the troupe!"

I looked at him and started laughing. "He's crazy. I'll talk to him."

They shook their heads furiously. "No, no say an'thing!" Attila said. "He be mad at us for saying an'thing."

Things were clicking in my mind now. Once I had asked Attila whether he wanted to accompany me to an amusement park for the day, and though it was clear he wanted to, he had shaken his head. I asked him if George had been the reason.

He nodded. "Das part of de reason. But George no like us to go to places like dat. He's afrai' we might get hurt. If we break arm or somet'ing, the act loses de finale. And you know how he is about being de best!"

I did know. George, with a bushy mustache making him look like a German toymaker, was a perfectionist and had a bitter rivalry with the other two teeterboard troupes in the show. He wanted his performers to be the best, and there was always a dispute about which troupe would do the double somersault last and garner the most applause.

George and his wife had worked for Feld several times over the years, traveling back and forth on a working visa whenever Feld offered them a contract. Their troupe was the most colorful of all the teeterboardists, with several changes of masterfully wrought costumes. They worked in ring one, and put enormous energy into their act—far more than the other teeterboardists. They didn't walk from one place to another in the ring between tricks: they moved with choreographed handsprings and cart-wheels.

George was a heavy-handed master and reigned sternly over his troupe. His fifteen-year-old son had the misfortune of bearing the brunt of his father's temper and was never able to play with the other kids. The poor teenager would ride to work on the bus with his parents and back to the train with them, too, spending the entire day at the arena in their dressing room studying the lessons Teach had given him each day.

The circus headed on to Charlotte, North Carolina. There, Attila promised to introduce me to the wonders of authentic Hungarian goulash. While we were between shows, he strode through my door.

"You got everyt'ing?"

"I bought everything on the list you gave me."

He raised his eyebrows. "Gut! I tell you I bring de paprika. You can't make true goulash vit'out special paprika from Hungary!"

He pulled out a jar and held it proudly for my inspection.

"Me mudder sent dis to me! Not like the stuff you 'mericans call paprika at all."

He proceeded to hunt through my cupboards.

"What? You no have a big pan?"

"Back home in New York," I said. "I couldn't buy a whole new set of pots just to bring on the road."

He looked at me with disgust, grumbled something, and scooted out through the door, returning in a few minutes with a large black kettle.

"Dis my prize possession. You should have one of dese," he said. "How can you do wit'out one? I cook everyt'ing in dis!"

"This is really something special," I told him as we finished our second bowls.

He grinned knowingly. "Like I say. Carrots tase de same here. Onions tase de same. But nowhere else do dey grow de paprika like Hungary!"

"Well, I'll look forward to some other Hungarian delicacies," I said.

His eyes shone with pride. "You will luf everyt'ing. Hungarian cooking is de best in de world."

I smiled. "Even though you love America, you really miss Hungary, don't you?"

Now his eyes got a faraway look as an inner scene played in his mind. "Budapesht is beautiful, magnificent! It is on de Danube, and ve say in spring dat God reach down and touch it."

"I'd love to visit it one day," I said, touched by his rapture.

"Really? Den I teach you Hungarian so you can go dere!"

And amazingly, over the rest of the year, I learned a little bit of his language. Enough to get around Budapest if I ever go.

Charlotte was a real circus town—full houses all week, thousands upon thousands of people, all lively and loud, applauding uproariously every moment that could possibly warrant it.

Robin Frye was pleased with the response and walked around with a smile plastered on his face. This was his hometown. When he had grown up as a gap-toothed, freckle-faced kid, with pockets full of frogs and marbles, "The Greatest Show on Earth" was called "The Big Show," which is what he still called it when he spoke. Every year, even through high school and college, he would camp out at the rear entrance, taking pictures of the performers, whose histories he knew intimately. His hobby was building elaborate models of colorfully painted, old-style circus wagons being pulled by prancing equine pairs. He had wanted to run away with the circus, and always badgered Tim Holst, who was performance director at the time, for a job. Robin could even remember seeing Holst as ringmaster before that. The difference in their ages, Robin about twenty-nine and Holst about forty, hardly mattered anymore. Now they were working together.

One night Robin's joy in being in Charlotte was shattered. He bustled into the dressing room we shared.

"Have you seen my wallet, Kristopher? I can't find it anywhere."

"I'm really sorry," I told him.

He pounded a fist down on the counter, making everything there jump. "Darn it! It's been stolen. Just like your hats! We have to start keeping these places locked." He sighed wistfully. "The worse part is, it happened here. I can't believe I came home to get robbed!"

The weather in Charlotte was cold and wet. The train was parked miles from the arena, so I never really got a chance to see the city. My memory of the place is further tarnished by a major fiasco that occurred there.

The sound man whom I'd had problems with in Daytona had never gotten any better at his job, and sometimes he made it almost impossible for me to do mine. The spotlight would hit me and I would make a grand gesture and hurl my voice into the microphone, but no sound would come out of the speakers. Not even a trained opera singer could fill one of those auditoriums without electronic boosting! Embarrassed, I would stand there in the light and do my bit, but no one in the audience could hear me.

In Charlotte, this happened again, just as I was about to introduce the Globe of Death. I looked out into the stands at ten thousand faces and spoke, making my words chilly with foreboding.

And my microphone was dead in my hand.

I couldn't announce the most hair-raising act. I spun around and glared at the sound man. He held his hands out in bewilderment, an idiotic puppy dog expression on his face, as if it were an act of God or something, and he a mere mortal who could not fight against such might.

There was nothing to do. I made a grand gesture at the Globe of Death sphere, the band started the intro to the act, and the trio readied their motorcycles.

I trotted over to the sound board, where the man was frantically flicking switches looking for the malfunction.

I tried to keep my voice calm. "What's the problem here?"

"I don't know! I just don't know!" His voice was high with panic as he randomly hit the switches. If the board had been working, who knows what havoc he would have created.

"I beg of you," I said. "Please get this microphone working for the finale. The finale just can't be done without the microphone!"

"I'm trying!" he said. His hands were shaking, and I could tell he wasn't thinking. There was about as much in his head as in the head of a rabbit fleeing danger.

So the band struck up the music for the finale and there I was in center ring, singing my head off about the animals and the wonder of the circus while the acts paraded around the ring, and not a word was heard. I must have looked like a raving lunatic out there. I kept looking at the sound man, but he only returned his same blank look.

In the final verse, my voice suddenly reverberated through

the arena. My microphone was live! I glanced over to the fellow and saw his face finally alight with accomplishment. I finished the show with relief.

After the audience had departed I walked up to him to find out what the problem was. I knew it would only be a few minutes before Robin and Sarahjane descended on him, and I didn't want to be there.

"So what was the problem?" I asked.

He spoke in a tone that seemed to imply that he was a genius. "It was easy. *Someone* unplugged the sound board!"

I could only stare at him, clenching my teeth so I didn't say anything. I knew right then that he was out of there. He had a habit of leaning back on his chair and accidentally unplugging the cord. I was just mad I hadn't thought to look myself.

Later on I spoke to Robin and Sarahjane about the incident. SJ smiled at me. "Don't worry about it, Kristopher. We have a replacement for 'Dodo' coming aboard in D.C."

"I can't wait," I replied.

In one way or another we were all anticipating Washington. I knew I was doing a good job and was hoping to get my $50 raise. Other performers were downright scared, because only a few jobs were secure. Understandably, tempers were frayed as people worried about their futures, knowing their lives might soon be changed, fretting about support for large families here or back in Europe.

The circus was ready to explode when we arrived in D.C., where the Ringling head office was, where Kenneth Feld waited.

CUNNING CONTRACTUAL COMMOTION

Washington, D.C.

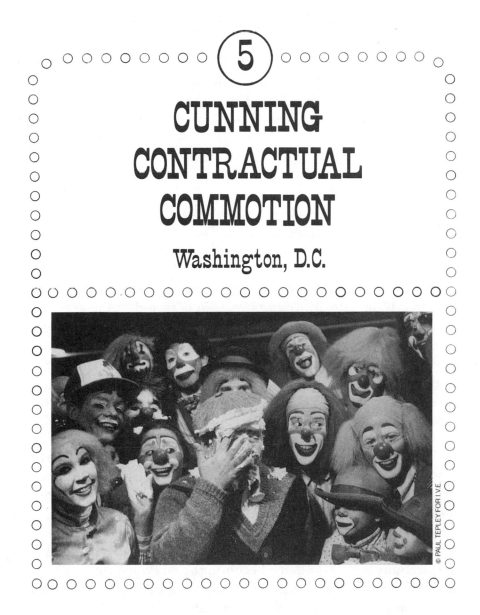

© PAUL TEPLEY FOR I.V.E.

The Potomac River flowed below as the train rumbled over the old iron and wood bridge toward D.C. The bad weather had dissipated, and now sunlight shone on the water. True to form, March had come in like a lion; now it was the end of the month and the "lamb days" were here.

Teach and I, wearing windbreakers, stood in the vestibule breathing the brisk wind as we gazed out on the scenery. In the distance, we could see the Washington Monument shimmering under the sun's rays.

"Ever been here before?" Teach asked, the rumble of the train all around us, drowning out the words.

"Last year to visit a friend in a show," I told him loudly. "But I never got time to take a tour. I mean to this time though!"

He nodded back.

"It'll be hard," he said. "It's two weeks straight with no day off."

"I'll find time!"

We stood there for a few minutes without speaking. I couldn't help but notice a decided droop in Teach's posture.

"You seem a little low on energy today," I said. "Is there anything wrong?"

He shrugged and continued to stare outwards. "I guess I'm getting a little over it, Kristopher." He gestured at the scenery. "I mean this must seem new and beautiful to you. But I've been over this route before, and it's all just one big déjà vu now. Traveling used to be fun, and I still love the people, but everyone is on edge about their jobs, and the whole feeling is tense around here now. It's just not the circus it used to be when Irvin was running it."

"Everyone says it was better," I said.

He sighed and looked thoughtful. "You would really have liked it back then. Irvin hated to fire anyone. He loved the circus and thought of it like a family. Everyone could be sure that if they continued doing quality work, their jobs were always secure. I mean Lou Jacobs the clown was eighty-two when he finally retired! Kenneth would have fired him years before. Nothing's the same anymore. Gunther's becoming a real tyrant, pulling rank whenever something doesn't suit him. I feel sorry for Robin as performance director. He really has his hands tied sometimes. Nope," he said. "Kenneth is really ruining things for the performers. I think I'll have to make this my last year."

As the train closed in on D.C., I couldn't help but wonder what I had missed in those golden years gone by. Teach gave his notice, and left us in Huntsville, Alabama, a few months later. His parting was amiable, and Robin and the Gebels threw him a nice barbecue going-away party where Sigrid thanked Teach for all he had done for her children.

The "animal walk" is a circus tradition. In the 1800s it was used as advertising. The ringmaster, manager, and performers would march the elephants through the town, followed by horses pulling cages containing lions, tigers, and whatever other creatures they had.

With a circus band playing, the parades became musical extravaganzas. The calliope, an instrument that can sound like an entire orchestra, was invented in the mid—eighteen hundreds, and was first used in a parade around 1859. The biggest calliope ever, dubbed the Apollonicon, was created by a New Yorker named Henry Green. The mammoth machine was so high and heavy that forty horses were needed to pull it down the street.

The wagons were specially built and wonderfully painted with battle scenes, stories from mythology, and panoramic views of Edenesque landscapes. Sometimes the parade would be a mile long! All this to whet the appetite of the masses to get them to come pay a few cents to see the show. Woe betide the circus that tried to get away without giving a top-rated animal walk: the townspeople would show their resentment at the box office.

Now, the animal walk had become a necessity. The train was often parked miles away from the arena, and it was quite frankly the easiest way to move the animals from one place to the other. Free publicity was also generated, because the walk was usually covered by local media.

The event was not the extravaganza it had once been. In some towns it was just a lazy stroll down narrow streets with lines of people watching from the sidewalks. But Washington was different. D.C. was the Ringling headquarters, and they planned something special.

I had never really awakened early enough to watch. When I did get up early it was to get my wash done or to do a promotional news spot. Gunther, dressed casually, would guide the animals down the street with his crew keeping everything in check.

I wasn't asked to participate in this special walk, so I decided to watch it like one of the spectators. Even so, I couldn't help feeling left out!

The animal walk had been widely publicized and crowds had gathered all along the proposed route. The throngs were heaviest near the train cars.

I stood among the inner fringes of the crowd and watched Gunther yelling more orders than were probably necessary just for the showmanship of it. Planks were fitted against the wide openings in the cars, and the big elephants trouped out one after the other, raising their trunks, eager to stretch, and see the sunlight.

The animal walk was under way. Elephants were formed in a line with local personalities riding each one. Workers driving tractors pulled wagons with the tiger cages on them. Clowns juggled and did comic antics, and showgirls in full costume strutted between the animals to the tunes of a fully uniformed marching band.

The crowds cheered loudly; children alternately stared and shouted. You knew they would never be quiet until their parents took them to the actual show. I added my applause to everyone else's, as thoroughly entertained by it as they were. It was fun being one of the audience for a change.

The crowd drifted away, most people following in the wake of the parade, and Teach drove up in a car he had rented.

He rolled down the window and stopped. "Hey, Mr. Ringmaster, you want to go for lunch at the Fish Market?"

"You talked me into it!" I replied.

The place was a few miles away, and we spent at least an hour there before returning to the train. As we drove back down a narrow street I saw something confounding.

"Hey, Teach, back up a minute. I think I saw something down that side street."

Teach dutifully stopped and backed up and rounded the corner. In front of us was a small park, and walking around in circles was a clown in full makeup wearing an oversized cowboy hat with an arrow stuck through it. The clown's name was Joe Strange, and he was shifting his head frantically from side to side as if he were lost inside some baffling maze.

Both of us in the car laughed.

"Can you believe it?" I said. "Not another human being in sight, and him wandering around like a lost puppy!"

"The Circus Has It All." © *Paul Tepley for I.V.E.*

Our Crazy Collection of Comical Clowns brings back those golden days of Hollywood (Uncle Soapy in red). © *Paul Tepley for I.V.E.*

CLOCKWISE FROM BELOW: Folderol at its Finest—the teeterboardists' *Charivari*. · Sabu! · Pyramiding Paragons of the Silver Strand—the Posso Brothers. · That elusive creature of fable and legend . . . the sensation of the ages . . . the Living Unicorn. © *Paul Tepley for I.V.E.*

CLOCKWISE FROM BELOW: A stupendous Spectacle . . . where the unbelievable and inconceivable pass before your very eyes (Notice how *no one* is looking at the audience or at the unicorn). · A clown stiltwalker during Spec. · A breathtaking display of precision and beauty aloft— aerial act Satin. · Sensations of the Springboard—the Dukovi Troupe. © *Paul Tepley for I.V.E.*

The Living Legend of the Circus—Gunther Gebel Williams.
© Paul Tepley for I.V.E.

I rolled down the window and shouted, "What's wrong, Joe?"

His head snapped around; even through the makeup I could see an embarrassed and confused look on his face. He hurried over, his voice strained when he spoke. "I lost the whole animal walk!"

"How can you lose sixteen elephants, two llamas, a team of horses, much less all the clowns and parade units?" I asked.

He shook his head and held out his hands. "I don't know. One minute I was shaking hands with kids and doing tricks. I guess I lagged behind a little."

"A little? The parade must have been through here a half hour ago."

"Well, you know how the streets here are. They twist and curve and don't seem to make a shred of sense! I haven't got a clue to where the Armory is!"

The Old Armory was where we were performing.

Teach leaned over. "Hop in. I know where it is."

"Thanks," Joe said, jumping into the car.

I shook my head. "All I can say, Mr. Strange, is you're aptly named. Who else could have lost an entire animal walk!"

Opening night at the Old Armory had the usual excitement of a "move in," even though the arena was large, old, and very dank. I had expected much more in Ringling's headquarters town. I could only guess that Kenneth Feld had some special deal worked out with this particular place.

Robin Frye called me over while the rigging was going up. "You have guest hosts tonight. You'll never guess who!"

"Okay, who then?"

He grinned. "Pat Sajak and Vanna White!"

"Hunh?"

He nodded his head. "Really, no kidding."

"What do they have to do with the circus?"

He shrugged. "I don't know. I'll have to call Publicity and find out. Something to do with a radio promotion."

Later, I put on my costume as instructed and waited at the front entrance. A limousine with dark windows slipped up to the curb. A chauffeur hopped out and opened the door, and Vanna White, dressed in a short, sequined blue dress, bounced

OPPOSITE: The Twenty-seventh Ringmaster of "The Greatest Show on Earth." © *Bill Atkins*

out of the rear seat. My first impression was of her legs. I couldn't believe how skinny they were.

Pat Sajak hopped onto the sidewalk behind her, and they both walked up to me. Or rather, I stepped toward them, so they just figured I was the welcoming committee.

"Hello there! I'm the ringmaster, Kristopher Antekeier."

Pat Sajak took the hand I proffered and shook it limply. He seemed a little aloof, and somehow nervous, not looking me in the eye.

"I'm Pat Sajak," he replied. "And this is Vanna White."

As I shook her hand I looked into her face at close range. Her makeup was so thick it was caked on her skin.

"Pleased to meet you," I told them. "So what exactly is this promotion for this evening?"

And Pat said in all seriousness, "Well, I'm a game show host on a show called 'Wheel of Fortune,' and Vanna is my assistant."

I wanted to say to him "Of course I know that! Who hasn't heard of your game show whether they wanted to or not!" The words that actually exited my mouth were "How do you tie in with tonight's festivities?"

Illumination dawned on his face. "Oh, that? There's a promotion going on at a local radio station."

Figures. The radio station had probably done some free advertising and promotion for the show and the circus, and now it was getting the reciprocal plug.

I ushered them inside and spoke while we walked. "I'd love to do some game show hosting. But I'm worried this ringmaster work won't help my career in that direction."

"Oh, no," Pat replied. "I don't think that at all. If anything, it's a great credit, a super stepping-stone. After all, it's a very similar position."

During all this I was aware that some of the male Eastern Europeans were lurking in the shadows and dogging our footsteps with cameras, mooning with lusty eyes at Vanna.

When I had shown them to an area where they could wait before the show, Little Laci pulled me over to the side.

"She is sexy, no? She is like a cat with those eyes. She makes me crazy!"

I looked around. There were a lot more guys hanging around than was usual.

"You and everyone else." I said. "But as far as you're concerned, she's too old for you!"

"What? I am man!" he said, all of seventeen.

I laughed.

Before the overture, I introduced the popular duo: "Ladies and Gentlemen, boys and girls, we have a special treat for you this evening! Direct from the number one game show on television, please welcome my honorary ringmasters, Pat Sajak and Vanna White!"

The applause was deafening, coming in waves. Just as I thought it was dying down, a new surge would come crashing down on us. You would have thought I had introduced the President of the United States. The two were escorted around the arena in the Pegasus Float. The audience didn't quiet down for several minutes, as the pair waved up at them. The house was packed, as it would be for every show of our two-week stint.

I was disappointed to find Kenneth Feld hadn't been at opening night. But he did make an appearance in his special seats on the second day of performances. There was a little girl with him who I thought might have been some young family member but turned out to be a Russian who was visiting the U.S.A. She had written a letter to President Reagan in reciprocation to the American girl who had written to Andropov a few years earlier and later died in an airplane accident.

I thought it was a great thing to do, amazed at how much goodwill could be produced from one small action by two little girls, and wondered how things might change for the better if a hundred or a thousand people could follow in their footsteps.

The consensus was that Kenneth Feld did not have the girl there to promote world peace. Or if he did, it was merely a side benefit. For him, having the girl there was good publicity and he expected the local news programs to film her feeding rose petals to the unicorn. They did. It turned out to be a very productive event for him.

He was very smart, with a great eye for what could turn a

profit, but I heard a story about his father that eclipsed anything I had ever heard about Kenneth.

Though the concessions company, called Sells-Floto, was technically a separate entity from the circus, Mr. Feld owned it too. Sells-Floto was an old mud show that had been bought by John Ringling North in the 1930s and been re-formed to handle the concessions, which were the real money producer. All the light-up swords, annoying spinning, whirring doodads, plush animals, and inflatable toys that sell by the thousands at every performance are sold by the concessions people who travel with the show and live aboard the train or in their own trailers. The popcorn, hotdogs, soda, cotton candy, and snowcones are usually under their jurisdiction too, depending on the deal with the arena.

It seems that in 1971, Mattel Inc. (the famed toy company) was looking for ways to expand their horizons and became attracted to Ringling Brothers, which on the surface seemed to be an immense money maker. After all, thousands of people see each show, already-steep admissions could be raised every year, and the performers were paid meagerly. Mattel offered Irvin Feld some $50 million in stock to take control. Since Feld had paid only $8 million for the circus and had run it profitably for years since then, the offer could hardly be refused. But Feld remained in control of Sells-Floto and kept the concessions.

Mattel strove to keep the circus profitable, but did not have the experience nor the easy concession money and sometime in 1982 went looking for a buyer to purchase the failing subsidiary. Who came to the rescue? Why, Irvin Feld of course! He bought the circus back, reportedly, at a low price of $22.8 million, a price that was not only less than half of what Mattel had paid him but which included a Las Vegas extravaganza and two ice shows as well.

There may well be more to the story, but no one has ever denied the main details. It was a sly business move.

I didn't get to speak with Mr. Feld that night, but everyone was very nervous because rumor had it that contracts were to be presented at the end of the week.

The next morning I had a kiddy show, then I had to race off

to do a radio interview and get back in time for the afternoon show. Days were often this hectic and could stretch on for fourteen hours.

The afternoon show proved to be memorable, for mishaps rather than for great production.

I was closely watching the progress of Susie Turcot, the new sound person who had been hired to replace "Dodo." She had worked for the now defunct Circus World in Florida and was acquainted with Joe Burt, the rigging foreman, who had also worked there and had recommended her for this position.

I feared she was exactly as incompetent as Dodo when the sound board blew up during the show, with only my microphone left working, but I was later relieved to find out that it was not her fault. A spectator had spilled Coca-Cola on some wires as he walked by! So all during Spec I was basically singing a cappella with the band hardly audible in the background.

Kenneth Feld was in the audience that day and couldn't help but notice how I kept the show going despite these problems. He had also seen a very good performance the day he had come with the Russian girl, so I was confident about getting my raise. I could only hope he had also received accurate reports from Tim Holst about my work on the previous two months of the tour.

Almost as if he planned to keep everyone on his toes, Feld did not immediately start calling people into his office to talk about their contracts when we arrived in D.C. Waiting made people especially edgy but also propelled them to new heights of excellence. Feld might be watching them at any time, evaluating them, making decisions that could change their lives.

Strange events seem to be attracted to such tension, or maybe tension helps cause them.

A workingman, driving a motorcycle, was killed in a collision with a car. Though the performers were not usually bosom buddies with the workingmen, everyone had something good to say about this guy. He was a nice fellow who always greeted me with a smile, one tooth covered in gold, and would often say, "Good show, man!" which I always appreciated.

Though I had only known the man in passing, his death had

a great effect on me and made me think about what I was taking
for granted. There are individuals in all of our lives who are more
like fixtures to us than people. His sudden death made me much
more interested in really getting to know the people I was working with and much more conscious of enjoying my time with the
circus as fully as possible.

Death, however, had not left us yet.

I had developed a rapport with Susie Turcot, the new sound
person, and she would visit me in my dressing room or my train
car. She was a sweet-natured, dark-haired girl who reminded me
a bit of MacKenzie Phillips. She liked to play games, too, so we
had something in common.

"I'm getting used to the size of my room," she told me. "But
there's a smell in the car that's really something awful."

"Which car are you in?"

"Two down from here."

I shook my head. "I've been in that car before. The clown
car's pretty bad, but yours seemed normal."

"I don't know, Kristopher. The porters have cleaned and
scrubbed, but it's still there."

A day later the foul odor had become noticeable outside.
Gunther Gebel Williams's car was next in line, and the animal
trainer finally realized the smell was coming from the room of a
concessionaire near the end of Susie's car.

Gunther asked around and found out that no one had seen
this guy for a couple of days, and he hadn't shown up for work.
Since he was a low-level worker, no one had thought to be concerned about his absence; people had figured he had tied one on
in town or flown the coop entirely.

A crowd gathered as Gunther pounded on the door.

No answer.

He pounded again and shouted the guy's name. Finally he
kicked the door in, and a stench blasted out into the hall, making
people run. The body was three days bloated, the skin having
turned a blue-green. Already, the flies were starting to get at the
rotting flesh. A syringe was stuck in the swelled arm.

Gunther slammed the door and fanned the air. "Somevone
call de police," he said.

I was not there to see it, but I can just imagine the disdain in Gunther's face. He did not like people weak enough to become addicted to drugs, and saw all human problems as deficiencies of character. He was a hard man, and probably felt that the concessionaire was stupid to have died this way.

Most people felt sorry for the guy, though. And I did too. You have to think that something you might have done could have helped the poor man. Maybe if you had cared just a little bit more, gone out of your way to say a good word, the guy would have felt just good enough about himself not to plunge that fatal syringe into his arm.

This became the hottest topic of conversation for the next week. Drugs were a problem with the show, as they were everywhere. Alcohol was the biggest problem with the workingmen, as it was often their primary reason for working—just to get enough money to buy a bottle on their hours off.

Hard drugs could be found among a few of the concessionaires, who were younger and earned a lot more money. Pot in particular was rampant.

I never touched any of it, so I was ignorant of the whole problem until then. Management decided to drug-test all the concession workers but never subjected the performers to the same procedures. I suspected they really didn't want to know the results. It might, or might not, have surprised them.

Now, Kenneth Feld had decided to deal his cards. Between performances, Tim Holst would step up behind the spokesman for each act and tap him or her on the shoulder. "Mr. Feld would like to speak to you now," he would say. It was not long before people started calling Holst "the henchman." Often, the person would come out of Feld's office with a white face and a blank stare. For many, it meant going back to their less-than-beloved Eastern Bloc homeland: Romania, Hungary, Bulgaria.

I remember seeing Eric Braun get the "tap." He followed Tim Holst into Feld's office, looking a little pallid. He was always nervous meeting with Kenneth, as he had been on much better terms with Irvin.

I liked Eric and did not fear for his status with the circus. He had been with Ringling since about 1969 and was one of the first graduates of Ringling's Clown College. Irvin Feld had loved Eric's work and taken a special interest in him, eventually encouraging the clown to develop dog-training skills.

Eric married Francine, a Canadian showgirl also in the show, and they had two children. Irvin liked the idea of circus tradition being handed down through the generations and asked Eric to put together a family act. Evidently, the old producer loved the two kids.

The act turned out to be tight and entertaining. In one trick, Eric catapulted his little French poodle, Peanuts, from a teeterboard onto his hand. Another was a comedy bellhop routine with his shaggy dog "Poopy." It was an act I had always thought especially funny.

In my mind, if anybody could feel sure of renewing his contract, it would be Braun.

The meeting didn't take long.

I was watching as the door creaked open and Eric stood there in a daze, having to be virtually pushed out of the office. My stomach fell as I watched him stagger out.

Apparently, Kenneth Feld was going to make radical changes. The next edition, the 117th, would be the first that he would produce alone since his father's death in 1984. He meant to put his own stamp on the new show that would start next year. Rumor was that his new idea included a punk-rock production number with break dancers, which did not sound very circusy to me.

From then on, you would see Eric on a pay phone during his spare time, trying to line up his next job. Of course, his need was not immediate, since this edition of the circus still had several months to go, but for an act like his, you had to have plenty of advance time to get booked. He had a family to support and had just bought an expensive truck and fifth-wheel trailer.

His wife, Fanny, was heartbroken. She loved the Ringling life-style, the friendships, and the partying. And she was always helping people think up new tricks, feats, and ideas for their acts. She was a real circus person.

One by one, the acts were ushered in to see Kenneth. And one by one they would exit in dejection. It seemed that Feld was cleaning house completely.

One day I saw Tim Holst walking in my direction. A gleam in his eye told me it was my turn. . . .

I walked casually into the office.

Kenneth looked up from his desk and motioned to a seat. "You play golf?" he asked.

"Why do you ask?" He already had me off-kilter.

"The green cardigan you're wearing. It's golfy."

"Well, my father used to play. But it's been years since I have. I was never into sports."

He nodded. Without changing a beat, as if he were still going on about golf, he continued, "So tell me what you're thinking."

I took a deep breath and leaned back in the chair trying to act more relaxed than I felt. "Well, it's only been eight weeks, but I'm liking it—and that's what scares me!"

Kenneth smiled grimly. He knew what I meant by that. The circus could be like a fever with no cure.

"Well, I like what you're doing out there," Feld said.

"My style is different from what you had before."

He nodded. "Exactly. I'd like to incorporate your specific theatrical talents into our new edition. The whole show is going to have a more theatrical feeling to it."

I perused his face, looking for more information. He had already approved my $50 raise, but just how badly did he want me to stay?

"I'd really like that," I said. "What are you offering?"

He chuckled. I could see he liked the way I got down to business. Unlike most of the others I was not scared of him because I had plenty of employment options outside the circus. I figured I had the upper hand since Feld was probably not used to dealing with someone he couldn't easily manipulate.

"Well, first off," he replied nonchalantly, as if it were un-important, "I'm asking everyone to sign a two-year contract."

That took me off-guard. I had been expecting a one-year renewal. As much as I loved what I was doing, I was unsure I *could* perform that long. Would my body hold up? Dancing on those concrete floors was hurting me already. I also did not know whether I could continue the life-style that much longer.

"I'll have to think it over," I said. "I wasn't thinking of a two-year contract."

He clucked his tongue and drew a breath in through his teeth as if my words really pained him. It was clear that it was a two-year contract or nothing. "Just so you know, I'm not going to have the usual five-week vacation in Venice during the two-year edition this time. I want the transition to be smoother between the tours."

Which is where I had come in.

I shrugged. "I'll need a week to think about this," I said.

"No problem," he said with a slightly disappointed tone.

I knew what he had wanted me to say was, "Oh, Mr. Feld, it's such an honor to be ringmaster of The Greatest Show on Earth I'll be your slave for eternity!" But no job was worth that to me.

"Talk to you later," I said.

"You bet," he replied.

A long week passed in which we had no day off, and I was in no mood to negotiate a contract. It didn't matter what the job was: when you're tired to the bones nothing seems worthwhile. But what I did decide was that if I were going to do another two years, Mr. Feld had to make an attractive offer. Thirteen shows a week, legs bandaged and aching, living in a shoebox, and not getting a cent extra for all the publicity I did on TV talk shows, radio programs, newspaper interviews, and personal appearances had to be worth more than I was getting.

Perhaps twice as much?

I deserved it. The job was demanding, especially the way I performed it, as I had great pride in giving my all for every show. So many kids were seeing the circus for the first time. Maybe they'd been trying to behave for a month so their parents would reward them with a visit here. After all the hoopla, I wanted it to live up to their expectations, and everything I could do to accomplish that wasn't enough.

I also thought about the parents themselves. After all, they had memories of the circus when they were children. And such memories are usually filled with more excitement than the actual event had been. Their adult lives were probably stressful and not as colorful as they had once dreamed. To the grownups, I wanted to give a few minutes of childhood back.

I ran into Feld at the backdoor of the arena. I was tired and wanted to go back to my train car, but he put a hand on my shoulder.

"Let's talk, Kristopher," he said in a firm tone.

We went back to his office and sat down.

"What have you decided?" he asked.

"Well, let me say this. I really like the job, Mr. Feld. But to stay on, and live in slummy train yards and give 110 percent every show, I'll need more than I'm making. At least twelve hundred dollars a week."

"Can't do it!" he replied simply.

I looked him in the eye and spoke in shaming tones. "You'll never get another ringmaster like me. And now I know what the job entails!"

"I offer my people the lowest cost of living of any circus show plus steady work!" he said.

I wanted to laugh. That might be true, but where else can people with chimpanzees and hyperkinetic dogs get a steady job? The work might be there, but it didn't pay much. And on top of that he charged them ten bucks a week to live in a closet.

He shook his head sorrowfully and scuffed the pavement with a shoe. "Contrary to popular opinion, I do not have a gold mine here!"

It was all I could do to stop myself from laughing in his face!

The problem was that the son of a gun was getting richer by the minute. At the time he had two circus units, three ice shows, and a highly successful Las Vegas revue starring illusionists Siegfried and Roy, famous for making large white tigers disappear during their act. And everywhere his Sells-Floto company sold those same high-priced souvenirs. I mean, the people who sold the souvenirs at concession stands each took home about $60,000 a year. As their boss, and owner, Feld's take must have been immense!

More likely, his problem was that if I got the pay I wanted, other people would demand a higher scale too.

We stood there staring at each other for a few moments until he said: "I'd insult you if I told you what I can offer. I can find someone else who'll do an adequate job. I wish you'd stay with us, though. So if you decide to change your mind before I find another ringmaster, let me know."

I knew he was bluffing. He might refuse to pay me, because his wallet was nailed together, but it was not because he thought someone else would do. He had auditioned hundreds of people all over the country to get me and knew exactly what sort of talent was out there. There might be another ringmaster, but not another who would do it the way I was doing it.

Calling his bluff, I stood up and shook his hand.

"We'll play golf sometime," he called, as I shut the door behind me.

Thoughts cascaded through my head as I walked down the hall. What the heck had I done? Had I held up against the shrewd producer? Had I done myself right out of a job? Only twenty-six other people in history had ever held my position, most staying five to ten years. Here I was, only two months into the show and already a marked man! But now, knowing what the job entailed and how hard I worked, I realized how incredibly underpaid I was.

The weather stayed achingly clear and fresh through Easter. One day between shows, I decided to get some sun in the rear parking lot. A little Hispanic boy skipped up to me. His name was Franky, and his mother, Liza, ran a concession stand selling stuffed toys. She was a single parent and was now dating one of the Dukovi teeterboard artists.

"Hi, Kristopher!" he called out.

"Hi."

He climbed a nearby fence and balanced on top. "Look at me, Kristopher. Look at me!"

I smiled. "That's good, Franky." He was six years old, already starting to perform. I could see him a few years from now starring in center ring.

I closed my eyes, trying to relax.

"Look, Kristopher, look!" came the high-pitched voice.

When I looked he started to walk the fence and pose—"style"—like a high wire performer.

"You see, I'm just like the Posso Brothers!" he chirped.

"That's right, Franky. You're a born circus star!"

"Do your announcement for me, Kristopher!"

"My voice is tired," I said.

It made no difference to him. He made the announcement himself. My act intro was, "On the highwire—the pyramiding paragons of the silver strand! From Colombia, South America— the Posso Brothers!"

Franky styled again and called out in a voice that tried comically to imitate my baritone:

"On the high wire—the pretty many pedigons of the silver stand. From Columbia, South Carolina—the Postal Brothers!"

I laughed and the kid laughed with me.

"I know all your announcements!" He said. "You want to hear them?"

"You bet!" I told him.

He made a magnificent gesture with his hands and screwed his face up trying to look dignified. "The Greatest Show on Earth presidents that exclusive feature of fatal and legend, the Living Unicorn!"

That killed me. The real announcement was, "The Greatest Show on Earth presents that elusive creature of fable and legend, the Living Unicorn!"

"Is that good, Kristopher?" he wanted to know.

"It'll do for right now. Do you have any more?"

He was proud to be the center of attention. He struck a pose and continued until I couldn't breathe because I was laughing so hard.

On April third I was invited by the two performance directors, Sarahjane Allison and Robin Frye, to visit Ringling's main offices, which were supposed to be rather grand.

Robin drove his staff car up New Mexico Avenue.

"Wow," I said. "These are some buildings!"

He nodded. "Most are foreign embassies."

"They look like capitol buildings."

They were brick edifices, with pruned bushes and freshly cut lawns. We pulled up to a building of impressive architecture, equal to any we had passed on the grand boulevard, but more in the style of an office building. It was three floors high, with a parking area underneath.

"I guess Ringling doesn't fool around," I said.

SJ inhaled from a cigarette and blew the smoke out the window. "Well, the Felds know just where to spend their money, and where not to!" she said.

I was almost expecting valet service here, but the place stopped short of that. We parked in the lower garage and entered the building. Doctors had offices on the first two floors, but Ringling occupied the entire top tier.

Not surprisingly, the head offices were similar to those of other major companies for which I had worked as an entertainer, namely Disney World, Cedar Point, Pepsi Cola, and United Features. They were big and gaudy, almost a monument to the company itself.

The first thing we saw when we entered was a four-foot-high wood carving of Ringling's most famed clown, Lou Jacobs. To one side was an antique circus wagon, ornately painted. And in a huge glass case was a stuffed gorilla, known once upon a time as "Gargantua the Great!" one of the legends of the circus.

For a second a chill went up my spine as I looked at these relics from the past.

I sucked in a breath before speaking. "You know, guys," I said, "I wouldn't put it past them to have an old stuffed ringmaster around here someplace."

SJ and Robin both chuckled.

"For God's sake, Kristopher," SJ said. "Don't give them any ideas!"

I conjured the image in my mind. "I can see it now. There I am, a hat in my outstretched hand and a smile on my face. Guys, if they do it to me, make sure they dress me in my green tux. That's my favorite!"

A woman named Mary showed us around and ushered us to the Public Relations Department, where we found several artists busy creating renderings for new posters for the ice shows and a few new designs to be painted on the sides of the circus trains. All would eventually be approved or rejected by Feld himself.

I created a ruckus when I entered because these were the people who had worked so hard to make the ringmaster search the national sensation of which I was the end product. They had placed the ads, created the posters, and written the information that had been released to all the newspapers. Now they finally got to meet the man they'd worked so hard to promote.

I had met Kenneth's longtime secretary, June, at winter quarters. She was an attractive woman, about fifty. She had a businesslike air but had always been warm when she had talked to me. She had seemed a little out of sorts in Venice, but here she was in her realm, her desk guarding entry to Feld's office.

She got up from her seat and spoke warmly.

"Hi, Kristopher! I hear you're doing a fabulous job! It's so nice to see you."

"Thanks. You too. Is Mr. Feld in?" I asked.

June shook her head and spoke reverently. "He's in a big powwow right now. Major people, you know. There's good stuff happening."

As far as I was concerned that was all right. I didn't really wish to see Feld himself.

"Well, can we sneak a peek at his office?" I asked. "I've heard so much about it!"

She shrugged. "I don't suppose he'd mind."

My first impression was of the masculinity of the office. If my memory serves me right, the carpeting was muted gray and mauve. Just inside the entrance, you walked between two large ivory tusks, ornately carved with incredible detail.

June spoke proudly, "Those were presents from Siegfried and Roy." (Those were the two Las Vegas illusionists whose show was produced by Feld.)

A sturdy glass-topped desk was at the far end of the room, a window directly behind it. On the desk was the telephone from which Feld conducted his business. I could see him there, feet propped up, while he negotiated with me on my original contract. It was strange to know this is where he had been at the time.

A few books rested on a peculiar side table, kept upright by two plaster casts of a gorilla's hands.

June saw me look them over. "Those are casts from Gargantua," she informed me. "Now if this stuff interests you, I'll have Mary take you on down to the merchandising room."

We thanked her for letting us in and again followed Mary, who had a nice southern accent. She led us to a room about forty feet long by fifteen feet wide. Not huge. But in it were displayed a thousand different items that had been sold to promote the circus over the years. A lot of the stuff was now collectors' items, and the place had that musty smell of a library filled with decaying books.

I recalled that United Media had a similar room that I had seen when I had worked for them in a Garfield Magic Show tour. Theirs had been mostly filled with "Peanuts" characters in a million shapes and sizes.

Mary smiled when she saw our eyes light up. "Would you three be interested in any old printed items?"

The three of us looked at each other like kids being asked whether they wanted free rein in a toy store.

"That would be wonderful," I said.

I watched Sarahjane, a model of jaded womanhood, suddenly start to giggle. "Yes, yes, yes!" she said. This new side of Sarahjane made me like her even more.

We went crazy in that room. It had five rows of shelves full of "printed items" from years long past: Ringling stickers, posters, and buttons. I found memorabilia from the show *Barnum*, which was some of my favorite stuff. We left the offices loaded with goodies, like kids coming home from a carnival with armloads of stuffed toys hard-won at the games.

I wanted to do some sightseeing, but getting the time to do it was difficult. We had one other day with only two performances, and I figured it was now or never. A subway ran right from the Armory to the Washington Monument area, and I took it.

One thing that really impressed me was the subway itself. It was immaculate compared to the dingy, rat-infested subways in New York. This might have been enough for me to see, but greater prospects loomed nearby.

Coming out of the subway, I noticed first an intoxicating

scent in the air. All around the cherry trees were in full blossom. I was not the only tourist, as the cherry blossoms are a famous spring attraction in D.C. It was great to be outside to experience this when so many days and nights had found me imprisoned in the Armory.

The big stone Smithsonian buildings were nearby, and I refused to come so close and miss the museum. When I got there, exhausted people were already sprawled out on the big stone steps, and hordes of students came bustling off parked yellow school buses. Lines of tour groups complained among themselves as they shuffled from one exhibit to another.

I fought the crowds to see the entertainment section and was surprised to find a bleak room with the displays virtually concealed by dusty windows. These people needed a housekeeper! The impact of the display was badly diminished because everything looked so grimy.

I was still thrilled to see the ruby slippers from *The Wizard of Oz*, even through a haze of dust. Archie Bunker's chair was there, along with Charlie McCarthy, Edgar Bergen's old dummy.

What really surprised me, though, was a pair of boots. They were old, faded yellow with well-worn soles—and had belonged to Gunther Gebel Williams. Lying beside the boots were an elephant harness with the Ringling logo (G.S.O.E.) and one of Gunther's old whips.

One of the circus's traditions is blowing a whistle to start the first and second acts of the show. Usually, it's the performance director's job. But it was about this time that Robin decided I was ready to do the whistle blowing, which was the signal that started and stopped all of the action during a performance. It is a hefty job, because the whistle blower controls the pace of the show. I was nervous at first, but slowly became more confident. Doing this gave me an even greater perspective on the circus: it is amazing that such a show could go without a hitch, run so efficiently by the mere sound of a whistle.

My greatest problem at the time was that Robin, Sarahjane and I were sharing a dressing room with the five band members who toured with the show. The band was actually bigger than that, but the conductor, Keith Greene, would call ahead to each city and line up union musicians to fill out the orchestra.

The five permanent members were just plain uncouth.

"Hey, did you see that fox in the second row?" one would say.

"Yeah, I could see right up her skirt!"

I hated listening to them talk. The conversation usually sank lower even than that. A few were having affairs with the showgirls, and they took pride in describing the most intimate and raunchy details of their sex lives.

Their one saving grace was that they were excellent musicians. The drummer in particular had to be sharp. He had to watch every move on the arena floor and accent the acts with cymbals and drum rolls at exact times.

Neither Robin nor SJ enjoyed the locker room talk either, and since Robin assigned the dressing rooms, he eventually alleviated the problem.

At the end of our two-week stint, you could tell the performers were just dragging themselves through their routines. Everyone was plainly exhausted. People were further depressed or openly angry about their contracts, for Kenneth Feld had not only cleaned house, he had gone through it with an industrial-strength vacuum cleaner.

Ninety percent of the acts—including the Braun family, all the teeterboard troupes, the Uriases with their Globe of Death, and the Flying Españas—had been told that they would not be rehired at the end of the year. Only Gunther, who was on a long-term contract, Satin, the two-girl black aerial act, and I were offered new contracts. And I still hadn't firmly decided which way to go.

The clowns and showgirls had more time to sweat things out, as their contracts did not come up for renewal until August.

People were very sad. Several acts had been with Ringling for years, and had virtually considered it a lifelong commitment. Now they would be looking for new work in a world where very few openings for their special talents existed. They would contact variety agents throughout the country, apprising them of their availability. They could also audition for some of the smaller tent shows like Circus Vargas, The Royal Hanneford Circus, Circus USA, and a few others that are still touring today. Many acts would also place advertisements in trade publications such as *Circus Reports* and *White Tops*. But whatever the case, people would be eating some meager dinners between now and their next jobs.

6

"THERE'S ONE BORN EVERY MINUTE"

My Circus-Style Birthday

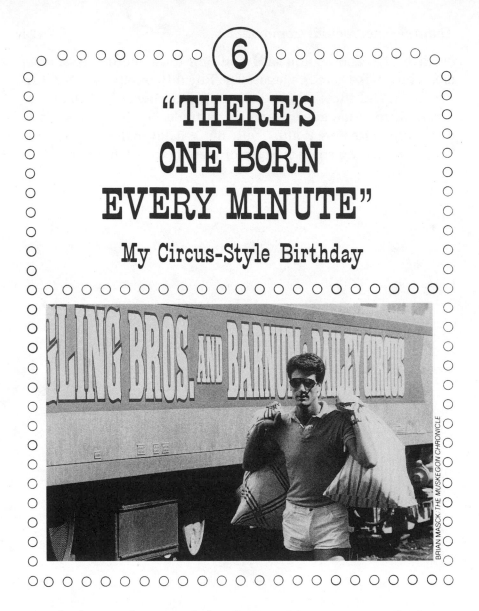

BRIAN MASCK / THE MUSKEGON CHRONICLE

"I've had enough!" David the clown told me. He waved a letter in the air. "I'm giving my resignation."

We stood in the parking lot behind the Armory, the elephants and horses snorting close by, shuffling at their tethers.

"Are you sure?" I asked him.

He laughed, but with little humor. "Is a bear Catholic?"

"Well, if you aren't happy," I said. "It's probably the best thing."

"Happy? The senior clowns are some of the meanest people

on earth! They make life miserable. You don't know what a new clown has to go through."

"Oh, yes I do. You've told me a thousand times!"

He shrugged and held up the envelope. "Well, I've made my decision. I'm getting out of here as soon as I can." He smiled. "Sooner, if possible."

We took a walk and he dropped the letter to Kenneth Feld into a mailbox. The letter explained, point by point, why he was leaving the show.

"Maybe he'll do something about the conditions," I said.

He shook his head sadly. "I wrote down what my problems were, but just for my own sake. I bet he's seen a thousand letters just like it. Probably gets a bigger laugh out of 'em than the funny pages! Probably frames them and puts them up in his office!"

I chuckled. "I've been in his office. I didn't see any."

Dave shrugged and his voice was a little weary when he spoke. "Probably uses them in the bathroom . . ."

We had survived the two straight weeks in D.C., and now the circus was moving to Cincinnati, Ohio. We were too close to New York for me to miss going home for a few days, so I rented a car to drive to New York and planned to fly out to Cincinnati to meet the show. David had never been to New York before, so I asked him to go along for the ride and see the city.

On the drive up the clown regained his humor. "This is great, Kristopher! Maybe I can audition for some clubs or something! The stand-up routine is for me."

I nodded and smiled during the entire ride, but I feared he would be disappointed. The circus is hard work, miserable work sometimes, but it has a thousand rewards as well. In the circus, you have plenty of time to communicate intimately with the crowds—before shows, during intermission, and after shows—and seeing a child's smile is about as rewarding work as I can imagine.

David, after visiting New York City for a few days, headed back home to Knoxville hoping to get a fresh start. I can only hope he found his niche somewhere.

For some reason I didn't think any run could be more eventful than D.C. had been. I was becoming complacent about the dangerous nature of many acts after seeing them performed flawlessly so many times. But accidents still happen in the circus, and we were to have our share during the year. They first started cropping up a few cities later in Hartford, Connecticut.

Our route had been through Cincinnati to Wheeling, West Virginia; then to a small town, Charleston, in the same state. From there we traveled north to Binghamton, New York, which was cold and dreary. I had to use the hot plates in my room for heat. Worcester, Massachusetts, came next.

None of these towns was without incident.

In Cincinnati I had severe sinusitis in reaction to the spring pollens and croaked my songs throughout the run. Of course, unlike the unicorn, I had no understudy. Worse, some friends from Cedar Point came to the show there, and I could only apologize for my condition.

In Worcester, I lost the train.

It had been a long trip, and I was eager to get off the train when we arrived. It could take up to an hour for the train to be spotted, which was the term for parking the brakes, and I was too impatient to wait. Usually, the train never strayed far from the place it first stopped in each city. Yet it would have to roll back and forth on the tracks, sometimes for hours, until the city train officials decided it was exactly where it was supposed to be on the designated tracks. Rather than wait out this lengthy process, I and a clown named Michael decided to find some dinner in town and hopped off during a brief stop.

We trotted to town around eight in the evening and, when we returned around midnight, the tracks were empty. It was dark in this desolate warehouse district, and a cold breeze was eating at our necks.

We started off along the tracks in the direction the train had been headed.

"It's impossible to hide a mile-long train!" I complained, as we trudged along.

"We've been walking an hour," Michael said. "It's one o'clock. Why don't we head in the other direction?"

"An hour?" I asked.

He nodded.

"But if we walk an hour back, we'll just wind up where we were, and we know the train isn't there!"

But the tracks looked empty as far as we could see into the gloom. It looked like the perfect place for two lost boys to be mugged or murdered by hoboes or something. So we turned around, cursing as we stumbled over railway ties.

At 2:00 A.M. we were back where we started, and it looked the same. Definitely no train. I had blisters on my feet, as I wasn't wearing socks, and we were so exhausted we thought we might fall down and not get up.

"This is like a scene from 'The Twilight Zone,' " I said. "We'll find the train and realize we've been dead all along or something. They'll be having our funerals when we get back."

"Do-do-do-do—do-do-do-do," Michael intoned the tune from the show.

We slogged back into town and found the police station, but they couldn't help us and were none too friendly. We must have sounded like a couple of nuts hunting desperately for a train full of acrobats and wild animals at that hour of the night.

Miraculously, a cab drove by and we flagged it down. The driver called the dispatcher, who remembered where the train had parked in the past and directed us. We found it parked beside a huge warehouse on some old "dead" tracks in a little valley.

We had passed it twice during our trek.

"One thing, Michael," I said, as we slunk off to our respective cars. "We can't tell *anyone* this happened!"

He laughed. "You bet I won't tell. We'd never live it down!"

As I rolled groggily into bed at 3:00 A.M., I promised myself *never to leave the train* before I knew for sure where it would be spotted. A few cities later I would forget my vow.

By the time we reached Hartford, I was really starting to enjoy the job. I was getting to know the people better and was feeling comfortable around them, whether it was the loudmouth, barbaric Constantin Josef—known as "Ugh"—from the teeterboards, or one of the shy España women from Mexico.

And I loved what I was doing. I had always wished for a job where I could sing, be a star, meet people, and travel. Well, maybe this wasn't exactly what I had had in mind, but it was darn close. Too, my bosses Robin and Sarahjane did not abuse their power, as many directors do, so that made the job easier as well.

We also respected each other. I felt Robin and SJ were doing a great job under tough circumstances, and they were very happy with my work. They also liked knowing they could trust me to be on time for every performance and, once there, to give everything I had to the show.

I was getting an unusual amount of press for a ringmaster because of the immense publicity generated the previous year by the now famous auditions, and because I was a lively performer who charmed the reporters. My insatiable appetite for reading the reviews in every city was further cultivated by glowing notices. A writer in Worcester described me as "boyish." Hartford said I was "zesty." Of course the other performers would pick up on these words, and that's what they would call me for the rest of the week.

"Hey Zesty!" someone would call.

"There goes Mr. Charismatic!"

"How you doing there, Handsome?"

I would take it with a smile, knowing it was all in good fun.

I did manage to do some shrewd business in Hartford. It just so happened I'd performed at the nearby Coachlight Dinner Theater the previous year. I invited the producers of the place to see me in the circus and provided them with "house seats." After the show I took them out for drinks and asked them whether they'd like me to play the title role in the musical *Barnum* after I completed my tour. It was an ideal hook, and they bit. We made a gentlemen's agreement right there.

The Posso Brothers—Jaime, Eduardo, and Alberto—were the high wire performers from Colombia. I never asked their exact lineage, but they looked like noble descendants of the Inca Indians with a small percentage of Spanish blood. They each had that sort of dark hair like crow feathers that seems to shine with other colors. They had large noses, wide smiles, and café au lait skin.

After watching their act a few hundred times, I had come to

the conclusion that it was a bit long. But the audiences didn't seem to agree with me. The Possos were real showmen, and the crowd watched spellbound as the three brothers performed tricks on the tightrope without the safety of a net underneath.

Their father had taught them to walk the rope when they were young, and in their late teens and early twenties, they had become so accustomed to the wire they had no fear of falling.

In person they were less charismatic than in their act. They seemed aloof, but I think they were all a bit shy. I tried to get to know them because I wanted to practice walking a wire myself in case I really did get to play the lead in *Barnum*.

They were always very patient as they instructed me on a wire strung about two feet off the floor. For them, it must have been like teaching a baby to walk. Here I was, tiptoeing across the wire, and they could do everything from pyramids to riding a bicycle.

The climax of the Posso Brothers' act was a combination of their previous feats. They made a pyramid with one man sticking out forward, his legs wrapped around the waist of the middle brother, who in turn supported the other brother on his shoulders. The man sticking out held a small unicycle on the wire in front of him, which would roll over the wire as the pyramid progressed outwards.

To heighten the tension they would "accidentally" drop the unicycle, which would fall somewhere into the ring below. (Sometimes into buckets of elephant dung scooped up after the previous act! When that happened, Robin and I would always laugh and tease them later.)

The audience gasped because the pyramid would always collapse and a couple of guys would end up clinging to the wire. Then they would have an extra unicycle handy and complete the trick to loud applause.

For good luck, each of them would shake my hand before heading up the rope ladder to the wire. In Hartford, the handshake didn't help.

The spotlights were on them, their red and white costumes glittering with silver sequins. Not only were they working without a net, but actually over a portion of the audience as well.

Eduardo placed a bicycle on the wire, carefully mounted it,

and rode slowly across. He made it safely to the other side and
styled. A storm of applause issued from the smiling faces below.
Alberto took the bike and began tying it to a perch.

I was watching him as the bike slipped from his hands. He
grasped for it, but his fingers closed on open air. A moan went
through the audience as the bike tumbled and fell. It all happened
so quickly, and you could hear a thump as it made an impact
with something in the stands.

I was already running forward, my mind crying "no!"

Whenever something wrong happens in the show, the cue
caller yells into the headset to the light technician, "Lights to
full!" and the lights on the arena floor blast on so in an emergency
you can see what you're doing.

The lights came on and we saw that the bike had hit a boy.
He rocked back and forth in his seat wailing, hands clenched
over his head, blood oozing from between his fingers. More blood
streamed from his mouth, running down his neck.

Arena ushers and medics raced down the aisles. The entire
audience was a blur of panicked faces as Robin and I ran to the
scene. The mother was screaming beside the boy as she tried to
pry his fingers apart to determine the extent of his injury. But
all the commotion, surprise, and pain had put the little guy into
shock and he was not letting go.

It was hard to see what was happening through the crowd,
which was now standing in order to allow the medics to pass.
The boy was laid on a stretcher and hurried outside to a waiting
ambulance. His mother followed behind pulling at her hair.

I was very shaken, and the Posso Brothers were miserable
up there on their perch watching the scene. Robin motioned them
to climb down, then turned to me and spoke in an anguished
voice.

"Just get the show over, Kristopher. Bring on the Globe of
Death," he told me.

"Yes, sir," I replied with a hoarse voice. My mind filled with
the irony of bringing out the Globe of Death just after an accident.

I strode back to the center ring to do my duty and try to
regain the audience's attention, which was virtually impossible.
The energy was gone from the show. The crowd was in shock

and no longer in a mood to be entertained. Before the act was halfway through, the aisles were filled with exiting people.

Twenty minutes later, after the show closed, the first thing we did was gather around the phone while Robin called the hospital. We were clenching our fists when a smile broke on our performance director's concerned face.

"They say he's going to be all right! His tongue's been severed, but the doctors managed to sew it back together. The head wound wasn't too serious and only needed a few stitches."

A flood of joy seemed to hit me like a wave at the beach, almost pushing me over. Looking around I saw smiling faces streaked by happy tears. No one was more relieved than the Posso Brothers, who grinned and hit each other on the backs when they heard the good news. Accidents like this have affected circus people for life and even prompted them to retire. I don't know if the Possos could have gotten back on the wire if the boy had sustained a horrible injury.

As far as the circus was concerned, the insurance took care of his bills, and there was no talk of a lawsuit.

Unfortunately, however, our travails were not over yet.

May 9 was my twenty-eighth birthday, and I had it circus-style—though had I known what was in store for me I would have voted for an alternative.

Robin and SJ threw a party for me in our dressing room before the show. A few performers stopped by and shared the sodas and cake.

Robin sidled up to me holding a paper plate and a piece of my cake on it. "You know what?" he said. "I just realized something. Your birthday is the same as Irvin Feld's!"

"You're pulling my leg," I said.

He shook his head, making his big pompadour wiggle. "No, really, it's true."

I thought that was really ironic. I wondered whether some astrologer could have predicted it.

Susie Turcot, the sound person, appeared with a smile on her face and a box in her hand.

"A present for me?"

She nodded shyly.

I tore open the wrapping as several people gathered around, some winking at each other. I think the rumor mills were starting to churn out grist about the two of us. We had become friends, but that was all.

Inside the box I found a hand-sewn, floor-length royal green robe. My favorite color.

"This is beautiful!" I said, meaning it.

She beamed. "I made it myself."

"You made it?"

She nodded, blinking her eyes coyly. And though it was a beautiful present, I cringed on the inside. I could see she had developed quite a crush on me. And though I liked her, I was not romantically interested.

Gradually, I noticed that even though there was a sizable crowd in my dressing room, all laughing, telling jokes, or talking seriously about their various love affairs, there was a distinct absence of clowns.

Then I saw Vogie, the boss clown, signaling me from the doorway. "Hey, Kristopher, come here!"

I put down my slice of cake and walked innocently forward. When I got to the door I could see twenty-six clowns crowded in the hall.

Tall and short, fat and thin, they grinned at me with un-nerving intensity and suddenly broke into the most hideous cho-rus of "Happy Birthday" ever rendered on this earth. I stood there, basking in the warmth of their delivery, even though I wished I could cover my ears. Then before I could escape, each and every one of them drew out a sock filled with God only knew what and started pounding me. White dust exploded from the socks at every impact and soon an impenetrable cloud sur-rounded me.

I took it bravely, realizing that the dust was the powder that the clowns used to set their makeup. The socks were always filled with it, and they patted their faces with them. When they stopped the barrage a few minutes later, I was completely caked with the white stuff. It was in my ears, in my eyes, ingrained in my scalp, covering every hair on my head; it was in every wrinkle of my clothing; it coated my mouth and throat and nostrils.

I didn't know whether to laugh or cry. I surveyed my poor body, blinking my eyes, seeing the clowns around me overcome by mirth.

"What did I do wrong?" I asked. The clown tradition was to "pie" or otherwise humiliate someone who had screwed up in some way.

Vogie shook his head. "Nothing wrong, Mr. Ringmaster. You've been 'powder socked.' That's circus tradition on birthdays!"

"But we have a show in an hour!" I sputtered.

He laughed. "I guess you better hope there's a lot of hot water left in the shower!"

That was the good day in Hartford. But Hartford was not over.

The leader of the Constantins, the Romanian teeterboard troupe, was Ugh. I was told that Robin gave him the nickname. But whoever coined the name, everyone in the circus had quickly taken to it. The word described him perfectly.

He was a very short fellow with a tremendous beer belly and a voice that scraped his throat. Robin and I both agreed that Ugh was a live version of the Tasmanian Devil cartoon character who always gave Bugs Bunny such a hard time.

He was fun when you first met him, because he was such a character, but after working with him on a daily basis, it was hard not to tire of his attitude.

He claimed to "know ever'ting 'bout ever'ting!" It didn't matter what you were doing: practicing in the ring, changing a tire, putting on makeup, Ugh was always there to step right in and tell you what you were doing wrong.

Bill Bradley, the director, told me one time, "I wish Ugh couldn't speak English!"

Ugh always called me "Ringmeister," and was always complaining about my announcements, telling me different words to emphasize. After a while you just had to get used to him.

His place in the act was on the bottom of the totem pole, absorbing the force of each member as he landed on the shoulders of the people above. Ugh's legs would wobble, and his face would get fire-engine red every time. We all wondered when he would have a heart attack. He was far too old and out of shape to be doing this sort of work, but no one dared to tell him this to his face.

Tricks would often be missed during performances. No one could do everything perfectly every time. But Ugh was not understanding. He would get frustrated and slap the performers right in the ring in front of thousands of eyes. Unfortunately, he was no worse than the other teeterboard chiefs, the Hungarians and Bulgarians, who all practiced this behavior.

The Romanians were earthy people, quick to laughter and quicker to anger. The women were beautiful but timid; the men were wild and promiscuous, bedding every showgirl who would let them. Like sailors, they had girlfriends in every town, and if the girls weren't already there, they met them. Their mentality about women was juvenile and a little sick. Any conquest was exploited by loudly told stories. The Hungarians were the same, but we never suspected how perverted they really were until the end of the year when the trainmaster discovered that two teeterboardists had placed a two-way mirror between their cabins so they could watch each other's sexual antics with the local girls.

Susie Turcot came crying to my room one night and told me that Ugh—who had a wife in the troupe—had appeared at her room wearing only a robe and expounded on the joys she would experience spending a night with him.

The Constantins were placed in the center ring by Kenneth Feld's order, because during their climactic feat—the double backward somersault to a five-man high—they did not use a "mechanic," a guide wire attached to a belt on the performer. The mechanic did not help the trick, but would break the fall should the performer miss his mark. Mircea (Meercha) was the one who catapulted to the top of the Constantins' stack.

After the aerial display by the Franconi Duo and Satin, I announced the troupes. As the performers leaped into action, wowing the audience as always, I noticed the routines looked particularly crisp tonight. A performer jumped onto one side of the teeterboard and catapulted his comrade into the air. The airborne man did his single somersault and landed on waiting shoulders. The acts progressed through their routines until it was my turn to announce their greatest spectacle.

"Now for the first time in each ring," I said, "you will see a double backward somersault to a five-man high!"

The drum roll cut in, and the audience hushed. The spotlights gushed over each troupe, who glittered underneath as they started the trick.

It was always a fight to see who would go last, but it was usually the Constantins who managed. No one wanted to go first because you got less applause.

Tonight the Dukovis were first. Stamen Alexiev was the fellow who vaulted, and though rigged with a mechanic, the perfectly executed maneuver was breathtaking and the audience clapped.

Immediately I watched little Attila Torok being sprung from the teeterboard in the next ring. His blond head tucked into his chest, he did two backward rolls in the air and straightened his body just in time to alight upon his fellows' shoulders. He grinned and gestured broadly with his hands. Again the audience went wild.

Now it was Mircea's turn. A troupe member jumped onto the nether end of the board and the small fellow catapulted into the air. He did his tuck and roll and spread out.

But he landed on air.

He was a full foot to the side of the totem pole. A gasp tore from my throat as his expression turned to horror when he realized his situation and watched the faces of his comrades disappear above him like windows of a building.

He plunged onto the cement floor with a dull thud.

The house lights snapped to full for the second time in two days and I could see Mircea writhing on the floor in pain. I hurried over but couldn't get close because his friends were already grouped around him. Ugh, red-faced, was hunched over the poor fellow, and I thought he might slap him for missing his trick. Medics dashed in and carried Mircea away. As they took the hurt performer through the door, Ugh watched in seething anger and bullied the other members into taking their bows.

The other teeterboard troupes watched with pale faces.

Whatever animosity or rivalry that existed between the different companies was temporarily gone. It took a dramatic event like this to make them pull together. It might have happened to any of them brave enough to attempt the trick without a mechanic.

For me, as for all the performers, it was pure misery to keep the show going. All this "show must go on" stuff seemed like pretty insipid philosophy. We no longer cared about entertaining the people and, for that matter, the people no longer felt like being entertained. We just wanted to know how Mircea was and if he would be all right.

From here on the spirit lagged from the show. The clowns missed their juggling routines and their frowns were real now. Even the elephants seemed listless, as they are in fact sensitive to the emotions of the humans around them, and trudged glumly around the track.

Accidents like the ones we'd been experiencing gave me the feeling of a stomach full of lead sinkers. Suddenly you think, "Why am I doing this? Why are any of us doing this?" The entire fantasy is shattered as abruptly as Mircea's leg, which was diagnosed as fractured in several places. The act was severely handicapped for several weeks because another member was already absent with injuries.

It was then that I realized how physically grueling it was to crank out thirteen shows a week. It was a hard job, and a dangerous one—and people were actually risking their lives. One time a broken leg. The next time could as easily be a broken neck.

We would not quickly forget Hartford.

Some circus people think Hartford should be taken off the route completely. It has always been a bad luck city for The Big Show. In 1944, a fire burned Ringling's big top to the ground. The death toll, adults and children, was nearly two hundred souls.

We were ready to have a little fun in New Haven.

The Blue Unit was making its spring debut at Madison Square Garden. Their schedule was slightly different from ours, and the performers were able to bus up to Connecticut to see our production. The ringmaster, Jim Ragona, was with them. I shook his hand before the show.

"I'm really eager to see you do the job," he told me.

There was a smirk on his face that told me he just wanted to see who was better.

"I hope you like it," I told him casually. I made a vow to do a really special job that night.

A few days earlier I saw Robin and Sarahjane, my dressing room roommates, whispering to each other and laughing. Their eyes gleamed mischievously as they headed over to me.

"Listen," Robin said. "We're going to play a trick on Jim Ragona. Make him think you've really got it made. He'll go back to the other show and drive them nuts!"

I smiled. "What are we going to do?"

"First," SJ said, "we'll move out of the dressing room and you pretend you always get your own room. We'll figure out things from there. You just play along. We'll call it 'operation Ragona.' "

"Sounds good to me," I told them. "I love a good practical joke!"

The show was energized that night, and I felt particularly pleased with my performance. Sweating in my sequined tux, I walked back to my dressing room. The first thing I noticed when I went to open the door was a professionally printed sign that said MR. K. ANTEKEIER—RINGMASTER. It looked very good.

I opened the door and found more surprises. A small table stood against the wall, covered with a red tablecloth. On top of it was a bucket of fresh ice, with cold sodas placed carefully on top. Beside it was a platter of assorted minisandwiches and cubed cheese and fresh fruit.

It looked beautiful and I couldn't help but laugh.

As soon as I had donned regular clothes, there was a knock at the door. It was Jim, and I was ready.

He bustled inside, and though he tried not to seem impressed, I could see his eyes register the accoutrements of the room.

I might have expected congratulations from someone else, but not from him, and I wasn't disappointed. The first words out of his mouth were "I can't believe what you're getting away with out there!"

I sucked in a breath. For him, a performing ringmaster was

somehow impinging upon the other acts. His own performance consisted of generic announcing with little personality, in the traditional style. I didn't respond as I could have. A fleeting thought did go through my mind, but I quelled it.

"Well, I try to add what I can," I said. "Feld wanted me to be more energetic."

We sat down, and during our conversation I could see his eyes flicking over to the snacks.

"Have a soda," I said. "Help yourself to a sandwich!"

Casually, I reached over and picked up the platter and offered him one.

He picked up a delightful-looking pastrami and looked at me searchingly. "They treat you pretty well here!" There was an underlying tone of disbelief in his voice.

I shrugged. "I've asked them to beef it up a little, you know. I like more fruit." I gestured with despair at the platter. "I mean, do you see any strawberries? I told them I wanted strawberries, and what do I get—cantaloupe!" I pointed grandly at the sodas. "And I told them I wanted Perrier. I can't drink Pepsi every night!"

He looked perplexed, and I really dug in here. "I mean you probably don't have any trouble, do you? I hope after a few years they figure out what you want, don't they?"

He nodded slowly and spoke in an irritated tone. "I'll take a Pepsi if you don't mind."

We never told him it was a joke, and I've always wondered just what happened when he got back to the Blue Unit!

As I had found out by experience, the train did not always park in the nicest sections of town. But New Haven was the worst so far. We were actually parked in the city dump. The smell was stupefying. You could almost see the stench wafting off the mounds of rotting garbage. Birds wheeled overhead. At first I thought they were vultures, but closer investigation proved they were seagulls. Below, thousands of birds pecked at the offal. It was a terrible place. Erwin Urias, one of the Globe of Death motorcylists, was practicing with his BB gun and stumbled over a decomposed body. I could only imagine that Kenneth Feld must have gotten a darn good deal to park the train there.

In spite of the disgusting scenery, the weather was beautiful and I decided to lie out in the sun on a flatcar. I closed my eyes and tried to forget the awful fumes as I got a "junkyard suntan." Never in my wildest dreams had I ever pictured myself here. Two years earlier I had been performing on cruise ships and sunning on tropical beaches. My, how our lives can change!

A dear friend of mine, Kim Kish, an actress in commercials, came up to see the show with a group of children from her church choir. After the show I changed clothes and went outside to answer questions from the eager children.

"Here's the ringmaster," my friend said when I arrived.

"Where?" came the chorus.

The kids looked everywhere but at me. I thought it must be a joke.

"Here!" said Kim, gesturing at me.

The small eyes narrowed on me, and one girl in front spoke for all. "He's not the ringmaster. The ringmaster wears a beautiful costume and always carries a hat!"

I laughed and spoke. "I don't always wear a costume," I said. "That's just for the circus. Out here, I'm a regular person."

"You're not the ringmaster!" the girl said.

It took a while to get them to understand. It was like seeing Santa Claus without his red suit. They thought I should always walk around in my sequined tails.

I had this problem a lot, and not only with children. It was a never-ending battle to get out of wearing my costumes to publicity interviews. Usually, I just wore a sport coat, and the newspeople always complained, asking me where my costume was.

I told them if they wanted to interview me at the arena, in the circus atmosphere, I would be glad to wear it. But away from the scene, it just didn't feel right.

My standard argument went: "You wouldn't have asked Alan Alda to wear army fatigues on your show, but on the set of 'M*A*S*H' he probably would have done an interview in complete Hawkeye character." Usually, they would understand. But they always seemed a little disappointed.

7

TITILLATING TOURING TURBULENCE

A Bumpy Road

BRIAN MASCK, THE MUSKEGON CHRONICLE

We were heading to Hershey, Pennsylvania, through pure Norman Rockwell America. It was Memorial Day, the last spring holiday, and you couldn't have ordered more perfect weather. We rolled through New Haven, Stratford, Bridgeport, and Darien. Each township had a parade marching down Main Street, with crowds on the sidewalks waving American flags. As the train passed through suburban neighborhoods, I waved to the families in their backyards. The dads flipped burgers, drank beer, and wore aprons with cute sayings embroidered on them like "Kiss the Chef!" The kids crowded picnic tables with plastic forks and paper plates, while the moms spooned out potato salad. It was almost voyeuristic seeing these people carrying on their lives. I couldn't help but wave at them, and they waved back, flashing Colgate smiles.

It made me miss a regular life I had not had in years.

When the train stopped briefly in the late afternoon, waiting to go under the river, I realized we were only two blocks from my apartment in Long Island City. It took an act of willpower not to pack a bag and jump off. The train arrived in Hershey sometime during the night while I slept.

We were parked several miles from the arena, so it was too far to ride the new bike I'd bought back in Providence. For some reason, even though it wasn't much money, it really irked me to pay for the bus ride, and I grudgingly dug into my pocket for a quarter to take the Ringling bus to work.

The arena, adjacent to an amusement park, had been built somewhere in the indefinite past, but I guessed the 1940s or 1950s. It had the same musty odor of old buildings in Coney Island. The smell of past crowds, hotdogs, and stale beer lingered in the stands. The place was the home of the local hockey team.

For winter sports you don't need air-conditioning, so the building had none. The weather was hot and humid, and the auditorium was stifling. My heavy, sequined costumes stuck to me and were dripping wet after each show.

Our dressing room was the office of the hockey team man- ager, and the walls were hung with dusty pictures of past teams and rusting trophies that had once been held in triumphant hands after a victorious game.

"This heat is unbearable, Kristopher!" SJ said, hands on hips. Sweat ran down her face and dripped over her chin.

"I wish we could do something about it," I told her.

She looked around the room, glaring at objects as if they were responsible for the heat. Her gaze rested on a refrigerator in the corner.

"I've got an idea!" she said.

She bent down and plugged in the machine and turned it on. It rumbled and shook but seemed to work. She opened the door and sat in front of it for a minute, then decided that wasn't good enough and left the room. She returned shortly with an ancient fan she had found somewhere, stationed it inside the refrigerator, and plugged it into the socket.

"Ta da!" she declared. "Instant air-conditioning."

I laughed.

"Sometimes you just have to be inventive," she said, as she set a chair in front of the contraption, plopped into it, and lit a cigarette.

I wondered what the manager would think if he saw his office now!

A letter was forwarded to me from the Ringling main offices in D.C. It turned out to be a fan letter from a woman in Binghamton who praised my work and thought she should "inform" Kenneth Feld what a "great addition Mr. Antekeier is to the show!" I wrote her a thank-you letter and enclosed a personalized, auto-graphed publicity photo of me from the circus. I received these sorts of letters throughout the year and found that what most impressed people were the little things I did. Just a wave to a child, a second of eye contact, or a few brief words during in-termission had an incredible impact on people.

Kenneth Feld made an appearance in Hershey. He was al-ready planning the 117th Edition of the circus and needed busi-ness and creative meetings with various members of the staff. The most I saw of him was a quick handshake and a few muttered words. We were both uncomfortable, wondering what the other was thinking. I still had not renewed my contract. I was hoping that more good reviews and enthusiastic fan letters would get him to up my scale.

Unfortunately, Kenneth Feld was hoping I would love the circus life so much I couldn't refuse what he was offering. Still, it was the two-year contract that was the brick wall for me. I knew it was just impossible physically to do the job so long. My knees and shins were in constant pain, and stairways were night-mares. If I get arthritis before my time, I'll know why.

I was handed a message to call home after a show in Columbus, Ohio. I didn't have good feelings about it, and when I heard the shaking voice of the friend subletting my apartment, I knew it was bad news.

"Tony, your landlord, was shot and killed today!"

"What?"

"He was delivering potato chips last night in the Bronx, and someone tried to rob him."

"Oh my God!" I said.

I was really close to my landlord and his family. They lived in the top apartment of a two-family home and rented the bottom half to me. They were Cuban, very tight with their two sons, and had sort of accepted me into the family. I had just seen them in May, and the news was devastating to me.

Later that night we had another performance. And while I danced in center ring singing my songs with clowns clowning, showgirls parading, tigers prowling, music blaring, thousands of people gazing down at me, the sadness in my heart could not be quelled. These people would never know my problems, and I would probably never know theirs. But while they were escaping their troubles for a couple of hours, it was not their duty to help me with mine. Now, whenever I see a show, and perhaps a bad performance, I have to be a little more forgiving. Who knows what is happening in that actor's life?

After the show a clown came up to me.

"Did you hear about Frankie the clown?" he asked.

I shook my head, hoping it wasn't more bad news. Frankie was a dwarf clown in the show. Almost all circuses have a "little person" as it's considered good luck.

"Well, during tonight's show, while all of us were piled on top of each other in the clown car, he announced his engagement!"

I smiled. "You mean he proposed to the girl he met back in Raleigh?"

"Yup!"

"But why did he tell you in the clown car?" It seemed like an odd choice, even for a clown.

He laughed. "Every night we try to up one another with news or a joke or something. It's tradition! Things get pretty rank in that car with fourteen sweaty bodies pressed together."

For the first time I really thought about the confines of that tiny car. "I imagine no one eats beans before a performance!"

He winked at me. "Au contraire, my innocent friend! Haven't you noticed how fast we get out of that car sometimes?"

Columbus was a good circus town. "The Big Show" had not played there for several years, so the press had a field day. When we first arrived I did four different interviews for competing TV stations in half an hour.

Lexington and Louisville, Kentucky, followed in quick succession. On the rodeo route we often have "split weeks," during which we play two towns in one week. The performers get an extra day of rest, but it's tough on the rigging crew, who have to load in and out.

In Louisville, the Españas had a party.

I rode my bike from the train to their trailers behind the arena. It was crowded with tired performers enjoying an evening after a day of shows. The Españas were from Mexico and had prepared their own recipe for guacamole. Salsa music blared from speakers. A half-dozen different languages made a babble all around.

The Españas were great hosts and loved giving parties for the show people. It was a great way to calm tensions among performers, too.

The Gypsy life-style suited the troupe well. Mama España, a tiny woman with a vibrant smile and happy eyes, sat clapping time to the music. Her son Noe (No-ay) danced with his girlfriend, a showgirl named Joanne.

Ugh was there too, telling them how to dance better. And when they wouldn't listen he recruited couples into an impromptu dance contest.

Except for the modern trailers in the background, we could have been a traveling Gypsy troupe back in Europe a hundred years ago. Or five hundred. Scenery changes, but people don't. People lived in their trailers now, just as they had lived in horse-drawn wagons of their ancestors. Papa España would sit outside, relaxing in his lounge chair and sipping a Bloody Mary while playing Spanish music on the radio. He had a round belly and two chins and sported a narrow mustache. Neither he nor Mama spoke much English, but they were always very warm.

Consummate circus performer Fanny Braun trains a showgirl between shows in a neck hang for the new edition of the circus. (Marc Lafontant)

The clowns mounted their stilts from tall ladders. Here, between shows, they get ready for a rehearsal of a production number.

Left: Attila Torok.

Below: Hungarian teeterboardist "Little Laci" and me on one of our many shopping sprees at a mall, holiday time.

Right: Robin Frye and Bob "Teach" Grote. (Courtesy Robin Frye)

Below: The Halloween party center ring in Buffalo, New York. (Check out the ringmaster at the upper left sporting the pig nose!) (Marc Lafontant)

Left: Clown Barbara's walk around—a kite flying a kid. (Marc Lafontant)

Below: Here's Uncle Soapy—in makeup, out of costume—getting his daily coffee from pie car, jr. You can see a drawing of him in full makeup on the front jacket of the book. (Marc Lafontant)

Opposite, top: The infamous Ugh never missed an opportunity to pose for a camera in his Spec regalia. (Marc Lafontant)

Opposite, bottom: On my last day, I finally broke down and touched an elephant—but not without trepidation!

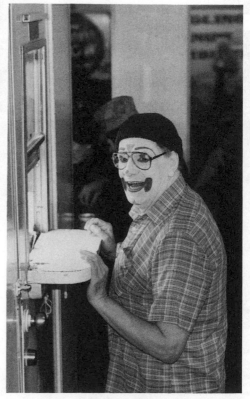

The train yard could look both ominous and almost romantic at
night. Here, a workingman says good-bye to a local girl just before
we pull out of La Crosse, Wisconsin.
(Brian Masck/*The Muskegon Chronicle*)

The three España sisters were small-boned and pretty. In shows, with their costumes and hairpieces, it was almost impossible for me to tell them apart.

The three sons were very different looking, slight, medium build, and large.

Ivan was the punk, only eighteen years old. A know-it-all with a tough-guy attitude, he was notorious for getting ready at the last possible moment. But none of them was ever on time. They were usually late for their entrance on the arena floor.

Once, Ivan stomped over to me after a show.

"It isn't very professional of you to announce us if you don't see us ready!" he shouted.

I shook my head. "It's not very professional of you not to be ready. You have plenty of time after the Liberty horses and clown walk arounds."

He huffed off, and nothing changed. I would announce them, and they'd come rushing into the rings, still adjusting their costumes.

Theirs was not as dangerous an act as others, since they worked with nets underneath them. But things could happen even when you thought you were safe.

During one show, a workingman accidentally dropped the wires stretching the net while the three sisters were taking their bows. The wire whipped across their faces and threw the women to the floor. It was a tense moment, while they writhed around, their hands covering their faces. Fortunately, they were not permanently injured. Ramon España was livid and had to be restrained from clobbering the poor rigger who had had one lapse of judgment and let go of his wire too soon.

The next leg of the tour was through the South. We hit Nashville, where we had a day off, and several of us went to see Opryland. Our audiences were sizable but were more used to their own brand of entertainment and did not respond well. Split weeks continued through Huntsville, Alabama, where the weather was hot and the people spoke in thick southern accents.

In Huntsville, the Urias Troupe gave me a jolt that would foreshadow later problems in their dangerous act. They rarely checked their motorcycles, and one machine was having problems as they sped around the steel mesh globe. The cycle sputtered and came down early, almost hitting the other performers as they buzzed around.

The old arenas in the South kept getting worse. In Little Rock, Arkansas, the coliseum had few dressing rooms and almost no back lot. Clown Alley had to be set up in a smelly livestock building down a hill from the arena. I could just imagine what would have happened if Dave had still been with us. This would have sent him packing for certain!

As it was, many of the clowns complained bitterly. Most of them had no clout so their protests fell on deaf ears. Robin Frye felt awful about the conditions and did his best to help matters and was able to move a few people to more comfortable quarters.

That's how I got to know Uncle Soapy, the oldest clown.

His real name was Duane Thorpe, and he had been with the circus for thirty-eight years. Because of his age and seniority, Robin Frye put him in an air-conditioned dressing room across the hall from my own.

I had not gotten to know the old fellow yet, as he was a bit reclusive. I remembered passing Clown Alley and peering in at the clowns in full makeup lounging near their costume trunks. Suddenly Uncle Soapy's voice would pierce the air: "Shut the door!"

Uncle Soapy's door wasn't closed now. He must have been lonely in the dressing room by himself since even though he was letting the cold air out, the door was substantially ajar. I could see him sitting near his trunk applying his makeup in front of the mirror. The trunk was a faded black with rusty hinges, scuff marks, and peeling stickers. A cigarette stuck in a long holder smoldered in an ashtray and sent a thin wire of smoke into the air. Soapy himself was a slightly plump fellow in his sixties with sagging jowls.

"Hey, Soapy!" I called. "You want this door shut?"

"Naw!" he said, without turning his head around. "It's all right . . ." His voice sort of trickled off. Not the usual terseness it could have. "Unh . . . how long till show?"

"Forty-five minutes," I told him.

"We got plenty of time, then."

"That's right."

I could tell he wanted some company. He might not be used to outsiders looking into Clown Alley, but now he was without the comfort of his comrades. I still didn't want to risk being rebuffed so I started to open my dressing room door.

"So Kristopher, you were in musical theater?" came his smoke-roughened voice.

"Yeah," I said.

"Well don't just stand there! Come where I don't have to shout, why don't you?"

I entered the room and sat on a chair against the wall while he continued to paint the makeup on his whitened face. Nearby, on the counter, I saw a *Playbill*, a theatrical publication.

"You like the theater?" I asked.

"Hmmph! Like the theater? I *love* the theater! When I was a young fellow like you I aspired to be an actor!"

He had a flamboyant way of speaking, though his accent was sort of like one of the Bowery Boys.

"I did a few plays, too, before I hooked up with The Big Show. I was in *The Greatest Show on Earth* movie, you know? Been here thirty-eight years now!"

"That's a long time," I said. "Don't you get tired of it?"

He smiled and winked an eye, watching me in the mirror. "I love it. It was my life's calling. I made some great friends here. Let me show you."

He got up from his chair and opened the trunk. Inside, the lid was plastered with old photographs held on by yellowing Scotch tape. "See here? This is Harold Ronk. And here? This is Ol' Count Nicholas!"

He proceeded to name a list of people. Some of them I'd heard of, as they were famous circus performers. But many others were clowns who had drifted in and out through the years. It was sad seeing these faces of yesterday. Soapy didn't know what had even happened to most of them.

"What about these pictures here?" I asked. "That doesn't even look like the United States!"

He smiled and ran a finger affectionately over the photos and spoke with a distracted voice. "That's right. These are from

Spain. I save my money every year and go to Spain when the circus is in hiatus in December.''

"Really?"

"I love the people," he said. "They're so happy. They're like clowns without makeup."

I had closed the door when I entered. Now it swung open, and a sweating fellow barged in. It was Jeffrey, one of the younger clowns. The heat outside was melting his makeup, which ran down his face.

"Wow! This air-conditioning is fantastic!" he said. "You know our dressing rooms in Clown Alley are in the pig stalls! How the hell do you rate an air-conditioned room?"

"Well," said Soapy. "You know what they say—pearls before swine!"

During our time in Little Rock, Soapy and I often discussed theater and made a pact to share our magazines, my *Backstage* newspapers a friend religiously sent from New York and his *Playbill* subscription, which was forwarded to him from the main offices.

"I really think I could have made it on stage," he told me once. "I had a real good singing voice. You know I used to be understudy for the ringmaster?"

"Really?"

"Sure. Ya wanna see a picture?"

"You bet," I told him.

He rummaged through his treasured collectibles secreted inside a hidden compartment in his trunk and pulled out a faded photograph of himself standing center ring in black tuxedo, wearing black horn-rimmed glasses.

"Old Harold Ronk would get lazy sometimes. He hated to sing in some of these old buildings, so I would go on for him."

Harold Ronk was a well-known staunchly traditional ringmaster who had been with "The Big Show" for many years.

It was amazing all the little things you found out about people. For instance, Soapy was the only man ever known to cancel a Spec when he was in charge because the floor was too muddy under the tent one day and even the elephants wouldn't be able to slog through it. That must have been way back before Irvin Feld started booking the circus into arenas! I could just imagine

Soapy doing the ringmaster job, loving every minute of it, just waiting for the time when Harold Ronk would tap him on the shoulder and say, "Hey, you want to go on today?' For a few shows he would put away the clown suit and take over the distinguished role of ringmaster.

But he was like many other people who don't appreciate what they are. Soapy was a hero to thousands of kids who had seen him in *The Greatest Show on Earth* movie, watched his antics in the ring over the years, and later grown up to be clowns themselves and considered it an honor to work with him. And besides those lucky few, he had made millions laugh over the years. I knew the impact of one wave to a kid. Who could tell how many people Soapy had made happy in his time?

With so many people traveling with the circus, there were bound to be a few that didn't mesh. A member of the band had rubbed me the wrong way from the very beginning. He was an abrasive fellow who tried to manufacture as much tension between people as he could possibly manage. I tried not to have anything to do with him, and Robin and Sarahjane loathed him too.

This guy was about six feet five inches tall, with long, gray, unkempt hair and a ratty beard. He had been with the show for fifteen years, so despite being a nut case, he was a pretty good musician. He had grown tired of the show, however, and had made it clear this would be his last year.

His obnoxious tone of voice and continuing crass behavior in the dressing room were most repulsive. The sad part was that no one ever told him how offensive he was. I guess we were all a little scared he would turn his tongue on us. Even so, I was not so lucky as to escape his notice.

One day in Little Rock he made a stupid, and really quite bizarre, comment about me to the band and it got back to me via my friend and companion Susie Turcot. Anger swelling my chest, I stomped to his dressing room at the arena and slammed open the door without knocking.

He looked down at me from his towering height, like a vulture peering down on a dying man. There was the same shrewd, amoral look that I see in that bird.

"Have I offended you?" I asked through gritted teeth.

He shook his head innocently. "No, why?"

"Is it true that during the sound check you had some negative things to say about me?"

A smile seemed to play on his lips without forming. His eyes narrowed and his posture straightened. His tone of voice was proud. "Yes, I did!" he told me.

"Well, I've got a few things to say about you too!" And I let go of virtually everything I had held in check these past months. I told him about his offensive mouth and his offensive breath, appearance, and odor.

And all he did was smile, arms tucked firmly together across his chest.

"And furthermore . . ." I stopped.

Looking at him, I suddenly realized nothing I said would affect him. He was an unhappy man, and his verbal abuse was a way of bringing others down to his level. My coming here, the words I was saying were playing into his hand. It was, somehow, the only twisted joy he got out of life.

I looked him in the eye and said, "You're just not worth it," and left the room.

Our concessionaires were a healthy mix of people: white, black, and Latin Americans, tossed in with a few Europeans. Many had gotten their jobs because they were married, or attached, to a person in one of the acts. Others had performed in the circus in previous years but had since retired or had their act canceled. But "The Big Show" was their home, and any other life-style would have bored them, so they took jobs in sales. Still other performers, clowns and showgirls for instance, had made the change simply to make more money.

Marc Lafontant was a young black concessionaire who spoke fluent French and had a striking smile and a strong build. His personality was always optimistic and outgoing. He and I both liked to explore the cities we were playing, and ended up getting fairly close as we happily played tourist.

Marc had a severe stutter, which amazingly would totally disappear when he got intoxicated—or when he was pitching his souvenirs from the concession stand. He was always one of the top-grossing salespersons, and made over $60,000 of his own during the year. His smooth talking, courteous demeanor could win over even the hardest-to-sell customers. Marc's greatest joy was gold, and he always wore long, thick chains. Every other day, it seemed, he came in sporting a new gold ring.

He asked me to help drive his motor home through bayou country to our next destination, New Orleans. Jeffrey the clown joined us, and together we made an uproarious "Three Musketeers."

It was a lovely ride across Lake Pontchartrain. Shacks raised on high stilts over the water lined the marshy shore, Spanish moss hung like thick cobwebs from the trees, and tall herons tiptoed carefully through the reeds looking for prey. The dilapidated old shacks gradually turned into concrete and glass as we got closer into the city. I had been here twice before: once for a Puppeteers of America convention while I was in high school, and again for the World's Fair several years later in a touring production of the Garfield Show—a job which I loathed.

We arrived in the morning and parked in a lot behind the Superdome. The gargantuan building was intimidating. I was further daunted when I went inside and stood in the middle of the place, with some hundred thousand seats tiering up so high they virtually faded from view. I was awestruck, knowing that even "The Greatest Show on Earth" extravaganza would be a tiny procession in this amazing space.

Marc came up behind me.

"It's all right," he said. "Don't let it get to you. We'll only be in one corner."

"It won't matter," I said. "We'll still look like fleas jumping around down here."

The advantage to driving here with Marc was that we had arrived a full day ahead of the train, and I got to spend my day off having fun instead of vegetating in my cabin. We went back to the lake, went swimming, and sat in the sun. Then, in the evening, we headed for the famed Bourbon Street. We ate a spicy Cajun dinner and then hit some of the clubs for the jazz.

I don't drink, so the next morning it was easy for me to get up for two radio interviews I had been asked to do. One was on location in the French Quarter, and the other was at a studio on a call-in program, my favorite kind of interview. Answering live, impromptu questions was a real challenge. By this time I had a lot of experience, so my answers were quick and to the point.

Inevitably, someone called in to have me do my "cry," as they put it, meaning the opening announcement—"Ladies and Gentlemen . . ."

I obliged, of course.

I don't think I did a single interview in which I was not asked to declaim those immortal words. If this was any indication, there were a lot of frustrated ringmasters out there!

The train arrived and parked in a muddy warehouse district. It was a rough part of town, and one of the Urias' motorcycles was stolen off a flatbed almost the moment the train pulled in. More than once, I was really sorry I had chosen train life over that of the motor home.

The Superdome was so big, it took ten minutes to walk from my dressing room to the center ring. I could have brought my bike inside and ridden it from one point to the other as sailors do on aircraft carriers.

The place did have its good points though. My dressing room was the most elegant, spacious, and private of any during the tour, certainly a whole lot different from those hothouses we had played elsewhere in the South.

One of the amenities was a huge bathroom with a bathtub.

"You have a bathtub!" Susie Turcot exclaimed when she found out. Her body almost went liquid. "What I wouldn't give for a nice soothing bath!"

"Well, you can use it," I told her.

If eyes can light up, hers did then. I had never realized how much people, maybe women especially, like a bath. A shower had always been fine for me.

Susie, of course, couldn't keep her delight secret, and word got around. Soon I had a slew of showgirls pleading with me for a chance at the tub. Eventually, I just left the dressing room unlocked every night, ostensibly for just Susie and one other showgirl, but who knows how many clandestine late-night baths were taken! Living on the road, you get what little pleasures of home life you can.

The immense space of the arena was definitely a problem. The circus is a very sensual experience. The audience has to smell the animals and see the glare in a tiger's eye to really get the excitement out of it. I mean, from the top seats, the unicorn must have looked like a sheepskin rug. When I stood center ring on opening night and made my announcement, my voice reverberated as if I were in an empty airplane hangar. I could imagine I was projecting about as much charisma as a dressed-up scarecrow. I felt sorry for the audience. They were just too far away.

8

A DYNAMIC DUELING DISCOVERY

Canasta!

BRIAN MASCK/THE MUSKEGON CHRONICLE

During our stint in New Orleans it became clear to me that I could not renew my ringmaster contract. It was a sad realization because this had been the most thrilling year of my life. As a kid, I had loved carnivals and had surrounded myself with circus paraphernalia. In addition my professional experience had groomed me for the job. If Destiny cares about us poor entertainers, it had taken special pains to get me the position.

With all of that, I felt a little traitorous when I thought about leaving the show. But in the back of my mind a thought popped up. What if ringmaster were a step toward a higher achievement?

The sudden thought was like an epiphany to me. It was like being a man who has been told he has only a few months to live. I started to enjoy my life to an even greater extent. I became intensely interested in all the people around me, in their jobs and their talents, their histories and their projected futures. And interestingly, I found that a lot of people shared my newfound joy. Kenneth Feld had told most of them they would not be returning in the new edition, and after the initial shock and disappointment, those people too were suddenly more "involved" than before.

I was luckier than most. My particular talents could be adapted to virtually any performance technique, from acting in film and theater, to emceeing, to becoming a talk show or game show host, to almost anything.

For a teeterboardist, an aerialist, a trapeze artist, or a tight-rope walker to find another job, he would most likely have to find another circus, such as one of the smaller shows still performing under tents. Of course, after performing in "The Big Show," almost any other circus would be glad to have these performers, so all was not lost. But these specialists had attained the highest ground of their profession, and any other production was a step down.

I was lucky. Opportunities for me were endless, and I was thankful for it.

The audience response in New Orleans was not great. Of course, dwarfed as we were by the Superdome, it was not hard to see why. When we moved north toward Jackson, Mississippi, things came back into perspective. Again, in a more homey auditorium, "The Greatest Show on Earth" looked like the triumphant production that it indeed was. Thunderous applause surrounded us after my opening announcement and it reached greater heights during the evening.

In my new state of heightened awareness I became so mesmerized by the gracefulness of the Flying Españas and the precise timing that made the act possible that I almost missed my cue. The drummer, however, started his roll and jolted me out of my reverie in time to announce their triple somersaults.

The two catchers for the Flying Españas were the only members who were not part of the family. One of them, Raul Segura, was from Sarasota, Florida. He blended in perfectly, however, because he spoke fluent Spanish and came from a circus family as well. His grandfather had been a popular clown, and most of the family had been raised in circus life.

The way I got to know many of the performers was through the games we played between performances. Raul and I started playing Yahtzee with Carolina España and quickly became friends. I enjoyed being in the midst of the big, chaotic Mexican family and learned some Spanish by virtual osmosis.

Playing games shortened the time between shows and kept boredom at bay during our long travel days. My friends have to watch out for me now if they want to play games. I have so much more experience than most of them.

I guess in the far north, during bitter winters, people play as much as we did. So if I play anybody from Minnesota I'll be wary!

After Jackson, we played Lafayette, Louisiana, the Cajundome. It was a real treat because it was a perfect size and only a year old to boot. Everything was clean and bright. It had sort of a "new car" scent to it. After the elephants left, I'm afraid, the scent was replaced by an odor.

The trip to Lafayette was a painfully long one. The scenes outlined in the windows were of rural poverty, dry weather, and cactus growing in the rocks beside the rails.

The train stopped with a tremendous jolt. I leapt from my settee, ran down the hall, and jumped down the steps from the vestibule. It was dim along the tracks and I hastened forward through high weeds until I came on a gathering crowd emitting a buzz of conversation.

"What happened?" I asked a figure who appeared out of the gloom. It was Claudia, a concession worker.

"The train derailed!" she replied.

We joined the people and jostled for a view. Sure enough, two cars leaned off the tracks at a dangerous angle.

"I was in my room," Claudia said breathlessly, "when it hit like an earthquake! Everything slid to the side. Me included!"

Tim Holan, the train master, stood nearby rubbing his chin and looking a little bemused.

"What happened, Tim?" I asked.

He shook his head. "I can't believe it. They told us to park the train on these old tracks, and it's obvious they haven't been used in years! No one checked them before we came in like they should have." He gestured violently. "Look at them. Any jerk could tell those rails couldn't support the weight!"

It was a long night. A giant crane was brought in to hoist the two leaning cars back onto the tracks. Luckily, no one was hurt.

I found out later that this was not the first derailment. Once in the 1960s the train had left the tracks at high speed, injuring many people. From then on, I never took barreling down the tracks for granted and always worried about an accident.

I have always liked Fourth of July. Fireworks exploding against the night sky remind me of brilliant, ephemeral flowers blooming in an instant and withering away.

This year the day was not memorable for me. I rode my bike to the arena for a show and saw a few scrawny fireworks sponsored by the local Jaycees. Then it was time for the show, and when we had finished, the fireworks were already gone except for a few "civilian" rockets flashing upward with the sound of firecrackers going off in the background.

The next day I really screwed up my lyrics. I repeated some in the wrong place and totally forgot others.

Sarahjane came up to me after the show, a cigarette in her hand.

"What's the problem, Kristopher?" she asked, smoke puffing out from her mouth.

I shook my head. "I don't know, SJ. I just couldn't concentrate."

She smiled and nodded her head knowingly. "You've got 'long-run-itis,' " she said.

"Oh my!" I said. "Is it contagious? Is it—deadly?"

She chuckled and took another long drag on her cigarette. "It can be deadly for a show, anyway."

I took a deep breath. "I'll get it under control. I hate messing up."

This was not my first bout with my "long-run-itis." After

you repeat a show so many times, paying attention becomes a real problem. It doesn't become mechanical as much as it becomes second nature. Then, suddenly a few synapses in your brain refuse to spark and you're out there in front of thousands of people and your lines just aren't there. You've said them hundreds of times—and suddenly they're gone. It's such a frightening experience, I don't think there's an actor who hasn't dreamed of forgetting his lines. The problem is that the nightmare often invades reality.

"You need to free up your mind," Sarahjane said. "Relax."

I smiled. "You're right, SJ. I think it's time for a game! I've got a few tucked away in my wardrobe box. Do I have an opponent?"

Sarahjane didn't miss a beat. "Name your poison! What's your favorite?"

"Well," I said. "My all-time favorite is a card game. . . ."

"Like what?"

"Well, you've probably never heard of it. It's called canasta."

Her eyes narrowed rivetingly on me. She tried to make her voice casual, but there was an edge on it. "Canasta? I play a little canasta. My mother taught me."

"I used to play with my grandmother. She said it was all the rage in the fifties."

SJ shuffled her feet. "Did you usually win?"

"Always," I said.

She inhaled, the cigarette glowing bright, now a mere stub. I knew I had found a real player. "Well, I'm not doing anything between shows. You want to try a game?"

"I could manage," I said.

Canasta is a variant of rummy played with two decks and all four jokers. It is a difficult game because of wild cards, melding tactics, and point strategies. There are just too many variables to master the game easily.

We sat at a makeshift table in my dressing room, as I shuffled the two decks and looked across at my competitor. There was a hungry look in her eyes, and her smoking rate had increased.

The cards slid across the table as I dealt them. She watched in silence as her pile added up. Then, when I had finished dealing, she snatched up her cards and shuffled through them with quick precise movements, putting them in order in a jiffy.

She glanced at me over her cards, and her eyes showed that she realized how intimidating her actions might be to an amateur. She cleared her throat.

"I'm always fast getting my cards tidy," she said in a cool, low voice.

"Right," I told her and then buzzed through my cards as quickly as she had hers. I looked up when I was finished to see a look of respect on her face. She nodded slowly, acknowledging my expertise. We were like two gunslingers sizing each other up.

SJ played the game with the cigarette hanging from the side of her mouth. We drew cards. During the game, I made all the right decisions with my combinations, often picking up the entire discard pile, a key factor in winning canasta.

"I'm out," I said, laying my cards down.

"Damn!" She threw her unused cards on the table. "I thought I had you."

I started to gather the cards and her hand closed over mine.

"My deal," she said gruffly.

We played the entire two-hour break and learned we were perfect adversaries. Our strategies clashed, and we would alternately chortle and curse as we caught each other at the other's tricks or learned new ways of overcoming a problem.

Canasta became our standard fare to get through those long Saturdays. Soon we taught Raul Segura and Susie the game so we could play partners—and things really started to pick up. We became fanatical, dodging back to the dressing room as soon as a show was over to play a game.

Evidently, Tina Gebel saw us playing once between shows. She told Gunther and he marched up to SJ the next day.

"You vill not play cards anymore!" he ordered, in his thick German accent. "It isn't ladylike or right for a director."

SJ gritted her teeth and remained cool. "What we do in the privacy of the dressing room is our own damned business," she told him. "A card game is not moral degradation! We're playing between shows, and we're not playing for money!"

Gunther sucked in a breath, stared at her for a minute, and

stomped off. Gunther and his family did not care for SJ, probably because she was not intimidated by them.

Gunther's dictatorial qualities really irked me. The German tamer didn't acknowledge us for a few days, and after that we always made sure the dressing room door was closed, or we played on the train.

I had enjoyed my overland trip with Marc in his motor home and decided to travel with him to Houston. Coming into the city, I couldn't believe how spread out it was. It is one of those cities of glass that are dazzling in the sunshine. I'd never toured through here before and was eager to explore.

On arriving at the arena, called The Summit, the other trailer folks were busy hustling around trying to find places alongside the arena. Noe España accidentally ran over a water main and a geyser spewed forth in the middle of the parking lot.

Never a dull day in the circus!

Besides the water gushing forth (it was eventually shut off at the street), everyone was jockeying for position trying to second-guess where Gunther would want to park when he arrived. There is a first-come, first-served basis about sites, because there was often a shortage of room available behind the arenas. But Gunther would often throw the whole shebang out of whack no matter when he arrived, because he got his pick of spaces, being the petty tyrant that he sometimes was.

So it would always be a race to get to the arena first and hook up water and electricity, hoping you weren't where Gunther wanted to park his megacruiser.

Marc hooked up his utilities and jumped into the shower, while I watched TV.

"Who's cut off my water!" came his voice muffled from the bathroom.

The door slammed open and he came scrambling out with a towel wrapped around his waist. Sudsy water streamed down his dark skin. He strode to the door and flung it open. Outside, one of the Bulgarians was bent over the water hook-ups.

"What are you doing!" Marc yelled.

The Bulgarian looked innocent. "I hook up de watter."

"Couldn't y-y-you knock on my d-d-door and ask before y-y-you splice in, for cripes sake?" He stammered badly when he was mad.

He slammed the door before the poor guy could answer and went to finish his shower.

I laughed. Anger didn't suit him. It was like watching a sheep suddenly sprout fangs, and it just didn't work.

Some people call Texas "God's country," but we called it "circus country." All year long, whenever I'd mention that we'd had a particularly responsive audience, people would always snicker and say, "Just wait till we get to Texas."

They were right.

The arena was packed for every performance, and the crowds were so enthusiastic they really made each show worthwhile.

The one thing I could never understand was the attitude of the performers during the Spec portion of the show. They would parade around looking gloomy, when I would be emanating energy.

"What's the problem with them?" I asked Robin.

"They hate Spec," he told me. "They feel like props. Plus it's the second year of the tour, they're bored, and they know they're not being renewed."

"It's hard for me to fathom. In legitimate theater you always give your all, no matter what. That smile doesn't come off your face until you wipe it off with your makeup!"

He smiled and tapped a finger on my chest. "That's why you were hired."

Most of the performers did come to life during their own acts. I did have to give them that. And Satin, the black female aerialists, were always "on" no matter what; that added to my respect for them. They were one of the few American acts, and it was very plain that their entire psychology was different than that of the Latins and Europeans. They knew the parade, the façade, was just as important to the audience as the tricks.

During the first show at The Summit, I found a dozen roses waiting for me in my dressing room. They were from an old acquaintance I'd toured with back in my Cedar Point days who was coming to see the show. I also found messages from some high school classmates who now lived here and would be in the audience.

All these people who kept popping up everywhere really amazed me. It made me realize how many people I'd come in contact with over the years while performing. It was like "This Is Your Life," all these past ghosts materializing in the strangest places.

In the middle of the show, Jane, my touring friend, opened a banner during the finale that blared at me in center ring: WORLD'S GREATEST RINGMASTER—KRISTOPHER!

I loved it, and the cast also got a big kick from it. My nickname for the week became "Mr. Greatest!"

Unfortunately, I did not live up to the title during our two-week stint.

It was too hot to keep the animals outside, so they were housed in the building. I could smell them from my dressing room, and their proximity revved up my allergies. I prayed I wouldn't lose my voice, but my cough persisted and by the first weekend my voice was completely shot.

It so happened that Tim Holst had flown in to check up on the show.

"Is there any way you could go on for me?" I asked him. "You were ringmaster once. You've got the whole show in your head."

He shook his head. "I couldn't do it."

"We could make up cue cards," I said, my voice cracking even now.

"It's not that," he told me. "There's just too much for me to do here."

I looked him in the eye and could tell it wasn't that. He just didn't want to go back in the ring and screw up, possibly making his underlings lose respect for him.

"This is worse than Cincinnati," I told him. "If I raise my voice I sound like a frog."

He smiled, not friendly. "Well," he said, "no one will notice another animal!"

Miserably, I went on that night. To her credit and my surprise, Tina Gebel actually showed some compassion and brought me some lozenges. Her brother, Buffy, however, looked at me with disgust for being so unmanly as to lose my voice. Sigrid was livid and complained to Tim that I should have an understudy. Boy, was that an understatement!

My performance was terrible, and I never felt more vulnerable in my life. Later I had a fever and sweated all night until it finally broke in the morning. My voice returned slowly over the weekend but continued to crack. The audiences were supportive the entire time, though, and SJ was always there to pep me up.

Gunther, too, was having troubles, with his teeth. His brilliant white set of choppers was man-made and was giving him pain. Tim came into the dressing room one day and was talking to the local promoter about flying in Gunther's dentist from Florida. It made me wonder what the tigers would do if they knew Gunther's teeth weren't real. I had always figured he intimidated them with his teeth. How else would you impress a five-hundred-pound cat with three-inch fangs!

I was a little miffed that they were so concerned about Gunther that they were considering the dentist's expense but had no compassion for my voice, which was much more evident during a show than a toothache, or gum-ache rather.

Those are priorities for ya!

I learned it was custom for the circus to make a special appearance at a prison just outside town. A minicircus was concocted to be performed in one ring with a few acts and clowns, and, of course, the ringmaster.

It was a terribly hot day when we arrived in two chartered buses. We set up in the dusty prison yard, with fences around us and guards packing guns and looking very mean.

The experience was very strange. The prisoners couldn't have cared less about the acts. All they wanted to see were the women. Whenever a female appeared, they would hoot and whistle and yell out various suggestions. The worst was during Carolina España's contortion act. It had been a while since any of those fellas had seen a woman in such unglamorous positions and they loved it.

It always seemed as if a city was either unbearably eventful or totally uneventful. Houston continued to be the former. The Urias Troupe had been having their problems throughout the South. If it was not the equipment it was the riders themselves.

The group was composed of Mama and Papa Urias and their two sons, Melvin and Erwin, who all hailed from São Paulo, Brazil. The extra man was José Medina from Mexico.

Melvin was a jolly, somewhat overweight ten-year-old who hated the circus and was not part of the act. He wanted to direct action films and pictured himself as the next Steven Spielberg.

His brother, Erwin, however, was more enterprising. Though only sixteen, he was bright and incredibly mature, seeming several years older. He and his father, Victor, along with José Medina, rode the motorcycles in the Globe of Death.

Mama Urias, Katja, stood in the middle of the sphere as the big machines buzzed in dizzying circles around her. As a mother, she was extremely industrious about taking care of her family and always had some aromatic concoction brewing on the stove for them to eat. She was not a pretty woman, but once she put on her makeup and donned her wig, the change was amazing, and she could look very regal inside the shining metal mesh.

In the final trick of the act all three cyclists revolve around the inside of the sphere as Katja stands, arms outstretched, in the middle of the noisy, frightening melee.

The timing of this final feat is crucial, requiring all three men to start moving simultaneously in different directions around the globe. Each revved his engine and throttled up, bursting forward, but Victor got his foot caught in the steel mesh. He and his motorcycle toppled sideways, pinning Katja down.

A low "ooh" emanated from the audience.

The other two cyclists were desperately circling the sphere while Victor, struggling, attempted to lift the bike off Katja. The lights had gone to full up, and the audience was craning forward. I rushed over, but I could only watch as the tires and chains on the bikes spun at ferocious speed as José and Erwin swerved around the mother and father.

Then Katja's scared eyes fell on mine. She was reaching for

me as if I could help her. No, she wasn't reaching for me. She was reaching for—her wig!

I couldn't believe it. About to be run over by two powerful vehicles, she was determined to save her hairpiece, which had fallen off.

Erwin and José continued to circle, getting dizzier by the second. You could only make so many revolutions before you had to quit. Just as I was sure they couldn't go around one more time, Victor pulled the cycle off his wife, and they both stood up straight, giving the others a place to let their cycles stop.

The next thing I knew, Katja was walking out of the globe, wig in hand, waving to the audience to assure them she was all right. Everyone walked out of the globe and took his bows to thunderous applause. As soon as they were out of sight of the audience, Katja was whisked away.

After this drama, I had to regain the crowd's attention. And with my croaky voice it wasn't easy! I was also worried about Katja, and was hard put to deliver a lively finale.

In fact, only her hand was injured, and the rest of the year Katja and I would laugh about it. There I was, thinking she was somehow reaching out to me for help, and it was her wig she wanted.

Though the crowds were great in Houston, I was glad to see it go. I had a feeling that we were keeping just out of the reach of something really bad happening and were getting out of town before it could overtake us. Luckily, we had only to tend our bruises on the way down to San Antonio.

San Antonio, however, proved to be a mixed blessing.

9

MALEVOLENT MANIACAL MANEUVERS

More Feld Mania

I had been eager to get to San Antonio, where my mother now lived, along with my sister, Kimberly, and her family. On the phone, my five-year-old niece, Rachael, was a chatterbox of enthusiasm and couldn't wait to see her Uncle Kristopher in the center ring of all this commotion. The plan was for me to stay at their house and forget the train life for a week. I was *really* looking forward to it.

San Antonio is famous for its magnificent River Walk, a downtown area modeled on Venice, Italy. Canals run throughout the town and under streets. At night you can ride in little boats past all the lights and waterside restaurants with couples dining in candlelight. Artists are selling their paintings and street entertainers are doing tricks. The atmosphere is very romantic.

The old coliseum was less romantic, though. Again we were without air-conditioning in hot humid weather. Here, the Posso Brothers and I shared one of those dressing rooms made from the blue dingy curtains. It was not an auspicious beginning.

Part of the news team from a local TV station came in as "honorary ringmasters." Earlier in the day they interviewed me and hinted they would hire me as their new weather man if I wanted the job. The way things were going, I almost accepted.

But when I thought about leaving the circus I realized I couldn't do it. Right now I held a unique position, one that I did not relish giving up despite all the hard work.

But I loved the family time I spent here, bringing my niece cotton candy every night, my mother waiting up to fix me a snack. A bit of normal life felt nice.

It was August now, and the big word was again *contracts*. Now it was the clowns and showgirls up for review, and after the cleanout in Washington, D.C., the tension was mounting. A lot of people were saying you couldn't have a circus without clowns and showgirls who could adapt to any new edition, but this did not serve to calm their fears.

Kenneth Feld, Bill Bradley, Crandall Diehl, and a slew of technicians all flew in for a production meeting for the new show.

I saw Bill Bradley hustling from one meeting to another and caught the breathless man by the arm.

"So what's the new show going to be like?" I asked.

He smiled slyly and spoke out of the side of his mouth, an old leprechaun telling forbidden secrets. "Well, it'll be like nothing you've ever seen before," he said. "It's really going to pull the kids in. The Spec will be centered around dancing Cabbage Patch dolls!"

He didn't look as if he were pulling my leg.

"You mean . . .?"

"Yep, kids love those things!"

"You're serious," I said.

He looked at me with the smile playing around his lips. "It wasn't my idea. But I'll have to give it my best shot."

Between shows I noticed that Uncle Soapy's hands were shaking and he seemed jumpy.

"Are you all right?" I asked him.

The old clown gritted his teeth. "I always get nervous when contract time comes around," he said. "You never know what Kenneth might do. Irvin was more predictable."

I patted him on the back. "I'm sure everything will be all right. You're an institution around here. No one with a heart would let you go."

He shook his head. "I'm getting old, you know; it's really getting hard for me to give it my all. But all I got is another two years, one more contract term, and I'll get retirement with full benefits."

I smiled. "What would you do with all that time off?"

His eyes took on a dreamy look. "I'd go and live in Spain for a while. That's the first thing." His eyes narrowed on mine. "I'm scared, Kristopher. If Kenneth fires me, I don't know what I'll do."

"Even Kenneth Feld isn't that heartless," I reassured him. "In fact you're probably due for a raise."

A clown told me he saw Kenneth storming out of a meeting room, his face red, jaw clenched, body taut. "They're not going to tell me how to run my circus!" he had said.

Later I caught up with Bill Bradley backstage.

"What's wrong?" I asked Bill.

The white-haired gent took a few deep breaths.

"Kenneth's scrapped the Cabbage Patch Spec," he managed to say. "Coleco just told Mr. Feld they wanted more creative control, and it sent him over the deep end."

"He was really that committed to it?" I said.

Bill nodded his head. "But Kenneth's been totally unreasonable. He shot down things that took us weeks to plan! Every time we go in with something he says the same thing: 'I don't know what I want, but I sure know what I don't want!' How can you reason with that? We've reached a total deadlock!"

Hot gossip was always boiling on the proverbial burner of the circus since it was such a small community. The next thing I heard, via the talkative wardrobe mistress, was that Kenneth Feld had fired both Crandall Diehl and Bill Bradley, who were seven- and fifteen-year veterans of the show. Feld said he blamed them for the creative problems, but everyone felt he was just making an excuse to cut more old hands from his father's regime.

"Fifteen years with one job is a long time in show business," Bill told me later. "It was fine while it lasted, but I feel like an enormous weight has been lifted off my shoulders! There was just no pleasing that man!"

The next day I caught a glimpse of Uncle Soapy in Clown Alley. I ventured in, and he looked at me in the mirror as I stood behind him.

"So did you get the raise?" I asked.

He tried to speak, but the words were choked. I gritted my teeth, knelt down, and put my arm around his shoulders. He put his face down and tried not to sob.

"I won't be returning," he said finally. "Kenneth says it's time for me to move on."

I hugged the clown tighter. "How can he do this?" I said.

It was a terrible feeling for me. I felt so guilty for building up his confidence.

"I don't know," Soapy said. "I guess he's just cutting everything he can. You know I'm getting a pretty good salary these days, and I've got a big train room to myself now. It'll be prime real estate for next season."

"I just don't believe it," I said. "I didn't think even Kenneth could be that cutthroat." I tried to imagine the entire cast staging a walkout in defiance, but that wouldn't work. Most of them had already been fired. "What are you going to do?" I asked.

He shook his head. "I don't know, Kristopher. I've been with this company most of my professional life. After making this my life's calling, you'd think the son of a gun would have at least let me finish my life as a clown!" The thought he was leaving drummed through his head and tears filled his eyes.

All I could do was shake my head. In twenty minutes the poor guy would have to go into the ring and make the children laugh.

We spent a few days in Fort Worth, and then it was on to Dallas.

Everyone was excited, especially the Europeans, because the cast of "Dallas" would be visiting.

Our show that night was energetic. My voice was in good form, the performers were tight, and the audience was loudly enthusiastic.

The "Dallas" cast had special seats: Larry Hagman sat like royalty with a large cowboy hat perched on his head. The showgirls, clowns, and other performers really mugged around in that area. Hagman seemed to be enjoying himself.

Clearly many of the circus people were real "Dallas" fans, and this was an exciting night for them. Unfortunately, during intermission, the television actors were hustled backstage to see the Gebels, and the rest of the performers were disappointed.

Robin Frye hurried up to me. "Come on, Kristopher; Larry Hagman wants to meet you."

He hustled me into a private room backstage where Hagman, Barbara Bel Geddes, and Sigrid and Tina Gebel were talking.

"Oh, Kristopher," Sigrid said, holding out her hand regally. "I want you to meet Mr. Hagman and Ms. Bel Geddes!"

Larry Hagman thrust out his hand and gave me a good ol' Texas handshake. He was still wearing the high, broad hat.

"Good to meet you there, young fella," Hagman said in his exaggerated accent. "Yes, sir. I'm a real circus fan, you know. You did a good job!"

"Thanks," I said.

Bel Geddes smiled. She was a small classy woman. "You're so energetic out there. How do you do so many shows? I'm a stage veteran myself, so I know what you go through. Is it as crazy as it looks?"

I laughed. "Every bit."

"I loved it so far," she said. Here she lowered her voice. "But tell me about the unicorn."

I winked. "It's a unicorn all right."

"Come on; you can tell us!"

"It's a unicorn," I told her again.

She gave me a steady gaze with a wrinkled brow and then

smiled, obviously letting herself believe. "Wow," she said. "I never thought I'd see a real unicorn!"

She had several other questions about the various acts, and I did my best to answer.

"So how long ya been ringmaster?" Hagman wanted to know. "I don't remember seeing you before."

"This is my first year," I told him.

Sigrid Gebel's voice cut through mine as I was about to go on.

"This will be Kristopher's *only* year," she said. "They aren't paying him what he needs."

Hagman looked down his nose at me. "How much they payin' ya, boy?"

"Not enough for the work I do."

He snorted. "You don't work the circus for money, kid. You do it 'cause ya love it!"

I couldn't believe this coming from a man who demanded so much money and personal concessions in his own contracts.

"You're absolutely right, Mr. Hagman," I said. "I do love it, but I want to leave on a high note."

I was thoroughly intrigued. It seemed that for all Hagman's success he had a certain envy of me. He was really a carnie at heart.

Another night we welcomed Roger Staubach as my guest ringmaster. To the crowd, he was a real live hero: a local boy who had done it all and did what he could to promote goodwill in the city. I have never heard such applause as when he followed me out to center ring wearing my green and purple tux. It was funny, though. Since his shoulders were so much broader than mine, it looked as if he were wearing a boy's jacket.

He had a dazzling smile and silvery gray hair. His young son was with him.

"I read the circus program," he told me during intermission. "It says you were in *Prizzi's Honor*. I'm really impressed."

I looked at his honest face, with piercing eyes, and couldn't lie. "I was only an extra. It does say that, doesn't it?"

He nodded. "Yeah. But that was a great movie. What part were you in?"

I told him the parts where he might possibly get a glimpse of me if he played a videotape slowly enough.

He said he would remember the parts.

"I've been watching you out there, Kristopher," he said. "I really like your style. You've got dancing feet. If a running back had your moves no one would catch him. Usually you see ringmasters just standing there doing an announcement or two, but you make it interesting."

"I appreciate the compliment," I said smiling. "Especially coming from you. You know my brothers would give their right arms to meet you. You're a real hero to them."

"It's nice to know they remember," he told me.

He was a modest, sincere man, and the respect the audience had for him was not misplaced.

For me, this was the best part of being ringmaster: not only meeting people of his "stature," but meeting so many different kinds of Americans. It's a big place out there, and the only way to appreciate the amazing variety of other lives is to get out and see how many there are.

Abilene was a complete dustbowl, but Austin was a pleasant surprise with the university there and a collegiate feeling throughout the city. Again I was plagued by allergies and continued to do the show with stuffed sinuses, though my voice was at least okay.

Grocery shopping on the road was tedious. I'd borrow Marc's or SJ's car to make it a little easier. In Austin I returned to the train with two grocery bags full. I tripped ascending the steps to the vestibule, slid down, and landed on the ground with a thud. A small crowd of circus people, all laughing, collected around me. I could only laugh along with them.

"Wouldn't you know," I said. "I can be so poised in front of thousands of people, but at home I'm a klutz."

Canasta became more intense, virtually a sickness with us. I cannot say how many thousands of hands we played. Though we were all great friends away from the table, we became very competitive while playing. I got terrible when I won and made a big deal out of it. One day I returned to my dressing room to find a sign erected on the makeup table, which was in Susie's unmistakable artistic calligraphy.

KRISTOPHER GLOATS, AND THAT'S NOT NICE! it said.

I knew it was in fun—but still, from that day on, I toned it down a little.

The Españas' act was so clean they had experienced no troubles. But the world is a dangerous place, and they were to be hit by a tragedy that no one could have foreseen.

Our next stop was Tulsa, Oklahoma. Again, I rode with Marc in his motor home and arrived before the train. We parked behind the arena, started a barbecue outside, and set some frankfurters to plumping.

Another one of the concessionaires, Jim, drove through the gates in his wheezing car and stopped next to us with squealing brakes, sending clouds of dust over our food.

"Come on now," I was saying to the guy when he jumped out.

"Did you hear about the Españas?" he asked.

"No. What's wrong?" I immediately forgot about the food.

"One of their motor homes blew up! The one Ramon and Peggy always drive."

"Oh no! Are they all right?"

Marc came bustling out of the trailor.

"Ramon and Peggy's motor home blew up!" I told him.

"Everyone's all right, though," Jim continued hurriedly. "José Medina was driving his car behind the trailer and saw sparks flying from under it. He called them on the CB and told them to stop and get out as quickly as they could. They did, and just as soon as they got clear the whole thing blew up right in front of their eyes!"

I leaned up against the motor home shaking. A tragedy had been narrowly averted.

"So they're all all right?" I said.

Jim took a deep breath, nodded, and wiped his brow. "Yeah. They'll be coming in pretty soon with some of the other families."

Soon the rest of the circus people started arriving, all talking about the Españas, who eventually rode in dispersed among other troupes.

Mama España was distraught.

"Deya lose everyt'ing!" she wailed. "Dat wasa Peggy and Ramon's home. Everyt'ing dey own wasa eenside. Money, peec-turres, scrapabooke, and cos'umes. Ees alla gone!"

I hadn't thought about that so far. The trailer was their home, and just like anybody else's house it contained all the memora-bilia of their lives. Everything material that meant anything to them was gone.

Then Mama brightened up. "But t'anks to Gode, we are all alife. An' t'anks to José Medina," she said, and she hugged her nearest family member to her bosom.

I don't think we ever found out exactly what the cause of the accident was. It's amazing how quickly these things can hap-pen. José Medina was not the most popular man in the company, but thanks to his keen eyesight and quick thinking he had saved the day.

In Tulsa we learned that Erma Bombeck would be visiting the show to do a story on the clowns. Well, the clowns finally met their match. Any one-liner they zinged her way bounced back with superior force. I think Dave, who was no longer with the circus, probably would have met defeat in a war of words. To go with her wit, she had a wonderful charm that sugarcoated any sharp observation.

She looked like a midwestern housewife in her polyester pants suit. There was something in her eyes that showed a swift intelligence. Like David Letterman, she had a space between her two front teeth.

"So you're the eighties-style yuppie ringmaster," she told me. "A little young, aren't you? I have dirty laundry older than you!"

I laughed. "Kenneth Feld wanted to update the show."

"Well, I like it," she said. "It really surprised me, though. The last time I saw the circus P. T. Barnum was still ringmaster!"

She kept me laughing nonstop for half an hour.

My dressing room in Tulsa was the size of a broom closet. In fact it was a broom closet. Susie Turcot and I were playing a quick game of canasta, knowing the fifteen-minute warning had already been called.

"Ah ha!" Susie said. "I'm out! How 'bout them apples, Kristopher."

"All I needed was one more canasta."

"I weep for you," she said. "Well, we better get out there."

She turned the doorknob and pulled. Nothing happened.

"You got this thing locked?" she asked.

I tried the knob myself. We could hear the band start to warm up.

"Come on, Kristopher!"

I rattled the door and jerked the knob, but it wasn't budging.

"Help!" I called and started banging on the door.

But there was too much commotion outside for anyone to hear us. The band's horns started up brashly, and the sounds of workmen lining up the elephants for the opening came from the other side of the door. I pounded and pounded, but the sound just echoed around our ears.

Susie looked worried. "Do we have enough air in here!"

"It's not that bad. Someone will come looking for us."

I let my eyes roam around the small room looking for anything that might help us escape. I noticed a curly wire sticking out behind a bunch of brooms and mops.

I stepped over and knocked the whole bunch of them aside. There was a phone attached to the wall.

"Oh please let it be live," Susie whispered behind me.

I picked it up and put the receiver to my ear, hearing a low steady tone. I dialed zero.

"Hello!" came the building operator.

I quickly outlined our predicament, and the voice told me she'd relay the information. In a few minutes we could hear a maintenance man on the other side of the door, trying in vain to unlock it. The band was about to start the overture.

Suddenly the door sprang open and let in a whoosh of fresh air. Apparently we now had the full attention of everyone around, because they were gathered in a circle around the door.

"Yep," said the maintenance man. "The lock was jammed."

A sudden thought burst in my mind and I blushed. It must have struck Susie at the same time, because her face flushed red.

Ugh stepped forward. "Hanky panky so close to show? You should be ashamed of yourself!"

The whole group tittered. We didn't bother denying anything. It just would have made matters worse. I ran to the ring and jumped out with just a second to spare, and Susie reached her position on the light board a moment after. As I was singing my song, and the clowns sprang out and the showgirls blossomed from their pyramid and everything looked so perfectly timed, I wondered what the audience would think if they had known the truth. Seconds earlier I was being sprung from a closet!

Susie and I laughed about it the rest of the year, and we both made sure that locks were working before we closed the doors behind us to play canasta.

There's an old maxim that says familiarity breeds contempt. When you work with dangerous tools every day, you can get careless. How many carpenters do you know with a finger missing? A buzz saw can take one off in an instant. Well, the same goes for any tool, and in the circus the animals are the tools we work with. You just plain forget how dangerous they can be after you've seen them perform so many tricks so docilely.

We had gotten through Wichita, Kansas, and Lincoln, Nebraska, without incident. Now we were playing Springfield, Illinois. One morning Robin Frye stopped me after breakfast.

"One of Gunther's men found a couple of human fingers outside the tiger cage!" he said.

"No!"

He nodded his head. "We called the police, and it turns out that a man checked into the hospital last night with fingers missing. The idiot must have climbed into the animal car last night! Can you imagine anything so stupid? Those aren't just big puddy tats!"

The newspaper carried an item about the poor ignorant fellow. He must have come to see the show and been taken by the apparent ease with which Gunther commanded the big cats. But the tigers are just trained jungle animals, and the operative word is *trained*, not *tame*. "Tame tigers" is a contradiction in terms. No animal that powerful with all those millions of years of instinct powering its cells can ever be fully trusted. Gunther exercises authority over them through sheer force of will and, like a concert pianist, he makes it look easy.

But try playing *Moonlight Sonata* without years of training and see if you don't end up short a couple of fingers.

The summer was ending, the days were getting shorter, and my time as ringmaster was dwindling. For a while I had almost forgotten I would not be here permanently, and the realization that it would soon be over really got to me. Sometimes I remembered what Larry Hagman had told me: "You don't work the circus for the money, kid. You do it 'cause ya love it!"

I could have worked out the money angle; I was sure about that, even though I knew Kenneth wasn't about to pay me the $1,000 a week that I was worth. But as soon as I thought about that, I could feel my knees start to ache at the thought of another year of concrete floors. Now I knew why I was the first dancing ringmaster. No one else had been so dumb!

You cannot cover so many thousands of miles doing shows, driving between cities in a state of exhaustion without risk. The Españas could attest to that. Now it was my turn to watch the inevitable.

It was Labor Day, September 1. I drove SJ's car overland following Marc in his motor home. We were on our way to La Crosse, Wisconsin. It was a long, dreary trip, and I had to sing along with the radio to keep awake.

In front of me was the stalwart hulk of Marc's motor home pulling his car on a trailer. Suddenly, the big vehicle dodged to the side and jumped over the curb. The trailer twisted as it followed its master. My heart skipped and the bottom dropped out of my stomach.

I swerved to the side and smashed on the brakes. Luckily, Marc was able to stop his trailer before it continued into the ditch.

I jumped from the car and ran forward. Marc opened the door and jumped to the pavement in a daze.

"What happened?" I said. "Are you all right?"

He nodded his head. "I j-j-just plain fell asleep, K-Kristopher. One minute everything was fine, the n-next I was jarred awake by the c-c-curb!"

"Well, I'm glad you're all right," I told him, really meaning it.

I calmed him down and we then inspected the damage as gawkers drove slowly by.

"The axle's bent," Marc said, climbing out from underneath the trailer. "It's not going anywhere. That was a fifteen-hundred-dollar nap!"

I let out a breath. "Well, maybe we can find help in the next town."

Once in SJ's car, I went to turn the ignition, but the keys weren't there. We determined that in my haste, I must have re-flexively pulled them out and lost them on the road around Marc's trailer.

We spent two hours looking for the keys until we finally found them in the crevice between the car seats. We were two frustrated fellows by that time. Poor Marc: all he wanted to do was get to the next gas station and we had to spend two miserable hours searching for the keys because of my carelessness. It was a bad Labor Day for us.

When we got to La Crosse, I spread out a blanket on the banks of the Mississippi that ran behind the arena and slept the rest of the day. The train wasn't supposed to arrive until late that evening, and the accident as well as the drive had exhausted me. Marc didn't have time to rest. He was out trying to get his trailer repaired.

The rest of our stay there was gloomy and rainy. If Texas enthusiasm had been "heads," La Crosse was the other side of the coin in all respects. The audiences were as responsive as cardboard cutouts.

To give them their due, it was September and the folks were readying the kids for school. Fall was around the corner and I had only two months to go.

Again I concentrated on my enjoyment of the show, telling myself to savor every moment. This part of my life would soon be over, and I wanted to make the most of it. I was also worried about slipping into a state of depression after all this excitement was over. The way to prevent that was to tell myself then that I had gotten everything I could out of my experiences.

To make matters harder, Kenneth Feld told me I still had the option of signing a new contract before he found another ring-master for the next season. My fingers itched to sign the contract, but my knees throbbed in dispute. My mind and body were playing a tug of war with me that could only end by ripping me apart.

I told Kenneth I would let him know.

Madison, Wisconsin, another fresh college town, followed, and then we trekked on to Kansas City and St. Louis, Missouri.

I was always after Attila and Laci to save their money for when they went back to Hungary. But the two teenagers were incorrigible consumers and were always begging me to borrow a car and drive them to a mall. The two boys were clotheshorses and were determined to take home a wardrobe bought from retailers throughout America.

I am a conservative dresser, and the boys were very flashy in their dress. Attila decided I should look more stylish and demanded I take him to a mall, where he proceeded to pick out an amazing array of clothes. I put several items back.

"That's more like it," I said.

"Come on, Kristopher, you need dis stuff!" Attila pleaded. "You de conference for De Greatest Show on Eart'! You mus' always look your best!" (*Conference* is the European term for ringmaster.)

I laughed. "No one's thrown me off their talk shows yet," I told him. "I think I can manage for the next few months. Honestly, I'll never wear all these things."

He gave up with a frustrated gesture of his hands.

We played Uno that night, and his eyes grew sad as he discussed his family back in Hungary. Here was a seventeen-year-old boy who'd been away from home for two years. His parents would not believe how much he'd grown up.

"I sad to leave de show," Attila said. "But den I go home and see my fadder an' mudder again. So dat's all right."

"What will you miss most about the United States?" I asked him.

He smiled. "I miss McDonald's and eatin' Cocoa Puffs!" he said. "We no have dos in my country."

McDonald's and Cocoa Puffs! The boy had traveled for two years through thousands of miles of America, seeing more cities than most native boys would in their lives—and the best memory we could give him to take home was fast food. That's America for you.

Or maybe it's just the circus.

10

THE GRAND
FINALE

BRIAN MASCK / THE MUSKEGON CHRONICLE

"Get yer soo-veneer programs heeere!" the booming voice announced through the portable microphone.

I'd heard it over and over throughout the year, yet I never
tired of listening. The words tumbled forth from the lips of Buddy
the Barker in front of the arena, his perpetual patter of banter
and hard-sell pushiness encouraging every patron to cough up
three bucks for a "truly valuable souvenir you will treasure for
years to come. A free unicorn poster in every one!"

You would have bought anything from him: a broken-down

used car, a swamp, a magazine subscription, an encyclopedia set—or a program. He was one of Kenneth Feld's most valuable assets.

He was a friendly balding old guy with hanging jowls and a bulbous nose seen last on the face of W. C. Fields. He reeked of the word *carnie* and loved hearing himself speak. For him, every sale was a wonderful accomplishment.

"Buddy," I asked. "How long have you been with the show?"

He smiled widely, showing gaps between crooked, yellowing teeth. "Over thirty-five years now and going strong!" he said. "You know, Kristopher, if you weren't ringmaster you'd be a damned good hawker yerself. We're the same under the skin, you and me, what they call the same *ilk*. We're both good talkers and that's the key."

"I'd never outsell you," I told him.

"I bet you could! One word like *only* is the key factor. Can you say the word *only*?"

"Only," I said.

"You got it, son; that's all it takes." He spotted a group of folks, two families, with kids leaping ahead of them heading in our direction. "Here, you get these people!"

I paled. "I wouldn't want to take your job away," I said.

He laughed and started his pitch. "Git yer programs. A free poster of the Living Unicorn in every one. Fer *only* three dollars today!"

The two men were already reaching for their wallets.

I patted Buddy on the back. "See you later, old-timer."

His voice trailed off as I entered the concessions area of the old Checkerdome (now called the Arena) in St. Louis. I made my rounds, as I did in each city, saying hello to the salespeople behind the stands who traveled with the show.

Little Franky's mother, Liza, was always there to greet me with a smile. Papa Page and his family manned the cotton candy maker, and he was busy spinning the confectionery sweetness in pinks and blues with pieces of it stuck in his hair. A wave from his hand, colored from the dye, made me chuckle.

The old arena had the damp, musty smell to which I was more accustomed than I would have liked. Here I was sharing a dressing room with Sabu, the single trapeze aerialist, in a basement area underneath the stands.

I opened the door. "How you doing, Sabu?"

"Terrible, Kris'pher! Looke at cossumes!"

We had both laid out our costumes on the table the night before. The sparkling sequins were sodden with a brown, sticky substance.

"Oh no, arena seepage!" I cried.

It was a combination of spilled Cokes, snowcones, and syrups that was spilled on the floor by the crowds. In some arenas, it would ooze through the floors at night and drip into the rooms below. This was not the first time it had happened.

We did our best to clean up the costumes before going on, but it was really a job for the dry cleaners.

We were to have our first celebrity clowns here. TV talk show host Sally Jessy Raphael and her husband, Carl Soderlund, would be making a special appearance. During our stint here, they planned to interview our clowns, showgirls, and other performers for a segment on backstage life.

I strolled into Clown Alley and saw Frankie the dwarf clown helping a couple of others with their makeup.

"So where's my ol' pal Sally?" I asked casually. I had never met her before in my life and was just being funny.

"Right here!" said one of the clowns whom Frankie was helping. "Funny thing, I don't remember you."

"Oh no! I'm sorry. I didn't recognize you."

"It's all right," she said, laughing.

She and Carl were put in the clown "come in," which preceded the show, and took part in a bit where a supposed "vendor" is chasing a clown who has "stolen" a bunch of balloons. Each time the vendor almost catches up, the clown passes the balloons to a new clown who in turn runs away. Sally and Carl jumped right into the fray and did some funny stuff keeping the balloons away from the hapless vendor. The two wanted to continue through the rest of the show but could not do it because of the danger involved should they mess up with their timing or accidentally be in the wrong place at the wrong time. They were definitely good clowns though, and could have ad-libbed some funny stuff.

Fifteen thousand people packed the arena that night. August A. Busch, Jr., of Busch Beer fame was on hand as my honorary ringmaster. It turned out he was a real circus fan, and his ardor was not dulled by his eighty-plus years.

He wore a cowboy hat and walked into the ring with the aid of a cane and a woman aide. He waved at the crowd and said a few words into the microphone and was then led to the house seats. He had tears in his eyes the entire show, as if we were helping him remember wonderful childhood memories.

At intermission he was brought backstage, where he shook my hand.

"Do you think the boys would like some of my beer if I sent it over?"

"The boys would worship you if you did that," I told him.

Mr. Busch smiled and glanced at his lady friend. "Have Harold send over a couple of cases for the gang."

"Thanks a lot," I said. "They'll really enjoy it."

There was a faraway look in his eyes, and again I could almost see half-forgotten scenes now playing in his head.

"Don't mention it. It's the least I can do," he said.

Cedar Rapids and Des Moines, Iowa, followed. For weeks, Little Laci had been telling Susie and me he was going to cook us an authentic Hungarian meal with "good bread." Remembering the goulash that Attila had prepared, we were looking forward to it.

It turned out to be a sort of pork stew that was nearly unpalatable. Laci wasn't the cook that Attila was. But we ate everything so we didn't hurt his feelings.

"You see," he said, glowing with hospitality, "I repay you for taking me to all those malls."

I'd sworn, after our last fiasco, never to travel overland with Marc again! But following Iowa he begged Susie and me to help him drive his motor home for one *final* trip to Detroit.

"C'mon," he said," it'll b-b-be fun! W-W-We won't have a chance to do it a-a-again!"

"I can live without it!" I said. But Susie and I could tell it meant a lot to him. Besides that, he looked a little ragged and we feared for his safety. We finally agreed to go along, if only to help keep him awake.

It turned out his gauges were broken and we ran out of fuel on the highway. Marc flagged down a trucker and went for gas, and Susie and I stayed in the motor home, where we nearly froze to death.

"I knew we should have taken the train today," I said as we sat there shivering, playing a few slow hands of canasta.

"Just think of all the headaches you avoided by not keeping your uncle's motor home," Susie commented.

That, at least, was a consoling thought.

It was the first of October and the weather was dreadful. I was in my home state, so quite a bit of press was done on me. My hometown paper ran a wonderful front-page article written by a woman who had followed me around for three days in La Crosse.

Muskegon, where I had grown up, was three and a half hours away, but it seemed as if half the town drove the distance to see me. It was really wonderful.

The train was parked in an awful place where so much rain collected that we had to wade through puddles nearly two feet deep. The mud was particularly slick, and those people with cars were constantly cursing it as their tires spun helplessly. For the tenth time that year I ruined a pair of shoes, as did many of us.

An uncle of mine organized a chartered bus to transport friends and family from Muskegon and Grand Rapids. They cheered and raved throughout the performance and generally made their presence well known. After the show I signed autographs for them and answered questions on the bus.

My uncle, who is a Catholic priest, was really intrigued when I introduced him to our own Father Jack Toner, who had been assigned to the circus for four years. (I guess the Church must have figured that a congregation of two hundred and fifty confined souls was worth it!) On Sundays he would hold Mass in the center ring (where else?), and every once in a while he would ask me to read from the Bible for him. He loved the way my voice resonated with the Holy Word. He was seventy-one years old, about six feet tall with white hair and a love for the circus and for circus people. He always watched performances from the wings and provided encouragement for anyone who needed it. He especially loved the Españas' flying act and would watch them in rapture. Maybe sailing through the air seemed to him like being close to heaven.

He told me once that he had been at the ringmaster auditions and had chosen me to win. I guess that made me *ordained* to be ringmaster!

Our next stop was Indianapolis Market Square Arena. I was supposed to cohost a local morning show there called "A.M. Indiana." They sent a limo to pick me up at the train yard, which was just as muddy as Detroit had been. It was very satisfying to see that sleek black automobile glide through the muck getting a coat of gray all over it.

At the interview, it again struck me that I had little over a month to go before my time as ringmaster would end. I felt that I was hanging on to a rope that was slipping through my hands in a tug-of-war as I tried to hold on to something precious.

Every time I would think of my final show and saying good-bye to my friends I would get depressed. So I came up with the idea of organizing a giant end-of-year party in Pittsburgh, which would be our final city at the end of November.

I approached Marc, who was always game for throwing a shindig, and watched his eyes light up with excitement. We drafted Susie as our "technical assistant," dubbing her "TA." The party we named "The Grand Finale . . . the one day a year you will recall," quoting one of my lines from the show.

We meant it when we said, "Grand Finale." It would take a lot to impress the cast of "The Greatest Show on Earth." A mere party room would not do. We needed banquet facilities!

It was a long train run from Indy to Boston, so I took the two days and flew home to New York City for some R&R. When I flew into Boston the trees were in full autumn splendor, framing the circus train in shades of gold.

Now Kenneth made it clear that he had acquired a new ringmaster to replace me. I knew my days were numbered. All the signs were pointing to the end of a good thing. As if to take our minds off the future, our canasta playing became fanatical. SJ and I played every spare minute we could find.

We were in the old Boston Garden. It wasn't much of a building, and the attendance was virtually nil because the Red Sox were playing in the World Series.

Most of the people who had come had only done so for their kids and were there in body, not in mind. They sat there with radios and little TVs and forgot about us entirely. Cheers would occur throughout the audience at weird times, and we knew a good play had just been made. Home runs were really unnerving. Attila could have done a thousand triple back flip somersaults onto a million-man high, and only the innocent eyes of children would have recorded the impossible event.

I had called some old acquaintances in Pittsburgh, one of whom gave me the number of a man who managed special events at a hotel there. It turned out he was a circus nut and wanted to host the party for us. We worked out a deal for two hundred people with dinner in their grand ballroom.

So the party was on its way, and I had the job to organize it.

First we hosted auditions from the various acts and showgirls who wanted to entertain. Marc spent a great deal of energy helping with the preparations but then found out he would be transferred to the Blue Unit the week before the party and would be unable to enjoy the fruits of his labors. We couldn't believe it! Evidently, his superior sales ability was needed to help boost concessions profits at the other show. Performers were rarely transferred between units. But staff and concessions people were occasionally juggled by the bosses if they felt such a change would be beneficial.

It seemed that the days were going by in a blur, and mental pictures of the previous nine months raced through my mind— all the special scenes of the year, the good times with people, and the special performances. I milked the lyrics of the opening and closing numbers at every performance, clinging to this fading portion of my life.

The train run up to Buffalo, New York, was magnificent. We

chugged through the winding hills of Connecticut bristling with flaming colors. The wind scattered leaves across the fields and turned them into meadows of oranges, reds, and golds. The air was cold and pure. As the wheels clinked endlessly against the rails, you could look around a bend and see a mile of unbroken train curving in a broad silvery arc amid the vibrant colors.

Another ancient building in Buffalo! There were, I guess, building booms in the twenties and forties, and these old auditoriums would be used until they crumbled.

Here, Kenneth Feld phoned me to say he was paying everyone to make a professional video production of the circus which would eventually be marketed to consumers. My pay would be a thousand dollars, so I said yes. I wanted a video of myself as ringmaster anyway, because it would be a valuable tool for my career. I planned to send it to casting agents in New York and Los Angeles who might be looking for an emcee or a game show host. A lively videotape is the fastest way to a casting agent's heart these days, because they can instantly see what your talents are in front of the camera. It is virtually a televised resume!

We were to tape in the next city—Richfield, Ohio.

While we were in Buffalo, I figured I had to see Niagara Falls, where my parents had spent their honeymoon some thirty years before. Marc, Susie, and Attila decided they would come with me, all of us tourists at heart.

"You know," Marc said, as we approached, "the Canadian side is supposed to be much more interesting. Why don't we drive over?"

"Sounds all right to me," I replied, and headed the car toward that exit.

Attila's voice came shakily from the rear seat. "But, Kris'pher, I'm no American cit'zen, you know."

I glanced at him in the rearview mirror. With his blond hair, blue eyes, and light skin he looked as American as Wonder Bread.

"Don't worry about it," I told him blithely. "They don't ask for your passports or anything."

We got to the border and the guard asked whether we were all American citizens and I replied yes and drove through.

It got very quiet in the backseat and when I looked, all the blood was drained from Attila's face, which looked suddenly haggard and much younger. I realized he was not enjoying himself. I made an immediate U-turn and drove back through the U.S. gate. The guard asked the same question and let us through.

"Thanks," said Attila when we were driving down the road.

"It's all right," I told him. "The American side will be plenty good enough."

It's so easy to take it for granted that U.S. citizenship enables you to pass easily to many countries. It takes a situation like Attila's to point up how great this freedom is. Poor Attila would have needed a Canadian visa and permission from his government to pass the border, and it was unthinking of me to have put him in that situation.

Seeing Niagara Falls in pictures, movies, or television just doesn't have the same impact as the real thing: the untold millions of gallons rushing past and plunging hundreds of feet, exploding into foam and dancing prisms of light. The sound is deafening, of course; the water splashes you; and the panoramic view is massive in scale. You feel tiny and insignificant compared to this force of nature.

We had a great day and played tourist and took lots of pictures in crazy poses. I could imagine Attila's telling the story to his friends back in Hungary a few months later, showing them these pictures of the crazy American ringmaster—or "conference," rather—the four of us outlined against the giant falls.

We had many children traveling with the show, and someone always organized a party for the seasonal events, such as Easter egg hunts and now a Halloween party. Ricky Braun decided he wanted the festivities in center ring between shows.

I planned a scavenger hunt for the kids. A few of the showgirls and other performers helped out, and the kids all came prancing in wearing elaborate costumes. For children reared in the circus, regular costumes wouldn't do: that was their daily fare!

My list for the hunt was composed of things they could find in the arena: an empty popcorn box, a Ringling Brothers logo, and so on. The hardest thing for them to find was a purple rhinestone. Only a few costumes in the show had that particular color, mine in Spec being one of them. The kids bobbed for apples and then participated in a costume contest for which I was the judge.

Here were all these kids, living this exciting circus life, and all they wanted was a normal Halloween party to make them happy! We did what we could to give them some normal childhood experiences but it was impossible to do so fully.

Afterward, they went trick-or-treating around their neighborhood—the dressing rooms and concession stands.

Three weeks remained, and I felt as if the sun weren't shining, blocked by a rain cloud that followed me everywhere. Tears would fill my eyes at the end of each production number. I had never displayed emotions easily, and mostly I kept my depression a secret.

An urge plagued me to pick up the phone and call Kenneth to say, "It's all right; I'll stay!" But I knew it was impossible. My shin splints were so bad now that I couldn't sleep from the pain. That reason alone prevented me from calling; I knew I just couldn't continue the show in this condition.

Leaving something while you still love it is better than sticking around and burning yourself out.

Richfield Coliseum sits halfway between Cleveland and Akron, Ohio. The train was parked in downtown Akron, twenty miles from the arena, a long bus ride back and forth.

The last time I played this arena was in the fall of 1979 in a touring group for Cedar Point. I had been forced to wear an orange dog costume in a half-time show for the Cleveland Cavaliers basketball game. No kidding. Now I was with "The Greatest Show on Earth," and I felt much better about what I was doing.

My first day there I had an interview at the arena with local TV personality Lynn Sheldon, known throughout the Cleveland area as "Barnaby." We had worked together a couple of times when I did a few sports shows back in 1980–81, and I wondered whether he'd recognized me.

"Hi," I said. "I'm Kristopher."

He squinted his eyes and pointed a finger at me. "Cedar Point and the sport shows!" he said without hesitation. "I'd remember that lanky form anywhere!"

We had a terrific interview for his children's program. I explained to the kids how our circus children were tutored and what sort of life they had.

"Well, Kristopher," Barnaby said toward the end of the show. "You certainly seem to be having the time of your life!"

"I certainly am," I replied. "I certainly am."

We got our first winter snow on November 11. It settled on the trees and the train yard like a thick coating of dust. This was the first time the yard looked picturesque, save for a few ominous nights with train lights dimly shining on the old warehouses or junked cars surrounding us.

Cedar Point was close by, affording the staff an opportunity to come and see me. I could tell they were really pleased with my performance. The first time some of these people had seen me work was back in 1976 when I was a green kid who couldn't keep time with the music.

The circus videotaping went on throughout our stint in Richfield. I was thrown into a few scenes with the Braun kids with impromptu lines, the majority of the dialogue being ad-libbed or read from cue cards.

The story line was that two kids, the Brauns, want to go see the fabulous Living Unicorn and are taken to the circus by Uncle Tim, played by Tim Holst. Between the acts, the kids get short interviews with some of the performers and see a little of the backstage area.

The production was terrible. The kids were wooden, mouthing their lines in a monotonous, uniform way like creatures in some bad sci-fi movie. Amazingly, Tim Holst was even worse. The video is worth the money for the unintentional laughs. The company which made the video, however, was as good as the actors were bad, and the high production values also make the video well worth watching, as the scenes of the actual performances were first-rate. It is as close to being at the circus as a video is going to get for a while.

Sarahjane and I sat in her train room playing canasta. Our decks of cards, which had once been shiny and new, were now oily, dog-eared, and easily pliable. An ashtray was filled with cigarette butts, though I had emptied it twice in the last hour. Smoke curled up from the cigarette between SJ's fingers, adding to the swirls that eddied about the room.

"You realize," SJ said, "this is probably our last canasta game."

I nodded and swallowed. "Yes, I know. I'm happy for you, but I'm sad too."

Sarahjane was being transferred to assistant performance director of the Blue Unit, with the hopes of someday being promoted to Robin's position.

"It's quite an honor, though," I said. "You'll eventually be the first woman performance director in the history of The Greatest Show on Earth!"

Our game was slow and a bit maudlin, and we reminisced about the year. I barely made it through the show, knowing it was her last. A few days later her bags were packed and she was off to her new job.

"You take care now, Kristopher," she said, as we hugged goodbye, tears streaming down our cheeks. "Think about me whenever you play cards."

I smiled wanly. "It won't take playing cards to remember you, SJ."

I had prepared myself to give up this life in one big chunk, but having it disappear in little bits like this was harder. I was losing a relationship, not only with one person but with an entire experience. It was like a summer romance that ends, not because things go sour, but because of the boundaries of time.

I could write to Sarahjane, I could see her later, but most people would be gravitating back to their mother countries where we would be divided by oceans. Now that the dream was steadily drawing toward a close, I did not want to wake up.

In Akron the weather was downright cold, and my train car lost its hot water, forcing me to shower in frigid conditions. I tried the arena showers, but they were disgusting. My circus friends might be great people, but they were slobs. Old razors, tissue, empty cans, and various flotsam and jetsam were strewn about in an awful mess.

It embarrassed me to know they would leave this for the arena custodians to clean up as they had all over the country. I guess it's sort of like living in a hotel room: no matter how dirty you make it, the next place you arrive at will be clean, and your old mess a mere memory.

I ended up heating water in pans on my hot plate, then running into my shower to pour them over my head.

Sarahjane was gone, and now so was Marc. Change was all around me, and we were heading toward our final destination on the train to Pittsburgh. I sat in my train room, the lights low, glancing out the window occasionally to see the blurred lights of small Ohio towns rush past, wondering what those people were doing in their homes, one minute thinking about how sad I was to be leaving all the excitement, the next minute thinking how nice it would be to abandon show business for a normal existence. Life in show business seems to engender more lows than highs, but when the highs come along they are so uplifting they are worth the pain of what comes between.

I entertained myself with plans for the big party. I had been on the phone constantly with my contact in Pittsburgh. When we arrived the next day, Susie and I drove out to the Holiday Inn, where we met Herman Hartman, the voice at the other end of the phone.

We discussed the arrangement of centerpieces on the tables, lighting for the show I'd organized, and a sumptuous buffet. We hoped at least half of the two hundred and fifty people who traveled with the show would attend.

I was an unbearably edgy person that last week, and poor Susie usually shouldered the brunt of it. We were in the last week of shows, and I just didn't want to give it up. And as bad as my depression was already, I knew it would only get worse after closing. Unfortunately, intellectualizing it did no good, perhaps even goading the depression into getting worse.

The worst part was realizing that show-biz friendships were

fleeting moments and were never the same once removed from the time and place. I had rarely become attached to people in the shows I'd done, but then I'd never done the same show for so long and traveled with people so closely. In spite of the idiots and personal problems between various performers, we had become a huge family. I was not only leaving a job but a home.

We decided to hold the party on November 19, the Wednesday of the final week. If we waited until the weekend with six shows to do, no one would feel like coming. We sold over 150 tickets at fifteen dollars apiece to cover the costs, which included a bus to transport everyone between the train and hotel, the music, the entertainment, and the huge buffet.

I emceed the evening as a ventriloquist, using one of my old puppets—a witch named Gertie. Her personality is cutting and witty, and I had the entire crowd in stitches. We raffled off prizes and announced the winners of mock awards, such as "cutest couple" and "most popular."

Gertie started running away from me, becoming lethal at times, poking fun at virtually everybody, including me.

We also showed a beautiful videotape created by Noe España, a carefully edited five-minute montage of our year's experiences. After it was all over, even Ugh was crying openly. The party was a complete success. Old hostilities were mended and friendships reinforced. When people left, it was with their arms around each other.

The camaraderie of those final few days was at its height. Flashbulbs were popping everywhere as people hurried to snap the photographs they had promised to take all year long. Backstage was an endless array of poses and cries of "Say cheese!"

Susie and I promised Attila and Laci we'd prepare them an authentic American meal, which we decided was pork chops and apple sauce. We all had a lot of fun that night reminiscing about the year that had just flown by in our lives and how it had affected us.

For many of these people the breakup was even harder than it was for me, as they had been with the show for a year longer. On the other hand, most of them would be leaving with their entire families, and that would soften the blow.

We capped our American evening by watching a video of *The Wizard of Oz.* It was amazing seeing these teenage Hungarian boys mesmerized by the fifty-year-old movie. We had to keep on explaining things to Laci, because his English wasn't so good.

"Dis very nice, Kris'pher," he said at the end. "But nex' time maybe we get *Cannonball Run?*"

We laughed. I guess that sort of movie, with car chases, smashups, and fight scenes would be almost as authentic a touch of true Americana as Dorothy and Toto.

November 23 finally arrived—the end of the season.

It started off as a sunny day. I got up early enough to spend a few hours packing. I couldn't believe all the mementos I had picked up along the way.

I took the photos from my wall and carefully piled them together in envelopes, leaving darker squares against the slight dustiness of the walls. Soon, someone else would be living in this room covering up the aged paneling with his own snapshots.

Each time I took a photo down it made me recall the instance. Here I was standing with Pat Sajak and Vanna White; another showed me with Marc in his motor home. That darned guy, I hoped he hadn't run out of gas on the ride to the Blue Unit. SJ and I smiling up from a table covered with cards. Robin Frye in his black tux—thanks, guy, you and SJ treated me like a pro and made my life easy. Susie sitting at the table in my room smiling wistfully at the camera. Attila and I at the arch in St. Louis and a couple at the Wet 'n' Wild amusement park.

Snapshot by snapshot I peeled the sticky tape off the memories that I would never forget.

I was the twenty-seventh ringmaster of "The Greatest Show on Earth." No, I *had been* the twenty-seventh.

A knock came at the door. I wiped my eyes and opened the door.

"Are you ready?" Susie asked, sniffling.

"In a minute. I've just a few more things to pack."

We were going to load my things into her newly purchased used car. The next show, the last, was in an hour, and after that she was going to drive me to New York. Then I would have to say goodbye to her too. She would turn around and head to Florida for rehearsals with the 117th Edition.

I signed a bunch of eight-by-ten publicity photos, personalizing each one, and left them on the dressing room tables of those who had meant a lot to me during the year.

I walked into Clown Alley just before the last show and saw Uncle Soapy slumped in a chair beside his trunk. This would be his last show of a thirty-eight-year run. If it was bad for me, it must have been devastating for him.

He too was looking at old photographs. He looked up at me with wet eyes.

"It's been a good life, Kristopher. I can't complain," he said.

"Knowing you has meant a lot to me," I told him. The words were awful things to force from my throat. I couldn't say anything else and just handed him my photo with the message on the bottom.

I thought to myself, "Dear old fellow, may all your days be circus days," and left the room.

Backstage, people were lining up for the opening number parade, and I took pictures of them. Gunther walked by and stopped to take a picture with me.

After the flashbulb exploded, he turned and shook my hand. "I tell you ven I first see you in Chicago, I picked you. You did a gut job dis year."

Coming from him, that was the ultimate compliment. I was about to tell him how his charisma and professionalism had affected me, and what I had learned from him over the year. But before I could say anything he was off yelling at an elephant to get into place.

The spotlight hit me as I announced those famous words for the final time: "Laadieees and Gentlemen! Children of aaaaall aaages!" It was tough at times to get the opening number's lyrics out, and I had to avoid looking any performer in the eye so I wouldn't lose my composure.

As the acts went through their routines, I could almost see the phantoms of past performances beside them, like watching a television station that's just a little out of whack so you see a second image superimposed over the first.

As Attila and Mircea did their somersaults, I could see the time Mircea missed and broke his leg. When the Possos were on the wire, I could see that bicycle falling down and almost hear the sickening crunch from below.

But there were good-time ghosts here too. I could hear the laughter of hundreds of thousands of voices across the nation as Uncle Soapy frolicked for the last time and Poopy toppled Eric Braun's luggage with the same glee as always.

I wondered what would happen to Sweetheart and his one-horned sibling now that his year was over? Would he find a green pasture or be sold to the highest bidder for some sideshow exhibit in a carnival?

Gunther Gebel Williams and family were the only ones out there whose sadness was not a virtual aura hovering around them. But in another way they were the saddest bunch, unable to care enough about their fellow workers to show sympathy.

As for myself, I could almost decipher another me over my shoulder mimicking my movements. He was a younger man with a spring in his step that my aching feet might never have again. But my phantom double was also a fellow who had known less about this world, the people in it, and had been less appreciative of life in this special country.

Attila, Little Laci, and their Eastern European troupes would all be going back to a home where they had to beware of everything they said, and where vending machines and candy were the greatest luxury.

Most of the clowns and showgirls were just beginning their show-biz careers and would have a lifetime to look back upon this crazy tour, living in hot, filthy train cars eating greasy food, eager for the next town so they could wash away the sweat and smell of their bodies. What about Uncle Soapy, though? Where would he go now? It made me sad wondering what would happen to him.

I could only hope that everyone, myself included, would prosper.

———————

Tim Holst had flown in for the final performance. He requested I make a closing announcement during the finale.

The band stopped at the appointed moment and I began with difficulty, "Ladies and gentlemen, boys and girls, may I have your attention, please. You've just witnessed the final performance of the One Hundred and Fifteenth Edition of The Greatest Show on Earth. Most of the performers and I will be moving on with our careers and returning to our native homes following tonight's performance. We thank you for being with us for this very special performance!"

The band kicked into the remainder of the closing number and I trailed off with "and that's what it takes to make a circus," concluding with the line "May all your days be circus days!"

Ricky and Neecha Braun, Eric's two children, were at my sides clutching my hands as they had hundreds of times before. We jumped off the ring curb and ran out the arena stage door with the spotlights following us. In the seats of the arena I could feel the children wishing they could run off with me. But they could have that wish again next year with a different edition and a new ringmaster.

I took off my sequinned tails, gloves, and whistle for the last time and hung them properly in my wardrobe box. Quietly, almost solemnly, I picked up my bags and walked across the arena floor one last time as the familiar cries of Joe Burt supervised the workingmen in lowering the rigging.

I waved to a few people who waved back and didn't turn around to see the magic fading behind me as the rigging and cables came down. Susie was waiting in the car, her eyes filled with tears.

"Take me home," I said. "It's time to go home!" *This dream was over.*

And so ended the most interesting year of my life. It took months for my body to recuperate. It took longer to adjust to real life again. Sometimes I could hardly believe I had done it.

"Would you ever do it again?" people ask me. They want me to say "Yes, in a heartbeat."

But my chance was there. I could have signed on at any time.

The 117th Edition would have brought me a new family and another two years of adventures. But that would almost have been harder than leaving.

So I say, "No, I wouldn't go back. The memories are good enough." But that's easy to say when the opportunity has passed.

Months later, in June 1987, the phone in my apartment rang.

"Hello?" I said.

"Hello, Kristopher, this is Kenneth Feld," came the familiar voice. "How would you like to be ringmaster of The Greatest Show on Earth again?"

"Oh, no, you sly fox," I said to him. Then to myself: "You're not catching me again!"

"But, Kristopher, you haven't heard my offer. . . ."

EPILOGUE

But Did They All Live Happily Ever After?

Things have changed since I left the circus. The good news is about Uncle Soapy. He was rehired by the concessions manager and is happily hustling programs at the arena doors along with Buddy the Barker. The two of them are quite a garrulous pair!

Sarahjane is still with the Blue Unit, and has become the first female performance director in the history of "The Greatest Show on Earth."

The "Henchman," Tim Holst, crept up on Robin Frye one day in 1988 and tapped him on the shoulder. "You don't need to come in tomorrow," he said. No explanation was ever given. Robin is currently living in New York City.

Susie Turcot was fired right after Robin, and is now working as a technician for concerts and conventions in Washington, D.C.

Little Laci is performing in a gymnastics revue at a resort in the Canary Islands.

Attila is touring Europe with the Kis Faludi—with $350 of my borrowed money in his pocket!

Marc Lafontant is back with the Red Unit and has recently purchased a luxurious new fifth-wheel trailer. He will admit to no casualties since I left.

Gunther Gebel Williams is on his final two-year tour before retiring.

The Kenneth Feld tradition goes on. For the first time in history, "The Greatest Show on Earth" is playing Japan. Tickets cost $40 apiece! What will he think of next?

GLOSSARY OF CIRCUS LINGO

ANIMAL WALK: Parade of animals through the city, which serves as a moving advertisement of the circus, and is also the only way of actually getting the animals from the train to the arena

BIG ROUTE: First year of a tour, composed of major cities in the United States (see Rodeo Route)

THE BIG SHOW: Alternate name for the Ringling Brothers and Barnum & Bailey Circus

BULL TUB: Pedestal used for elephants to stand on top of and perform tricks upon (the ringmaster occasionally uses one to stand on)

BUNK CAR: Workingmen's train car composed mostly of bunks

CATS: Term used whenever referring to the tigers and lions

CIRCUS WAGON: Trailer specially designed to fit on the flatcars to store wardrobe, rigging, and props

COME IN: Preshow antics performed by the clowns while the audience is entering the arena

CONFERENCE: The European term for ringmaster (Attila and Laci's name for me)

DONNIKER: Portable toilet on the train or in a trailer

FLATCAR: Flat traincar used to transport wagons, bus, and equipment

GYPSY BOX: Large wooden box with breakers used by those traveling by motor home or trailer to hook up electricity

KIDDY SHOW: The morning matinee

LIBERTY HORSES: Untethered horses used in performances

MECHANIC: Safety wire attached to a performer executing a difficult or dangerous trick or feat

MENAGE (pronounced "man-age"): The Ringling elephant production number/display

MUD SHOW: Any circus performed under a tent

"NUREMBERGS": Clown presentation of new bits and gags performed for Kenneth Feld in hopes of being put into the show (as in "Nuremberg Trials")

PIE CAR: Greasiest greasy spoon diner on the circus train. (I never ate there even once!)

PIE CAR, JR.: Trailer parked at the back arena door that served the same greasy food. (Don't ask whether I ever ate there, either!)

RIGGERS: Men who hang the cables and wires

RING CURB: Actual wooden ring creating the performing areas

RODEO ROUTE: Second year of the tour, composed of smaller cities

ROOMETTE: Small six-by-four-foot cubicles that clowns and showgirls call their homes on the circus train

SIX-PACK: Weekend performance schedule composed of three shows on Saturday and three on Sunday (as in "the dreaded six-pack")

SPEC: Extravaganza, or *spectacle*, usually performed at the end of a Ringling show's first half

SPOTTING THE TRAIN: When the train has been officially set on the tracks where it will remain for the duration of the engagement. (In other words, don't hop off the train until you know you're there!)

TO STYLE (STYLING): A circus performer's particular way of bowing and posing; their acknowledgment of the audience

TEETERBOARD: Seesaw used to catapult performers onto the shoulders
    of their comrades
TRACK GAG: Stationary clown act performed on the track of the arena
    that is used as a diversion while another act is being set up
WALK AROUND: Minigag performed by a clown while walking around
    the arena floor; usually a visual pun or play on words (for instance,
    a kite flying a kid)

RED UNIT
115TH EDITION
1986 OFFICIAL TOUR

DATE	TOWN	STATE	LOCATION	TRAIN MILES TO NEXT CITY
Jan. 23–26	Venice	Florida	Circus Arena	
Jan. 28–29	Lakeland	Florida	Civic Center	104
Jan. 31–Feb. 2	Daytona Beach	Florida	The Ocean Center	327
Feb. 5–16	Atlanta	Georgia	The Omni	467
Feb. 18–19	Chattanooga	Tennessee	UTC Arena	136
Feb. 21–23	Columbia	S. Carolina	Carolina Coliseum	376
Feb. 25–Mar. 2	Raleigh	N. Carolina	Dorton Arena	202
Mar. 4–5	Fayetteville	N. Carolina	Cumberland County Memorial Arena	157
Mar. 7–9	Asheville	N. Carolina	Civic Center	325
Mar. 11–16	Knoxville	Tennessee	Civic Coliseum	126
Mar. 18–23	Charlotte	N. Carolina	Charlotte Coliseum	269
Mar. 25–Apr. 7	Washington	D.C.	D.C. Armory	374

Date	City	State	Venue	
Apr. 10–13	Cincinnati	Ohio	Riverfront Coliseum	562
Apr. 15–16	Wheeling	W. Virginia	Civic Center	299
Apr. 18–20	Charleston	W. Virginia	Civic Center	256
Apr. 23–27	Binghamton	New York	Broome County Arena	774
Apr. 29–May 4	Worcester	Massachusetts	Centrum	300
May 6–11	Hartford	Connecticut	Civic Center	80
May 13–18	New Haven	Connecticut	Veterans Memorial Coliseum	37
May 20–25	Providence	Rhode Island	Civic Center	117
May 27–June 1	Hershey	Pennsylvania	Hersheypark Arena	361
June 3–8	Columbus	Ohio	Ohio Center	467
June 10–11	Lexington	Kentucky	Lexington Center	234
June 13–15	Louisville	Kentucky	Freedom Hall	87
June 17–18	Nashville	Tennessee	Nashville Municipal Auditorium	188
June 20–21	Huntsville	Alabama	Von Braun Civic Center	145
June 23–24	Little Rock	Arkansas	T. H. Barton Coliseum	356
June 26–29	New Orleans	Louisiana	Superdome	485
July 1–2	Jackson	Mississippi	Mississippi Coliseum	183
July 4–6	Lafayette	Louisiana	Cajundome	324
July 8–20	Houston	Texas	The Summit	217
July 22–27	San Antonio	Texas	Joe & Harry Freeman Coliseum	188
July 29–30	Fort Worth	Texas	Tarrant County Convention Center	325
July 31–Aug. 10	Dallas	Texas	Reunion Arena	31
Aug. 12–13	Abilene	Texas	Expo Center	193
Aug. 15–17	Austin	Texas	Special Events Center	399
Aug. 19–21	Tulsa	Oklahoma	Convention Center	576
Aug. 23–24	Wichita	Kansas	Kansas Coliseum	198

Aug. 26–28	Lincoln	Nebraska	Pershing Auditorium	419
Aug. 30–Sept. 1	Springfield	Illinois	Prairie Capital Convention Center	488
Sept. 3–4	La Crosse	Wisconsin	Civic Center	372
Sept. 6–7	Madison	Wisconsin	Dane County Expo Center	132
Sept. 9–14	Kansas City	Missouri	Kemper Arena	639
Sept. 16–21	St. Louis	Missouri	The Arena	285
Sept. 23–24	Cedar Rapids	Iowa	Five Seasons Center	285
Sept. 26–28	Des Moines	Iowa	Veterans Memorial Auditorium	133
Sept. 30–Oct. 5	Detroit	Michigan	Joe Louis Arena	652
Oct. 7–12	Indianapolis	Indiana	Market Square Arena	299
Oct. 15–26	Boston	Massachusetts	Boston Garden	955
Oct. 28–Nov. 2	Buffalo	New York	Memorial Auditorium	486
Nov. 4–16	Cleveland	Ohio	Richfield Coliseum	232
Nov. 18–23	Pittsburgh	Pennsylvania	Civic Arena	129

52 Cities
15,751 Miles

CHRONOLOGICAL LISTING OF RINGMASTERS

P. T. BARNUM'S CIRCUS
1870–78   Dan Castello
1879–81   James Cook

BARNUM & LONDON CIRCUS
1882–89   R. H. Dockrill

BARNUM & BAILEY CIRCUS
1890–91   William Ducrow
1892–94   R. H. Dockrill
1895   John O'Brien
1896–1902   William Ducrow
1903–04   Frank Melville
1905   R. H. Dockrill
1906–07   William Ducrow
1908–10   Edward Shipp
1911–12   William Gorman
1913–18   Fred Bradna

RINGLING BROTHERS CIRCUS
Founded 1884

1910   William Gorman
1911–15   Al Ringling
1916–18   John Agee

Ringling Brothers and Barnum & Bailey Combined Circus

1919–46	Fred Bradna
1947–48	Arthur Springer
1949	Harry Thomas
1950	David Murphy
1951–55	Count Nicholas
1956	Preston Lambert
1957	Harold Ronk
1958	Don Forbes
1959	George Michel
1960–68	Harold Ronk

Blue Unit		*Red Unit*	
1969–72	Harold Ronk	1969–73	Bob Welz
1973	Tim Holst		
1974–76	Harold Ronk	1974–76	Tim Holst
1977	Bill Witter	1977–82	Kit Haskett
1978–80	Harold Ronk		
1981	Lawrence Kelly		
1982	Dinny McGuire		
1983–86	Jim Ragona	1983–85	Dinny McGuire
		1986	Kristopher Antekeier